paige press

THIS
Boy

JENNA SCOTT

Paige Press
Leander, TX 78641

Ebook:
ISBN: 978-1-953520-06-7

Print:
ISBN: 978-1-953520-07-4

ALSO BY JENNA SCOTT

This Boy

This Hurt

This Love

PROLOGUE

*A*s far back as I can remember, my life has been a series of moves. From Long Beach to Seattle to Medford, from Petaluma to Sacramento to Fresno. Up and down the West Coast, one cramped, tiny apartment after another. No place ever seemed permanent or solid enough for me to really put down roots or make true friends.

I guess that's why I ended up so obsessed with reading. Mom never lets me forget that when I was a toddler, I insisted on carting around my entire collection of Dr. Seuss books to each new city, begging her to read me one every night before bed (until I learned to read on my own when I was five). The characters and stories I soaked up formed a found family for me, giving me the stability I craved. Places and people I could always return to, no matter how many miles we put behind us.

It seemed like every time I started to get comfortable in a place, my mom would be telling me it was time to pack up our stuff and go somewhere else. So when the days in La Jolla slowly added up to months, then a year, then four years, I thought that we'd found *the* place. That nothing would convince her to leave.

Then, a few months ago, the Incident happened.

Afterward, my public high school kicked me out halfway through my senior year, and with my plans to attend the college suddenly looking shaky, I started wishing my mom's drunken antics would force us out of here as they'd done so many times before. It didn't matter that I'd been on track to be valedictorian, or that—thanks to my Advanced Placement classes—my GPA was over a 4.0. Unless I graduated, no crap college would take me, let alone a great one like Stanford, my absolute dream institution of higher learning. The only place I could transfer to was Oak Academy, the ritzy private school where tuition would cover our rent for half a year.

It seemed like a long shot, but my mom stepped up and made a few calls to OA anyway, then met with a few administrators. I still have no idea what she told them, but soon after that, I got a letter on fancy embossed Oak Academy stationery saying they'd reviewed my case and were willing to offer me admission thanks to my good grades and otherwise clean record. That if I wanted to finish my senior year with them, I could—and that they had need-based scholarships available for students just like me.

Luckily, I was able to keep my job babysitting for the Becks, a family of real-estate magnates. Either Mr. Beck doesn't know what happened at my school, or he doesn't care. Or maybe he just kept me on because I'm great with his kid. Either way, it means my salary is safe, and I can keep socking away the majority of my paychecks into my secret college fund.

My job is practically perfect in every way, a light to hold on to during these trying times, and Harrison is the sweetest kid a part-time nanny could hope for. I took to calling him Harry from day one since he looks like a six-year-old Harry Potter.

But there's one challenge at the Becks' that I still haven't triumphed over.

Hunter Beck.

He's a senior like me, six-feet-and-change of blond, blue-eyed, homegrown SoCal hotness, and he's got an actual six-pack—which I can't help ogling every time he's shirtless, which is far too often—to boot.

The way Harry talks about his older brother, you'd think Hunter could walk on water. I know he doesn't. Every week, it's a different girl I catch doing the shimmy of shame through that big house, and every week, I have to find new ways to keep Harry from finding out what his brother is *really* doing to them. Sorry, Harry; it's not tickling.

Besides being a total manwhore, Hunter also happens to be exactly the kind of spoiled, arrogant asshole cliché that you'd expect an entitled rich boy to be. He has this way of watching me out of the corner of his eye whenever we're in the same room together, yet he rarely deigns to speak to me. As if I'm so far below him, he can't even muster up a simple hello every now and again.

Obviously, there's no point in pursuing anything with Hunter myself for about a million really good reasons, but even knowing full well how horrible and narcissistic he is, sometimes I still feel like he's my kryptonite. Every time he walks by in his swim trunks, slung low over his hips and tight, tanned abs, his hair slicked back and damp from his nightly laps in the Becks' pool, I have to practically wipe the drool off my chin.

Like I said, it's a challenge.

And because the sandwich that's my life isn't covered in enough shit already, it just so happens that Hunter goes to my new school. I can only hope we won't see each other in the halls, or God forbid, have actual classes together. That would be way too distracting for me, and I'm committed to maintaining my GPA.

Because Hunter Beck might be pure fire, but I know better than to let myself get burned.

Or at least, that's what I keep telling myself.

Chapter One

CAMILLA

I wipe my hands on a dish towel and survey the Becks' kitchen one last time, making sure I haven't missed any stray popcorn kernels or cookie crumbs. The dishwasher has been emptied, the floor swept clean, and the granite on the island is basically a mirror. All that's left is putting an adorable six-year-old to bed, and then I can finally go home.

When I get to his room upstairs, I find him already in his pajamas. He's focused on the latest *Adventurers* graphic novel, his lips moving as he reads and his signature cowlick sticking up on the back of his head. My heart melts a tiny bit.

Harry still reads picture books most of the time, but I've been trying to get his reading level up a bit. The last time I was at the library, I checked out a few *Adventurers* for him, thinking he'd take a few weeks to get through the first one.

Turns out I'd underestimated the kid. He's been devouring volume after volume on the weekly ever since I introduced him to the world of one of my favorite series growing up. Watching him fall for those characters the same way I did makes me love the little guy even more.

A smile is on my lips when I ask, "Did you brush your teeth, bud?"

"Yep." He puts the book on the night table and slips under the covers. "I used my blue Batman mouthwash too."

"Wow, I'm impressed," I say honestly.

Kneeling by the bed, I tuck him into sheets that are so soft he must feel like he's surrounded by cotton clouds. I can't help envying him a little bit. The ones we have at home are worn so thin, I swear they've been around for five generations. My mom's priorities have always leaned more toward her liquor cabinet than our linen closet.

"All set?" I ask, reaching for the bedside lamp.

"Wait!" Harrison looks under his pillow and around the room, the worry on his features intensifying every second. "Roo isn't here," he finally says and looks up at me in a way that guarantees I'll come to the rescue. He knows all too well I can't say no to that pout, just like I know he can't sleep without that stuffed kangaroo.

"I'll get him," I say, already halfway to the door. "Do you remember where you saw him last?"

A frown crosses his face, and tentatively, he says, "Roo was watching me swim. And then you called me in for dinner, and I didn't want to get him all wet, so..."

"Say no more. I'll be right back."

"Thanks, Milla," he says, clearly relieved.

"You're very welcome."

Downstairs, the living room is as dark as we left it after our Disney+ session. Using my cell phone as a flashlight, I carefully weave around leather couches and the big glass coffee table. The heavy drapes on the floor-to-ceiling windows are still drawn, but I slip between them and go out back through the French doors. My light reaches a few lounge chairs lined up facing the pool, a lagoon-style monstrosity that's so big, I can't even see the far end of it where a small waterfall pours over fake rock formations.

I take a moment to look out over the city of La Jolla stretched out in the distance. Cozy golden lights twinkle from other hillside mansions, the shining expanse of the Pacific Ocean reflects the crescent moon above, and I catch the heady scent of night-blooming jasmine. But what would normally be a beautiful scene quickly turns all sorts of mortifying when I hear the telltale sound of splashing.

I freeze in place, and that's when a harsh gasp reaches my ears.

Oh God, no.

Other girls might worry some creep had broken into their boss's home—babysitter home alone with a small kid is a textbook trope of horror. But other girls don't work for Hunter Beck's family.

Unfortunately, I know for a fact that there's no serial killer in that enormous pool because after three months of my mom working as the Becks' housekeeper and me babysitting Harrison, I've already lost count of how many girls eighteen-year-old Hunter has brought home to hump and dump. There's a new one every week.

Then again, those are just the ones I *see*.

In a panic, I duck behind the lounge chairs. Although it's hard to see exactly what's happening, the continued sound effects confirm what I already know.

As my vision adjusts to the darkness, I can make out the moonlit figures in the water. The long, wet hair of a girl with her back pressed up against the side of the pool, facing Hunter with her arms locked around his neck. Him facing my way, his tan biceps taut and his lower arms under-water, hands probably wrapped tight around the girl's hips or ass as she bobs up and down.

While I'm worried at first that he can see me crouched here on the deck, the splashing and gasping keeps on going. Surely they would've stopped if they'd realized I was here.

I consider making a run for it, going back upstairs, and telling Harry that I couldn't find Roo. But the kid is stubborn, and he'll want to come out here and look for himself. Meaning I won't be the only one forced to witness Hunter's sickening debauchery.

Unacceptable. Harry is so sweet and precious. I won't be the one responsible for shattering his world with the ugly truth about the shameless horndog of an older brother he idolizes.

So, yeah, there's no way I'm going back without the stuffed animal.

Which means I have to turn on the floodlights to find this goddamn plushie.

Which means I'm about to get a fully X-rated viewing of Hunter Beck's latest live porn show.

But the more I debate my options, the more a fresh emotion begins to spark in my chest, quickly burning everything else away. Anger. With a dash of dismay and a whole lot of protectiveness toward the kid waiting upstairs.

Harry swims in that pool. Hunter *knows* that, and yet he's still pounding away at some random girl in the same water his brother sometimes straight up swallows.

When I finally get up and flip on the lights, there's nothing but anger left in me.

Any hope I had that they'd stop and be even remotely ashamed of themselves is dashed instantly. The girl looks over her shoulder, sees me by the French doors, and giggles. The splashing grows even more frantic, and she starts to moan. And when I stalk back toward the lounge chairs with the biggest scowl I can muster, Hunter's eyes lock on mine, and I suddenly find myself going complete deer-in-the-headlights status.

His gaze is intense, glazed over but still fully connected to mine. It's impossible to look away. Common sense screams at me to run inside, but it's as if he's physically holding me in place. Like he wants me to watch him. Like he's getting off on it.

The staring contest continues, me still glaring, Hunter's blue eyes burning with a combination of lust and what I'm guessing is self-satisfaction. He knows exactly what he's doing, putting on a show with this girl, and how horribly uncomfortable this must be for me. A smirk plays at his lips. I think he's actually about to say something to me when his expression changes, his eyes rolling slightly. *He's about to come*, I realize with a flush of heat to my cheeks. Oh God, this can't be happening.

He pumps faster into the girl, driving her into the wall of the pool, bouncing her hard with his thrusts. I can't believe I'm still standing here watching. He's disgusting. But there's something else going on inside me, something I don't even fully understand. A tight feeling in my lower belly; heat radiates from it, and my pulse races hard.

The girl starts moaning his name, sounding fake as hell, her voice pitching higher and higher. "Hunter, Hunter, Hunter," she whimpers in that obnoxious baby voice. Give me a break. She probably picked that up watching internet porn.

I guess it's working though. With his eyes still on me, Hunter braces himself against the pool's edge, groaning a little as he climaxes.

The sound makes me shiver, and then he pulls away from the girl, and the spell on me is finally broken.

Spotting Roo at the base of a palm tree on the other side of the pool, I bolt over, grabbing the stuffed animal and tucking it under my arm. Then I stalk back toward the house, my phone gripped tight in my hand, desperate to get away.

In the pool Hunter says, "Looks like servant girl got a kick out of watching us."

If my mouth wasn't so dry, and my job wasn't on the line, I'd tell him to have some basic human decency and consider the fact that his little brother is right upstairs, probably within earshot. But I keep quiet. I need the money.

Meanwhile, the girl giggles like Hunter just said the funniest thing ever.

"This was probably very educational for her," he goes on.

My cheeks are burning, and I want to die.

In some sick, twisted way, he's kind of right. I'm not the most sexually experienced person in the world. But this isn't the way I imagined getting educated.

That's not even the worst part of all of this, either.

Because tomorrow, I'll be starting school at the same private academy that Hunter goes to. The girl he just screwed will probably be there too. With my luck, the two of them will tell the entire senior class that new girl Camilla Hanson is a pervy voyeur, and I'll have yet another fantastic high school experience being the resident loner who people love to gossip about.

I didn't think things at my new school could start off so badly, but at this rate, I'm going to end up worse off than I was at my last school, where the Incident That Shall Not Be Named took place.

"Should you pay her extra?" the girl asks. "Give servant girl a bonus?"

"This was her bonus," Hunter quips.

The rage that was so strong a moment ago gives way to

embarrassment again, only this time, it brought a friend: sheer humiliation.

They think themselves so above me, like I'm dirt under their shoes, just because I work for the Becks. They're not even ashamed I walked in on them. Yet I'm the one who feels like she's about to sink into a hole of shame. Stopping with my hand on the handle of the French doors, I whirl around.

"I'm not your *servant girl*," I say, keeping my voice steady.

Then I go inside, slamming the door behind me for effect. I know it's childish, but it's all I've got.

I head up the stairs, trying to calm down with a few deep breaths before walking back into Harry's room. He beams at me when he spots Roo in my hands, and I get him settled in again quickly, leaving his door open just a crack on my way out.

My heart's still beating madly, and before I realize it, my feet are taking me down the hall past Mrs. Beck's office, which always reeks of floor polish and that plasticky smell of toner. The hallway light spills in just enough that I can see papers piled on every available surface. I have no idea what exactly goes into real estate development, but it seems to involve mountains of contracts and other legal documents. Paperwork which Mrs. Beck no longer keeps up with ever since she went from executive assistant to Instagram influencer, thanks to her marriage to Mr. Beck... her former boss. Not judging. Those are just the facts.

At the end of the hall is the master bedroom, the door wide open. I've been in here before with Harry, quick dashes to look for toys or speak briefly with Mr. or Mrs. Beck, but it's the view of the pool that I'm after as I cross the empty room and go to the sliding glass balcony doors. If Hunter and his female friend are still down there, I can slip out the front door in a hurry without crossing paths with them again. The last thing I need tonight is more harassment from a couple of privileged trust fund babies who'll probably never have to work a day in their lives.

When I look down, I see them in the hot tub, facing the view of the ocean. The girl is drinking from a bottle that I hope doesn't contain actual alcohol, but then again, I'm sure she can afford an Uber home. I'd better get going while the going's good.

As I hurriedly cross the room back toward the door, I see a walk-in closet to my left, full to bursting with designer clothes and shoes, a low sofa, and a full-length mirror that dimly reflects my shabby jeans-and-T-shirted self right back at me.

I also see Mrs. Beck's makeup and jewelry strewn all over the dressing table, her diamonds shining in the stray moonlight coming in through the balcony doors. Everywhere I look, thoughtless luxury looks back. Standing there in my ratty Chuck Taylors, I feel exactly like what I am: a dirt-poor girl who doesn't belong in this space.

Without wasting any more precious time, I go down to the first floor, grab my backpack from the coat closet, and rush out of the house.

Chapter Two
CAMILLA

$\mathcal{T}$he whole bus ride home, I can't stop thinking about what I saw: Hunter and his flavor of the week, going at it in the family pool. The humiliation I felt when he called me "servant girl" is still there, raging under the surface, but as the indelible image of his athletic, tanned body comes back to me, I'm faced with one question I still can't answer. Why was he looking at me and not the girl he was literally inside of? Because I'm pretty sure I didn't imagine his eyes locked on me while he was finishing.

As I fumble for my keys outside the door of our tiny apartment, I'm relieved to find the lights are out, but any hope I have that my mom is asleep gets dashed as soon as I step inside and the stench of cheap bourbon invades my nose, carried on a warm wave of musty old carpet and the bleach-and-lemon smell of cleaning supplies that always lingers around my mother.

Thoughts of having a quiet evening at home quickly scatter when my mom, sitting on the couch in complete darkness, speaks from across the room.

"Look who finally decided to show up," she slurs as I

drop my bag and set my house keys in the bowl by the door.

"Harry went to bed a little late," I tell her, holding up my phone—a.k.a. my emergency flashlight—and she hisses, throwing up an arm to cover her eyes.

She's slouched against the worn cushions with a glass clutched in her hand, and I don't need to look at the floor to know there's an almost-empty bottle sitting there.

"Turn that thing off. I have a migraine," she says. "And get me more ice."

"Sure," I say. It's easier than arguing.

I walk into the small galley kitchen, feeling like I'm enabling her, but I already know nothing I say or do will convince her to stop drinking—believe me, I've tried. For *years* I tried, until eventually I got tired of having her yell and slap the effort out of me. Hopefully my ice-fetching will be the extent of our interaction tonight. It's always hard to see her like this, no matter how many times it's happened before. Because I've seen her in the brief periods where she gets herself under control, and she's vibrant and energetic and *present*. So it hurts even more every time she backslides into...this.

Setting my phone on the counter, I flip the light switch, but the bulb stays dark overhead. I try the switch for the garbage disposal, and that's dead too. Lovely. The power's out. With a sigh, I grab a clean glass from the cupboard, but when I turn around, I realize the fridge has also gone silent thanks to our localized blackout. Shit.

As soon as I open the freezer door, water pours out. With a single touch, I realize all our frozens—which is most of our food—have defrosted.

I swallow the growl rumbling at the back of my throat. The water is dripping from the open freezer down the front of the fridge, so I soak up what I can with kitchen towels, then twist them out in the sink, then repeat.

As I clean, I think about how I'm going to have to grab some groceries this week, maybe cereal and canned goods to get us by for a few days. I'll need to use savings from my secret stash again. I hate dipping into my college fund, but when it's between that and starving, I don't have much choice. These are all things I shouldn't have to worry about, but someone in this house has to.

Lucky for Mom, the ice tray in the back of the freezer still has a few chunks of ice in it, so I drop them into the clean glass, then head back out to the living room.

"This is all that's left of the ice," I say, handing her the fresh glass and taking her empty one.

"Hmm," is all she musters, pouring the rest of the bourbon into the glass.

"So...what happened to the electricity?" I ask as gently as I can. "And why are you still up? It's after ten."

It's her daily ritual to drink herself senseless as soon as she gets home from her long hours of cooking for other people and cleaning their houses, and her shifts start so early that she's usually passed out in bed long before now.

"I didn't pay the bill, and it's too hot to sleep without the AC," she says.

Then she shrugs, like it's no big deal she ruined the majority of our food supply, like we don't need things like light and ceiling fans and alarm clocks.

"Okay," I say. It's not worth fighting over it. "We'll figure it out tomorrow."

"I don't have the money," she murmurs. "For the bill."

I take a long breath. The whole reason we moved to La Jolla—a ritzy seaside community where we can barely afford even the crappiest, most run-down apartment—is all the mansions. Mom had bragged she was going to be making major bank cleaning houses here. But what she didn't factor in was how much higher the cost of living would be, how often her piece of crap car would break down, and that no matter how good her paychecks are, she always manages to drink away the majority of them.

"Fine. I'll take care of it," I tell her. "Just try to get some rest soon, okay?"

She obviously can't afford to miss work, but I still feel like a brat for telling her what to do. As I grab my backpack from the floor and then walk past her to go to my room, I feel her eyes following me.

"Are you gaining weight, Milla?" she asks.

In the hallway, I freeze. "I don't know," I say, trying to deflect. "I'm tired."

"You need to exercise more. Men don't marry thick women," she reminds me, as if I haven't heard it all before. As if the cheap processed food and ninety-nine cent drive-thru menus we live off of should have turned me into a supermodel by now.

She may be skinny, thanks to a strict diet of booze and Diet Cokes, but she definitely isn't healthy. And if she's so concerned about my body, she should start caring about hers too and how the alcohol is ruining whatever's left of it, inside and out. But those words won't ever leave my lips.

There are fights worth getting into and fights you walk away from. This is the latter. Especially because we've rehashed the subject so many times that I know exactly how she's going to turn everything around on me, and then I'll just end up apologizing.

"Maybe someone will love me for me," I finally tell her softly, tugging at the hem of my shirt so it covers the curve of my belly.

She laughs, and it feels like a kick in the gut. It takes

everything I have inside to just clench my jaw, go in my room, and lock the door behind me.

My room is smaller than any of the Becks' walk-in closets, but at least it's mine, and I'm grateful for that. Most of the apartments we've lived in have only had one room for me and Mom to share, and sometimes all we could afford was a one-room studio. As shabby as this place is, it's a palace compared to some.

I sink onto my twin bed in the dark, hot tears stinging my eyes. Anger is what I should be feeling, but instead I just feel worthless.

The criticism feels especially cruel coming from someone as stunningly beautiful as my mom. There's no way I'll ever measure up to her. Even with the alcohol taking the soft curves out of her cheeks and hips, she still turns heads wherever we go with her dark hair, long legs, and pouty lips. She's the kind of mom who wears high heels and hoop earrings to go to the grocery store. The kind that teenage boys call a MILF. I have her same hair and deep brown doe eyes, but where she's always somehow glamorous and edgy-looking, I'm just...me. A mousy, mostly average teenage girl.

She's never understood why school matters so much to me or why I always have my nose in a book. In her point of view (which she swears is supported by actual scientific study), the world is easier on attractive people—and it's stupid not to take advantage of your natural assets. The thing is, I don't want to perpetuate that. Even if I could get ahead in life simply by being beautiful (which, ha), I'd rather know that my successes are the result of my own hard work. Beauty isn't everything to me the way it is to her, and I refuse to believe that only a rich guy can rescue me from poverty.

It makes me wonder what kind of chip she has on her

shoulder from her own parents, whom I've never met. Maybe they tried to drill that Prince Charming crap into her head too, and when it didn't pan out, she decided it should be *my* life goal.

Or maybe she truly and honestly believes that marrying rich is my only viable prospect for a stable future. You'd think she'd support my college plans more, given my stellar GPA and the fact that my eventual job prospects could mean more money for the both of us, but no. She has zero faith in my ability to make something of myself on my own terms. The reminder is like a sledgehammer to the chest every time.

Of course, it hasn't escaped me that she isn't married to my own father, whoever he is—his identity is a topic that's completely off-limits, though I'm not sure if it's because he didn't do right by her when she got pregnant or because she actually has no idea who he is. Either way, I can understand why she'd want me to avoid the same lonely fate. I just wish she'd back off and let me figure out my life on my own.

With a deep breath, I wipe my cheeks, pick up my bag, and set it on top of the desk in the corner. Then I use the ugly streetlight coming in through the window to take a look at my class schedule for tomorrow. I practically have it memorized by now, but my anxiety keeps me checking on it every single day anyway, as if it might rearrange itself behind my back when I'm not looking.

I start to build out a mental picture of my day as I go over each time slot. Classes start at 8:00 a.m., which means I have to be up at 6:00 a.m. to get to school on time to see my counselor, earlier if I want a shower. Which, after tonight, I definitely do. In fact, I'd be taking one right now if Mom wasn't outside my door ready to pounce.

I switch out my jeans for sleep shorts in the dark, but when I go to set an alarm on my phone, I see the remaining battery—a whopping eight percent—and start to panic. What if my phone dies in the middle of the night and I don't wake up in time for school? There's no way I'm showing up late on my first day at Oak Academy.

Knowing me, I won't sleep a wink now. Though with all the pre-school jitters, I doubt I would have anyway.

The truth is, I'm not looking forward to tomorrow at all. But how can I waste such an amazing opportunity? I can only chalk up the generous scholarship that OA offered me, supposedly from "an anonymous benefactor," to an actual act of God—especially after the Incident I don't even want to think about got me kicked out of my last school. And Oak Academy has the kind of pedigree that will go a long way toward getting me into my dream college: Stanford. I'd be a fool to turn down a free ride at this place, regardless of how much I'm not looking forward to going.

A fresh wave of panic rolls through me, and I press my palms to my eyelids, forcing myself to breathe. I need to get it together. This is my future on the line.

One last to-do on my list before bed. The uniform.

Popping open one of the Rubbermaid bins that acts as my dresser drawers, I pull out my new clothes and drape them over my desk chair. Because of course the fancy private school has a mandatory uniform, just like you see in every movie adaptation of a YA novel that involves a boarding school.

But although *Vampire Academy* had cute black skirts and jackets, and Hogwarts had cool robes and ties in striped house colors, Oak Academy...well,we get a white shirt, a navy tie, and a navy jacket on top. The khaki pleated skirt is knee-length, and girls are required to wear tights underneath, lest the sight of our bare knees lead anyone's dirty mind astray. The whole ensemble is completed by nondescript dark flats with short heels (no taller than an inch and a half) allowed if desired.

As I slide my collection of stuffed animals aside—a plush Hedwig, old Mr. Bear, and the even older Rudolph—and slip under the comforter and my scratchy old sheets, I take a final look at the uniform I'm going to be wearing every day. At least I won't have to worry about being dressed in my worn Target brand jeans and a thrift store button-up while everyone else is walking around in Ralph Lauren or Gucci. The only thing they can ream me for are my shoes. My gut tells me they're going to.

On top of that, Hunter Beck may already be planning to sabotage any chance I have at fitting in anyway. Maybe the whole school will be calling me "servant girl."

Just like that, the image of him in the pool earlier tonight comes back to me full force. I should be thinking about nothing except what a scumbag he is, but instead I'm stuck on the way he groaned when he came, breathless and desperate, stirring something in me that I can't put words to.

The scene plays out in my mind, over and over again, in minute detail. Why can't I stop thinking about it? About the way he moved, slow and then faster, harder, grinding into that girl until she was moaning his name. The way his mouth parted, his lower lip full and soft, the way he never took his eyes off me.

The lust and hunger I saw in his gaze stays with me, and soon I feel a deep ache between my legs that won't go away. Hunter Beck, pumping into that girl, groaning softly, dark eyes burning into mine.

It's all I can think of as I drift into a restless sleep.

Chapter Three

CAMILLA

irst days of school are always the worst. And I'd know—with all the moving I've done in my life, I've had plenty.

After a quick shower (thankfully, the landlord pays for our heat and hot water) and a breakfast of cold strawberry Pop-Tarts, I run to the bus stop in my brand new uniform with my stomach in knots. Mom somehow got up on time for work without an alarm clock this morning, which is a blessing.

As I wait for the bus, I make a mental note to call San Diego Gas & Electric about our overdue bill as soon as my phone is charged. I grabbed two hundred dollars from my secret stash this morning, which I'll have to deposit at my mom's bank after school in order to make the payment. I hope it's enough to cover what we owe.

Forty minutes later, I get dropped off down the street from the most prestigious school in a two-hundred-mile radius, and as I walk toward it, a sense of awe hits me all over again. Though I've passed the Spanish-style, red-roofed complex many times, I never thought I'd be crossing the hallowed marble steps of the main entrance. The uniform helps me blend in, but I can feel several pairs of eyes on me, which I try to ignore as I follow the signs to the counselor's office.

When I get there, I see a shiny plaque next to the door that reads Alaine Warren, PhD, and underneath, in much smaller letters, Guidance Counselor.

My knock is as frantic as my breath, which I'm trying to catch after running up the stairs and across two corridors. I shift my weight from foot to foot until I hear a "Come in."

Stepping inside, I see a youngish woman in a tailored pinstriped blazer with a wristful of chunky gold bracelets sitting behind the desk, an expectant look on her face.

"I'm sorry I'm late, Ms. Warren. I got—"

"Dr. Warren," she pointedly corrects while she motions for me to take a seat. "I didn't spend all those years in college for nothing. Camilla Hanson, isn't it?"

"Yes, ma'am." I look over the desk that separates us, taking in the gold-framed diplomas on the wall, the fancy pens, and the neat stack of files at Dr. Warren's elbow.

I wonder if one of those is my student file. The thought makes me feel sick.

If she knows about the Incident, however, she makes no mention of it as she looks over my transcript from La Mesa High, and if she's surprised at my straight As and high standardized testing scores, it doesn't show on her face.

"Do you need a copy of your schedule?" she finally asks.

"No, thank you. I already printed it out," I say.

She cracks a smile, and for the first time today, I feel myself relax. "You come prepared. I like that. Did you get all your college applications in for the January deadlines? Where did you apply?"

"A few UC schools, a few CSUs, and Stanford, which is my dream," I tell her, knowing the question was probably her polite way of asking if I was even considering college, given that I'm a charity case here.

"What about backup schools?" she asks. "Just in case."

"I applied to a few of those too," I tell her. "Just waiting to hear back now. Acceptance letters start going out soon. Fingers crossed."

"Wonderful!" she says brightly. "Let me show you to your locker."

Dr. Warren leads me to a loud, busy hallway on the first floor, hands me a Post-it with my locker combination written on it, and waits to make sure I get the locker open. It's as good as having a flashing neon sign over my head that says "New Girl," but I'm grateful for the kindness.

Just as she finishes explaining where my first class is, the warning bell rings.

"That's the five-minute bell. Better scoot," she says, gesturing vaguely toward the stairwell. "Good luck, Miss Hanson. I know you'll do well here."

The second bell has already rung by the time I get upstairs and find my classroom, desperation making me breathless as I rush through the door. The first thing I notice is that the teacher is running later than me, which, small mercy. The second is the instant pause in the hubbub around the room—I can just feel everyone staring at me. And I know what they must be thinking: new girl, scholarship charity case, looking sweaty and anxious in her somewhat-tight blazer and cheap shoes.

My pulse kicks up as my eyes flit around the room, desperately seeking a place to sit and blend in before the teacher arrives and makes a big deal over me.

"There's a seat here," a boy in the third row says, nodding to the empty desk next to him.

A relieved smile plays on my lips, and as I head over and sink into the chair, I let out a quiet, "Thanks."

Once I'm seated, everyone's interest slides off me. I slip my bag off my shoulder, and the boy waits for me to dig out my notebook and pen to speak again.

"I'm Emmett, by the way. Nice to meet you."

I have to remind myself that the chances of him knowing about the Incident are low; that he's being genuinely nice. His hazel-brown eyes look warm, at least, and not like they're about to turn judgy and scornful.

"Camilla." I try my best to come across normal, to seem like I don't have a huge cloud hanging over me, like my mom isn't an alcoholic and I wasn't expelled from my last school. "Nice to meet—"

"All right, young ones. To your seats, and put those phones away," an overly-caffeinated voice commands.

Our World History teacher strolls in, an older man so tall and lean he might have once played in the NBA. He's wearing designer glasses and a suit—the guidance counselor had been wearing a suit too, so I guess it isn't just the students who Oak Academy forces to wear a uniform. Faculty gets the treatment too.

Chairs drag across the floor, and Emmett sits up straighter. I do the same, watching in silence as our instructor sets his leather laptop bag on the dark wood desk and gives the room a cursory glance.

Cursory, that is, until he finds me.

"Right. I was told we'd have a new pupil today." Adjusting his glasses, he looks over at me. "I'm Mr. Robertson, and this is World History. Remind me of your name?"

I stand up and fold my hands in front of me. "Camilla Hanson, sir."

Students are turning in my direction, checking me out again, but I pretend not to notice. Mr. Robertson just nods, and I'm glad to return his neutral eye contact.

"Great. Are you familiar with Indian maritime history?"

His tone is that of someone who's assessing me, which I expected. Everyone wants to know what the new girl is capable of as soon as possible.

But while I've technically been out of school for a month or so, I've been keeping up with my studying. "Yes," I answer.

"Tell me about how it began, then." He's saying it casually, but it's obvious he's trying to gauge both my knowledge and how accurately I've presented myself.

I pause, feeling my cheeks burn with all the attention that's on me right now. "Do you want me to start with Before the Common Era? Indus Valley trade with Mesopotamia and all of that, or the later establishment of the navy...?"

"You can skip ahead to the fifteenth-century European discovery of India's spice wealth and subsequent trade routes," Robertson says, but his tone is less searching and more interested now.

"Sure," I say, mentally choosing my words carefully. "The official start of the spice trade is generally credited to Vasco da Gama's voyage from Portugal to Calicut, or Kozhikode, in 1497, when he initially returned with a cargo of," I think for a second, then nod to myself as I continue, "pepper and cinnamon. After that, Portugal had a monopoly on the ocean route to India for almost a decade unchallenged. But in terms of 'discovering' India's spice wealth, as you put it, sixty-five years earl—"

"That's enough." Mr. Robertson, who's been raising his eyebrows along with every word I speak, cuts me off before I can finish. "You may sit back down."

My mouth closes at once, and I wait for him to turn his back to the class and begin writing on the blackboard to mutter under my breath, "Sixty-five years earlier, the Chinese Muslim adventurer Ma Huan visited India on one of his expeditions. He wrote all about their spices and other aspects of their economy, politics, and culture in his book, *The Overall Survey of the Ocean's Shores*, published in 1451."

I'd read about Ma Huan in a high-adventure historical YA novel, and after falling into a Wikipedia hole, realized a lot of it was actually true—except for the part where Huan was a girl. Whoever said you can't learn anything about the real world from YA clearly never read the right books.

Beside me, Emmett lets out a quiet chuckle, and when I glance over at him, I realize he has a cute set of dimples.

"This class should really be called *Eurocentric* World History," he whispers.

I grin. Ally acquired.

The remainder of the class passes without anything eventful happening, and after I pack up my bag, I find myself walking out along with Emmett. He's been nice to me so far, so when we break into the corridor, I ask, "Do you know where Lab 4 is? I have AP Bio with Domnizky next, and I don't want to get lost on the way there."

"Sure thing," he says brightly, pointing as he starts to direct me. "Just go left at the end of this hall and across the glass walkway to the science building. Once you're there, you'll see the numbers on the doors. Pretty easy."

Laughter trickles into my ears, background noise that grows into what sounds like a full-on taunt. A shiver runs between my shoulder blades when I look toward the source. It's a group of girls, all with shining hair and perfect white teeth, some hiding their smiles behind well-manicured nails, others not even bothering.

At their center, with a pretty girl on his arm like an accessory, is Hunter Beck.

I freeze. My eyes meet his, and there it is again—that familiar lazy smirk spreading across his lips. Why is he looking my way? Are they all laughing at me? Did he tell everyone I saw him screwing some random girl in his pool last night? That I didn't run? That I liked what I saw?

Or is it that both my mom and I work for his family? That I'm "the help"?

Shame rises in me, flooding my cheeks with heat and crushing the breath in my lungs. Hunter whispers something into the ear of the girl he's with, and she looks at me and throws her head back in a throaty laugh.

I'm not imagining it. They are talking about me.

Is there a sinkhole that can suck me underground right now? An invisibility cloak I can put on? I want to run, but that will probably just make it worse. My shoulders start to slump when I feel a comforting weight wrap around them. It's Emmett's arm, I realize.

"Hey, Camilla?" he says, pitching his voice low and steering me gently in the other direction. "Don't pay attention to them. They act like that every day. A bunch of hyenas in lipstick, with Jockface McGee as their sidekick."

He seems genuine enough that I let myself relax a little, and he pulls his arm away to adjust his messenger bag, like he's suddenly all shy about touching me.

Smiling over at him, I say, "Thanks for that. I just—it's my first day, and I don't know anyone here, and it feels like everyone is staring at me."

"Honestly, they kind of are. But it's just because you're new. It'll wear off."

I nod and realize we've reached the glass walkway to the next building. "Well. Guess this is my stop," I joke awkwardly, gesturing at the corridor.

"Cool. Good luck in bio," Emmett says, turning to go.

"Wait!" I call out. "Um, do you know if there's someplace I can charge my phone? I just realized it's dead."

"There're outlets in the lab, and you can just plug it in

there. Domnizky won't mind." His brow crinkles. "Do you want to borrow my lightning cable?"

"That's okay, I have what I need." No need to tell him it's because my phone is so ancient that a standard USB cord won't actually work for me.

"Cool cool," he says, then hesitates. "Do you want to maybe give me your number? Since we have that group project for history? I'll text you so you can save me to your contacts once you're powered back up. I mean, if you want. No pressure."

Aww, he really is nice, isn't he? "I'd love that. I already consider you a friend."

He grins, and I tap my cell number into his phone before we part ways.

It's only as I turn around to head to the science building that I see Hunter out of the corner of my eye. He's leaning against a locker as if he's got nowhere else to be right now, and I can't help wonder if it's just a coincidence or if he stood there watching me give Emmett my phone number.

Either way, I hope Hunter saw the exchange—maybe it will make him realize that I'm perfectly capable of making friends here and that his shit-talk is a waste of time. God knows I have enough to worry about at my new school already.

I wish Hunter would just leave me the hell alone.

Chapter Four

CAMILLA

I've never been the kind of student who can just goof off in class, stare out the window daydreaming, or doodle in my notebook and then still do well on homework and exams. Nope. My straight As are the result of treating school like it's my job. I stay focused, hit the books hard, and never lose sight of my long-term goals. Luckily, I love learning—I'm a total Ravenclaw. In other words: nerd alert.

For the next few hours, I'm so engrossed in my courses that my classes fly right by, and then suddenly it's my lunch period.

The Oak Academy cafeteria is packed with faces I don't know and so loud I can barely hear myself think. I'm sure Emmett wouldn't mind if I joined him, but I can't spot him *or* an empty table, and there's no way I'm going to walk up to a bunch of complete strangers and ask if I can sit with them. The thought of getting rejected is way too humiliating, and I have no idea what kind of rumors the gossip mill (a.k.a. Hunter Beck & Co.) have already managed to spread about me.

As I stand in the serving line, I debate my options. I could send Emmett a text with my freshly-charged phone, but it feels desperate. I just met the guy. I don't want to be sticking to him like glue already because I'm pathetic when it comes to social skills.

My stomach growls painfully, reminding me I've had nothing to eat since those Pop-Tarts four hours ago. As I look up at the menu on the wall, I'm totally overwhelmed. They have made-to-order salads and sandwiches, grilled organic veggies, a selection of steak, tuna, and chicken, vegan and gluten-free options, a wok and sushi bar... It's like a Las Vegas buffet. And since my scholarship covers all my meals and supplies on top of my tuition, I can choose whatever I want. But then my mother's jab last night about my weight echoes in my mind, and my appetite disappears.

In the end, I grab a granola bar and a banana and wolf them both down on my way to the library, where I plan to spend my lunch period studying. It seems like my best bet for now. Especially since my genius plan for getting the students at Oak Academy to leave me alone and forget I exist is to keep a low profile.

After what happened at my last school, I need to be as invisible as possible.

The library is in the east wing, and it's love at first sight for me. Huge floor-to-ceiling windows let in tons of light, and the tall wooden bookshelves are packed with volumes but still neat as a pin. In the center of the room, gleaming silver MacBooks sit open on study tables to offer students access to the library's card catalog, the internet, and word-processing programs. More tables and chairs are placed at intervals along walls hung with framed art, and there are comfy couches you can sit on to read—a far cry from the library at my last school, which was a harsh fluorescent bulb-lit room with hard plastic chairs and a handful of particle board bookshelves.

As I work on my lab bio homework, I breathe in deeply, basking in this reprieve from my pent-up nerves and tension. As much as I'd like to chalk it up to first day jitters, I know deep down that Hunter is the real reason I'm wound up so tightly.

What has he told people about me? And how many Oak Academy students already know I walked in on him and some girl *in flagrante* in the Becks' pool?

Ugh, why am I even thinking about this right now? The only Beck that deserves my attention is Harry, not his manwhore of a brother.

I leave a few minutes before the bell rings and make that call to SDG&E's bill pay line, only to find out we owe $150 for our overdue bill, the late fee, and the reconnection charge. It stings to know I'm going to have to cover it with my babysitting money, but I know that if I leave it to my mother, it'll be days before we have electricity again. Thankfully, the Becks pay me well. It'll only take a few days to earn it back.

Heading through the halls toward English, the temptation to constantly look over my shoulder returns full force. My ears are pricked, listening for the whispering and giggles that surrounded Hunter this morning, but mercifully, I make it to class without running into him again.

In fact, I don't see him for the rest of the day. Luck is on my side.

My last class is debate, which I've been looking forward to. I've always hated public speaking, but this is more about articulating a specific point of view against an opponent—while having to think on your feet—which is a skill I'd love to have when things get ugly with my mom. Not to mention, the class will look great on my transcripts for college, especially if I make it to any of the big debate competitions around the county this year. Let's just say my nonexistent athletic abilities have left my list of extracurricular activities a bit lacking.

The teacher, Ms. Spencer, welcomes me with a smile and a textbook when I walk into the room and tells me to take any empty seat, which puts me instantly at ease. Then she tells the class my name and leaves it at that—no corny introduction, no "Why don't you tell us a little bit about yourself, Camilla," no on-the-spot interrogation in front of the other students to see how smart I am (or am not).

As she begins her lecture, pacing around the room to make eye contact with each of us in turn, I can't help but notice her hoop earrings have little skulls dangling from them. I love her. My hand quickly starts to ache from all the notes I'm scribbling.

"And now it's time for the fun part," she announces. "You all should have studied the handouts you received last week on the imaginary country of Spencylvania, so let's debate the pros and cons of admitting them."

Ms. Spencer then calls up a student named Sarah to advocate for Spencylvania's entry into the United Nations, assigning her the title of speaker for the United Nations Security Council. Her job is to recommend Spencylvania to the General Assembly (the rest of the class) and explain why. A tall, visibly shy kid named Jazz is then assigned the opposing position of a General Assembly member seeking to block the rest of the assembly from achieving a two-thirds majority vote to admit Spencylvania.

We, the class, are supposed to vote after the debate has concluded. But halfway through, Ms. Spencer makes Sarah and Jazz switch places and debate the opposing side.

Even though I'm excused from participating today, Ms. Spencer gives me a copy of the handout from last week, and

I find myself completely engaged in the exercise. We're not just learning how to present arguments, we're learning how the United Nations works and what kinds of things go into their decision-making processes. My brain is firing on so many levels.

For the second half of class, we're supposed to split into groups of two and research an assigned topic in preparation for a team debate exercise later in the week. My stomach is all butterflies with excitement, but then the door creaks open, interrupting Ms. Spencer's words.

Every set of eyes in the room turns toward the door, including mine. To my abject horror, I see Hunter Beck stroll in like he's walking down a red carpet in front of an adoring crowd of fans rather than showing up twenty minutes late to class.

A smug smile curves his lips, but none of his charm seems to carry any weight with Ms. Spencer. She's frowning, and I catch her shaking her head to herself before she says, "Please take your seat, Mr. Beck, and know that this is your third strike. The next time you're late, I'll be sending you directly to the principal's office."

"Just came from there, actually," Hunter says with a shrug, sliding into his seat.

"We were about to start on a group activity." The teacher's sharp eyes scan the room. When they settle on me, my heart begins to pound, my thoughts a panicked circle of *please not me, please not me.* "You can be Camilla's partner."

I nod at Ms. Spencer, every ounce of focus I have going into keeping my face neutral. This class had started out so well, but now it's taken a turn for the worse. The teacher hands out our topics and then instructs us to get into our groups and begin.

Hunter's eyes meet mine from across the room, and I

bristle under their bright blue sparkle. What is it about me that's always so damn amusing to him? God, he's so full of himself. Nothing but scorn and arrogance for us "little people." I can't stand him.

I'm already on high alert as he saunters over to the desk next to mine. Every ounce of him oozes pure confidence, from the way he carries himself to how his blazer hugs his perfect shoulders and biceps. The haphazardly knotted tie and casually disheveled hair only add to his obnoxious hotness in a way that should be criminal.

It takes everything I have not to get up and leave. I can't believe Hunter Beck has once again found a way to ruin the brightest part of my day.

"How's it going?" he says, dragging the adjacent chair closer to mine. My fingers are clutching my pen so tightly it hurts.

"Fine," I say. "We should start on the assignment." My voice is steady and controlled as I start to unfold the slip of paper with our debate topic on it.

"Hey, um, Hunter?" the girl sitting behind Hunter interrupts. Her golden hair falls in perfect beachy waves, and she tucks a strand behind her ear with a smile.

Lazily, Hunter cranes his head around to look at her. "Hey, um, Hillary?" he replies, copying her speech pattern exactly.

She giggles at this, and so do two of her equally pretty friends at neighboring desks. "I was just wondering if you'll be at the party? On Friday?" Hillary touches Hunter's shoulder, then trails her fingers down his arm. He doesn't flinch, and judging by her casual groping of him, it seems like they've hooked up before. "I was thinking of going, but...I don't want to if you won't be there."

"Me neither," one of the other girls chimes in. "Maybe we can all hang out together. All *three* of us."

The innuendo is anything but subtle. God, has he slept with the whole school?

Hunter just shrugs noncommittally. "If you want to go, you should go. I might stop by."

I clear my throat loudly and give them all the side-eye. "We have work to do."

Hillary makes an irritated huffing sound and whips around, blonde hair flying. Her friends lean closer, and they all start whispering. Probably about what a troll I am.

Turning back to me again, Hunter crosses his arms over his chest. "So why are you even taking debate? You want to be a lawyer or something?"

"I might," I say just to spite him.

"Ha." The laugh is short and clipped. "Sorry to break it to you, but only money-hungry liars and scumbags are allowed to be lawyers. You're way too good a person to be going into law."

Heat reaches my cheeks at the backhanded compliment. "You don't know what kind of person I am."

"Yeah, I do," he says. "You babysit my brother, remember?"

"Hunterrr," Hillary interrupts again, passing her phone to him. "This is what I was thinking of wearing to the party."

He looks at the photo on the screen, that lazy, rakish smile back on his lips. "Yeow. You really want me to go that badly?"

I can only imagine what he's looking at. Some trashy minidress and spike heels? Lacy lingerie? Handcuffs?

"Do you mind saving this conversation for later?" I say to Hunter. "Believe it or not, some of us actually care about our grades."

"Excuse me, who even are you?" Her nostrils flare, and

she waves her hand in front of her made-up face. "Never mind. I don't care."

She turns back to her friends, and they resume chatting —not about their debate topics, might I add—and shooting me some powerful stink eye. I pretend not to notice.

Meanwhile, Hunter doesn't even bother to hide the fact that he's texting on his cell phone under the desk. I know I could tattle to Ms. Spencer, but then I'd have to deal with him retaliating later, and that's the last thing I want. Still, I'm not going to let him ruin this class—or the entire school—for me.

So I do what I've always done: keep my head down and work my hardest. If he's not going to participate, I'll just start researching our topic by myself.

I'm not going to let Hunter Beck throw me off my game.

But as I smooth out the folded scrap of paper, I can't help letting out a dry laugh at our assigned topic: *Is marriage an outdated institution?*

I have a feeling I know exactly where Hunter's opinions on the subject lie.

Chapter Five

CAMILLA

 hen the bell rings, I'm the first to shoot up out of my seat, and I immediately begin packing up my things. Reaching the door as fast as humanly possible is the goal. But after slinging my bag over my shoulder, I only make it two steps before Hunter says, "Aren't you going to say goodbye?"

I halt, pivoting to face him and totally confused. Seriously, what is up with this guy? Why does he even care when he's been nothing but rude to me?

Then, in his hands, I see it. My spiral notebook, held out like it's a peace offering. "You forgot this."

My eyebrows draw together—is Hunter actually being decent to me?

Still unable to interpret his intentions, I tentatively reach for the notebook. "Thanks," I murmur, taking it.

Other students are looking over, and some—like Hillary —don't even bother to pretend they're not interested in watching Hunter slaughter the new lamb at school.

"No problem," he says. "See you later, Camilla."

Hearing him say my name makes my stomach twist. His

eyes burn into me as I slip the notebook in my bag, and I can still feel him watching me as I dart out of the classroom.

After a quick stop at my locker, I head out of Oak Academy along with the other kids who are streaming down the front steps and then start walking toward the bus stop shelter. The plastic enclosure stands next to the school's parking lot, but all the benches inside are taken. I'm left standing outside sweating in the direct sunlight, head bent over my cell phone as I wait.

Before I even realize what I'm doing, I'm navigating over to Stanford's familiar cardinal-and-white website, sighing as I scroll through pictures of the campus and all its smiling college students sprawled out on the grass. My dream of going there is half the reason I babysit and hoard all my earnings—and I say half because I genuinely like taking care of Harrison. But even with my babysitting money, I'm still going to need a scholarship. Tuition is $50,000 per year, and that's before housing and living expenses. The state schools are a lot less expensive, sure, but they're also less prestigious.

Suddenly, loud music blares, and I see a flash of white in the corner of my eye. My head snaps up, and I find myself looking at a tinted-window BMW that I've seen enough times to recognize it immediately. Hunter leaning back in the driver's seat isn't unexpected, but the fact that the passenger-side window is down and that he's looking right at me is.

I'm not sure if I should wave or wait for him to say something, so I just stand there like an idiot, unable to tear my eyes away from his, thinking he might actually offer me a ride. We're going to the same place after all, and it would be a nice change not having to ride a hot, packed bus that takes twice as long to get to his neighborhood.

He'd been nice to me at the end of class, so maybe...

With a squeal of tires, he zooms onto the street, his windows rolling up before he speeds off. God, what a jerk. He saw me waiting here, and he knows exactly where I'm going. Guess he didn't want anyone to see him fraternizing with "the help."

I remember the girls from class, glaring and whispering, and the ones in the hall this morning, all laughing at me. By the time the bus rolls up, I'm full-on stewing.

In the end, I'm glad I didn't get a ride with Hunter. After all, I have some urgent personal errands to attend to —the kind I'd be embarrassed to have to explain to him.

Hopping off the bus a stop earlier than usual, I duck into a branch of my mom's bank and deposit cash into her checking account, then immediately dial the power company and spend the walk to the Becks' house on my phone. I've had to do this kind of thing so many times that I've got my mom's debit card memorized at this point, and I'm beyond relieved when the woman at SDG&E confirms that the payment went through. She assures me that a tech will reconnect us within the next few hours, which means our electricity will be back on by the time I get home tonight.

I make one more stop at a corner store to grab a bag of salt and vinegar chips and an iced tea. It isn't the healthiest after-school snack, but it's what I'm craving, and besides, I need fuel for the long, sweaty walk I have ahead of me.

My school bag feels like an anvil on my back when I finally turn on to Hunter's street. His neighborhood is all giant houses that resemble modern art made of steel and glass and perfectly manicured landscaping, which none of the owners actually maintain themselves. That's what they pay people like my mom and me for. And Mr. Martinez, whom I wave to when I spot him mowing the lawn at the Becks' neighbor's house.

Sweat trickles along my hairline as I walk down the Becks' long driveway of fancy paving stones, and I remove my blazer and loosen my tie so I can breathe a little easier. I see Hunter's BMW parked in front of the garage, and I linger next to the car for a moment as I fish the house keys from my bag. I'm sorely tempted to drag their sharp edges across the flawless, pearly-white paint, but of course I'd never actually do it. The CCTV would incriminate me, and having a record for destruction of personal property probably wouldn't impress the Stanford admissions committee.

Unlocking the door, I step into the Becks' foyer and hang my bag and jacket on the fancy rustic wood coatrack. The ice cold air conditioning envelops me, and I let out a sigh of pleasure. I'm excited to see Harry, but I can't help praying his older brother stays out of my sight for the rest of the day.

I've had it up to here with Hunter Beck.

Chapter Six

CAMILLA

he thing that has always struck me most about the Becks' house is how impersonal it is. They had this place custom built over a decade ago, yet it gives off a vibe similar to a luxury hotel. Expensive abstract art on the walls, sleek, modern furniture, lots of neutral beige and black tones. There's a big family portrait hung in the front foyer, but everyone is stiff and posed. Even little Harry has a serious face in it.

What's missing? Personality, I suppose. I've seen the places where my mom has kept house before, homes for the upper middle class ranging up to the very wealthy. They usually have some indication of human warmth; splashes of color, little tchotchkes on the shelves, or messy piles of books and magazines. Not here.

Then again, I can't really speak from my own experience. My mom and I never stay anywhere long enough for our apartments to feel like they're more than just places to eat and sleep and breathe. Half the time, I don't even unpack my moving boxes. And to be honest, there's no previous town I'd want to return to; no four walls I truly miss.

As I pass the living room, I see Hunter kneeling on the floor with Harrison.

"You're late," Hunter says, barely glancing at me as I walk by. "It's 3:30 p.m.."

The urge to point out the fact that he could have easily given me a ride is strong, but I push it down. "I had a few errands to run. And I'm technically not late, I just usually get here early because of the bus schedule. Harry, I'll be right back."

"Touché," Hunter responds, but I'm already heading down the hallway toward the huge kitchen.

My mom is there, rinsing dishes in the copper farmhouse-style sink. I'd randomly mentioned to Mrs. Beck how pretty it is one time, and she told me the name of the company that made it, but when I looked online just to dream about owning such a fancy item myself someday, I found out that it costs twenty-five hundred dollars. Yeah. For a kitchen *sink*. It boggles the mind.

"Hey, Mom," I say, putting my half-empty iced tea bottle in the fridge.

I'm practically drooling at the smell of chicken roasting in the oven, and I see a pan of wine sauce on the stove and chopped vegetables on a cutting board waiting to be cooked. This is part of her job, I get it, but I can't help wishing she'd make dinner at home once in a while. She's good at it. But I guess it's too hard to work all day and then come home and work more. I'm lucky I get to have leftovers at the Becks' sometimes.

"Mom?" I repeat. "How's your day going?"

She hasn't acknowledged me. Just keeps rinsing the dishes, then loading them into the dishwasher, going back and forth on autopilot. When I step closer, I notice how her eyes are glazed and distant. It's how she usually looks after several glasses of bourbon—like she's somewhere far away and just totally numb to reality. Except she doesn't smell like booze, and as far as I know, she doesn't drink on the job.

Which means she's either ignoring me on purpose or something entirely different is giving her those unfocused eyes and mechanical movements. Maybe she's stressed about SDG&E.

"I called the power company and got the bill taken care of, so you don't need to worry," I tell her.

Suddenly, she whips her gaze in my direction, zeroing in on the bag of salt and vinegar chips in my hand. "Are you really eating those, Milla? Fried foods have carcinogens. Did you even check to see how much saturated fat is in them?"

"I didn't eat the whole bag," I say defensively, dropping what's left of them in the trash before she can inspect the nutrition label and give me a lecture about the evils of processed snack foods.

She shakes her head. "You need to pick something healthier next time. And fix a snack for the kid. He said he was hungry earlier."

"You couldn't make him something?" I ask, immediately worried for Harry.

A scowl of indignation crosses her face. "That's *your* job, not mine. You should be grateful I'm here to cover for you during the week."

No *How was your first day at the new school?*, no *Thanks for covering that electricity bill*. Just the usual criticism and straight-up judgment.

She's right about one thing, though. Harry gets home from school at 1:30 p.m., and I usually don't get here until three, though my shift "officially" starts at 3:30 p.m. If my mom wasn't able to keep half an eye on him for that crucial time gap, the Becks would just hire another nanny, and I'd have no job and no income.

Still, she has zero excuse for not cutting up an apple or even handing the kid a banana. Harry's probably starving.

As I start slicing kiwi and strawberries, I have to bite my tongue to keep from pushing the point with my mom any further. If we start arguing, I know it'll escalate, and when my mom is pissed, she gets loud. I'd die if any of the Becks walked in on us.

On top of that, we'd probably be fired, and we can't afford to lose our jobs right now. Especially after the Incident—though I'm sure the only reason we haven't been given the boot already is because Hunter's father doesn't know what happened.

"Take the chicken out of the oven when the timer rings." Mom wipes her hands on a dish towel and smooths her shirt down. "I need to head out to the Muirwoods'."

"Sure. See you later."

After checking that the timer still has almost an hour left to go, I arrange the fruit I've cut up in the form of a smiley face on the plate. Kiwi slices for eyes, strawberries for the lips, and some goldfish-shaped pretzels and cubes of white cheddar for the hair. Harry will love it.

I head out with the plate to go find him, hoping Hunter is gone. The route from the kitchen to the living room takes me past a room called the study, even though there are hardly any books, and I never see anyone studying there. Through the closed door, I can hear Mr. Beck's laugh, his voice smooth and confident as he talks real estate business with someone he's got on speakerphone. Mrs. Beck's been away on a wellness retreat in Idlewild, but she'll be back Wednesday morning.

These parents—even when they're home, they're still a

million miles away. It's sad how alone Harrison is all the time. And Hunter, too, although I assume he's old enough at this point not to care.

I smile when I spot Harry sitting on the floor in the living room, Legos spread out on the rug and sorted into piles according to color. But one look at his downcast eyes while he absently snaps Legos together, and I deflate. He'd looked perky when I first walked in, but left here all alone, it's almost like he's shrunken into himself.

This shitty day has spared no one, it seems.

"Hey, Harry." I kneel on the rug across from him and hold out the plate with the fruit between us. "Look what I brought."

He grins at the happy face on the plate, then up at me, his small fingers immediately reaching for a slice of kiwi. "Thanks, Milla."

"Sorry my mom didn't make you anything. Sometimes she's worse than Umbridge." I snag a pretzel fish and pop one into my mouth. "So what are you building? Can I help?"

I receive a very enthusiastic nod, which tells me I'm on the right track to perking him up. "It's a castle! But I don't think I have enough Legos for the second tower..."

"Hmm, let's see." I take in the scene, doing a quick mental calculation. "Does it have to be this big of a castle? If we make it smaller on the bottom, you'll have enough bricks left to build another tower on this side."

He considers. "That could work," he says and proceeds to dismantle the base he'd built. We snack on cheese and fruit and get to it.

It's when I'm watching him reach over to grab a blue brick that I notice it.

The inside of his bicep has a red mark on it. I instinctively grab his wrist and gently turn it so I can get a better look at his upper arm. Looks like a handprint almost, and the more I look, the harder I frown.

"What happened here, bud? Did someone grab you?"

"Um..." He looks down and bites his small lip. "I think it was at school. When I was playing in the jungle gym with my friends."

My breath leaves my nose in a sharp hiss. I have no reason to doubt him, but still, I can't help worrying that he's not telling me the whole truth.

"Harry?" I say, fussing with his hair a little. "You know you can tell me if there's ever anything wrong. Right?"

He nods but doesn't meet my eyes. "I know," he says. "I'm okay."

I want to say more, but then the timer in the kitchen goes off.

"You wanna go see if dinner's ready to come out of the oven?" I ask.

"Sure!"

He jumps up and bolts down the hall, leaving me to hurry after him.

I need to talk to Mrs. Beck about his arm, but it'll have to wait until Wednesday. It could be that I'm overreacting, but I'd rather be safe than sorry. And unfortunately, I know Mr. Beck will just brush my concerns aside—the last time Harry got hurt (spraining his ankle while we were playing badminton), I'd begged Mr. Beck to take him to the doctor to get checked out, but he'd insisted that Harry was fine. He said you had to "let boys be boys" rather than coddling them every time they scraped a knee.

Actually... I can't believe I'm even considering it, but maybe Hunter is the one to talk to. He might act like a total jackass to me, but he doesn't screw around when it comes to his baby brother.

After I get the chicken and veggies out of the oven and

leave them on the countertop to cool, I set Harrison up at the table with his math workbook from school and tell him I'm going to run upstairs to the bathroom, which I'm not entirely lying about—I am going to go—but I'll be making a slight detour first.

I tiptoe up the stairs to go talk to Hunter, but halfway there, a faint sound slows me down, and I freeze on the steps.

A harsh breath, and then another one. A slight moan.

Is someone hurt? Is that Hunter?

Mrs. Beck is out of town, Mr. Beck is on a work call, and Harry is down in the kitchen counting out two plus two on his fingers. It has to be Hunter.

Another quiet moan, and now I'm positive he's the culprit. I'm also positive it's not an injury forcing those sounds out of his mouth. He sounds exactly like he did last night when he was screwing that girl in the pool. Breathless, desperate, and undeniably taking pleasure in whatever he's doing. Or I guess I should say, *whomever*.

God, who'd he bring home this time? Do I even want to know? He left the door ajar too, and to get to the bathroom, I have to walk past his room and risk being seen by whomever he's banging in there. Or worse, risk getting an eyeful of another gross display of Hunter's exhibitionism.

But as his breathing starts to get faster, I realize there aren't any female moans accompanying his, and if last night was anything to go by, no girl stays quiet when he's pounding her. Which means he's alone in there.

Which means he's masturbating.

Suddenly, I'm too embarrassed to move, worried that the stairs will creak and he'll stick his head out into the hall and see me standing here like some pervert.

What is his problem, anyway? Couldn't he at least wait until tonight when everyone is in bed and I'm all the way across town? Are his hormones really raging so hard that they obliterate any sense of common decency?

Still, there's a part of me that's straining to listen to him make those noises. And a tightness, low in my belly, aches like a hunger pang. I hear a slight hiss and then realize it was me who made it, so I turn on my heel and run back downstairs where I belong, hoping Hunter's too distracted to catch the sound of my retreating footsteps.

Chapter Seven

CAMILLA

ll the way home, my thoughts are a swirl of moans and explicit images, and there's nothing I can do to erase what I've seen (and heard) of Hunter Beck over the past few days.

I see him finishing inside that girl in the pool last night, hard and fast; fingering another one in the front seat of her car while they sit parked at the curb; and groping yet a different girl in the billiard room in the basement, though that one was a month ago. Each time, I've noticed that he seems distant, detached... Still, I figure he must know what he's doing—the girls always sound like they're enjoying themselves, at least.

What would happen if I let him do something like that to me?

The question is there before I can stop myself from wondering, and just like that, the ache between my legs grows stronger. I'm ashamed to admit it, but facts are facts: I'm horny, and Hunter Beck is responsible. That's what I truly hate about all of this. Because he's not a good person. I don't even like him. It's just pure animal lust.

God, he's irritating. At least he can't read my thoughts.

With a squeal, the bus stops a few blocks from our apartment, and I let the cool ocean breeze snap me out of my helpless state of arousal. I still have forty dollars left in my wallet, so I stop at the little grocery store on the way home and grab a few essentials: milk, eggs, bread, cheese, some fresh produce, and a few frozens. It'll tide us over until Mom gets paid on Friday, and I can whip up some pasta and tomato sauce for dinner tonight.

When I get home, I see a few bright yellow envelopes on the floor that must have been pushed under the door earlier. I drop my keys in the bowl and set my bags down before gathering the envelopes up, eyeing the property manager's return address stamp in the corner. I'm guessing by the alarming color of the envelopes that this can't be good news. They're all unopened, though, and I can't read any of these letters until my mom does. Which probably won't be tonight, judging by the sound of her faint snores echoing off the walls of the living room.

Dread cuts into my gut as I tiptoe to the kitchen to put away the groceries. I can see the empty bottle of Jim Beam she left on the counter, which means she's out and will be in an extra bad mood if I wake her up.

I should rip into those envelopes right now, find out if we're being evicted rather than waiting for her to dump the bad news on me on a random day. But the memory of her hand hitting my cheek, leaving it hot and throbbing afterward, holds me back.

Slowly, I pad to her side and unfold the blanket draped over the couch to cover her with. She stirs but doesn't wake. I grab her empty glass and take it back to the kitchen, where I wash it and then put the liquor bottle in the recycle container. Then I make a quick dinner of spaghetti and frozen peas and pop the leftovers in the fridge.

My shoulder radiates relief when I drop my book bag on my bedroom floor. It's after nine now, and I wish I could just turn in early, but I have homework to do first. Unfortunately, the Wi-Fi, unknowingly provided gratis by our neighbors (whose password is *password*), is acting spotty. Yep. It's definitely not my day. Still, it was a smart move to spend my lunch period doing homework. Maybe I'll be able to finish up before midnight.

I change into pajamas and then sprawl out on my bed, flipping open my notebook to look over my list of assignments. AP Calc is going to take the longest, so I tackle that first.

My schedule is brutal sometimes, but school is all I have going for me to see myself out of this shitty life. Getting into a college like Stanford or one of the UC schools—or even one of the Cal State universities—is my best bet at being able to take care of myself and build a life of my own. I'd love to not constantly be moving from place to place all the time, stressing about money and whether my mom is going to need a new liver one of these days. If we're evicted right now, will we even stay here in La Jolla, or will we have to go somewhere else entirely?

For once, I actually want to stay where we are, though it's only because I know a diploma from Oak Academy will go a long way toward getting me into one of my dream schools. On the other hand, moving away would mean I'd never have to deal with Hunter's bullshit again.

Hunter.

I bury my face in my hands, trying to will away the image of his bare chest in the pool. The way he'd looked at me. Those damn sex sounds yesterday and today.

There's that burning tightness between my legs again as

soon as I think of him. The moans I heard hours ago flood into my head, making my pulse race, and suddenly I'm thinking about what would've happened if I'd been brave enough to interrupt him. He'd have zero shame about it, I'm sure, and would probably use the moment to humiliate me some more. I know that, and even still...I'm curious. He was looking at me while he fucked someone else in the pool. Was he thinking about me when he jerked off too?

Why am I even pondering this?

Of all people to have this effect on me, why does it have to be Hunter? And why do I have to keep running into him when his dick is out of his pants? And why does my traitorous body keep responding like it's something erotic and not utterly mortifying?

Suddenly, I realize why my mom hasn't opened those letters. Sometimes it's just better not to know the truth. As long as doubt exists, the things that we're most afraid of having to face can be both true and false.

Maybe I should start calling those unopened envelopes Schrodinger's mail.

My phone vibrates with a notification, and I see a preview of a text from Emmett on the screen. I swipe it open and smile as I read, *How'd the rest of your day go? Find all your classes okay?*

He's so nice and in that genuine way that comes from growing up with a healthy, well-adjusted support system. I bet Emmett's mom asks him about school over the dinner table, bakes him cookies, and doesn't tell him he's getting fat.

Then I berate myself for being jealous of things I don't even know are true.

Rather than get involved in an hours-long textversation, I figure it'll be faster to just call Emmett and have a quick chat, so I dial him. He picks up on the first ring.

"How goes it, new girl?" he asks.

"Ha. It's fine," I tell him, keeping my voice low. "I'm dying over some AP Calc so I can't talk long, I just figured a call would be faster."

"I feel you on that, and I'm only in Algebra 1," he says. "Speaking of which, wanna come over and study sometime this week? We should get started on that paper for World History."

"Are your parents cool with me coming over late?" I ask. "I babysit this kid after school, and I don't get out till 7:30 p.m.."

"Seven thirty is fine. They won't mind. Actually, don't laugh, but the whole thing was my mom's idea. I told her about you, and she said I had to invite you over."

"Oh really," I say. "What exactly did you tell her about me?"

"Nothing. Just that you're new and you didn't really know anybody. She said to ask what your favorite kind of cookies are."

Ha! Called it. "She doesn't have to do that. I don't want her to go through all the trouble..."

"It's cool. She loves mothering everyone. So when are you free?"

"Wednesday is good," I tell him. "And any cookies containing chocolate are fine in my book."

"Wednesday it is."

We talk for a few more minutes and then get off the phone. I may have had a day from hell, but I'm grateful to find that I've made a real friend, and when I turn back to my homework, I still have a smile on my face.

Chapter Eight

CAMILLA

*E*mmett's gorgeous, Spanish-style house is in one of the family-friendly neighborhoods a few blocks from downtown La Jolla, and there are so many palm trees in the front yard that I turn to him and joke, "Are you sure your house is back there, or are we going on a jungle adventure?"

"This'll be an adventure, all right," he jokes back.

As soon as we step through the door, I can feel the warmth of the place—and not just because his mother is waiting there to greet us with a smile.

"You must be Camilla!" she says, sweeping me into a surprise hug. "Come in, come in. I have the cookies all ready."

"Thank you so much. You really didn't have to do that," I say.

She waves my comment away. "The only thing I don't seem to burn to a crisp is baked goods, so please enjoy them. They're my pride and joy."

"She's not kidding," Emmett tells me under his breath. "Next to her cookies, I'm chopped liver."

"Oh hush, you," his mom says, playfully whacking him on the arm. "So Camilla, where did you move here from?"

"L.A.," I tell her. "And lots of other places before that. But we've actually been here for almost four years now. I'm only new to Oak Academy."

"Well, I hope you love it. It's a great school," she says.

We follow her into the kitchen, which is done up in brightly colored Mexican tiles and smells like heaven. The glass doors to the backyard are open, and even though it's dark out, I can see a little fountain out there that's making soothing trickling sounds. I sink into one of the chairs at the table and let out a deep sigh. This is nice.

Emmett's mom bustles over to the fridge and asks us, "Would you rather have milk, coffee, or tea?"

Glancing over, I notice she's tall, like he is, with the same big hazel eyes and high cheekbones. She's in designer jeans and a vintage Rolling Stones T-shirt, which makes sense since Emmett mentioned that she works from home as a CPA.

"Coffee would be great if you have decaf," I say. "And cream. Thank you."

"It's just from the Keurig," she adds. "Nothing fancy, if that's okay?"

"That's perfect," I tell her.

"Make me one too, pretty please," Emmett chimes in, loading up a plate full of cookies from the cooling rack on the stove.

The chocolatey, sugary scent is making my mouth water, and I want to devour them immediately, but I remind myself to wait until the coffee finishes brewing.

On the walls, I see pictures everywhere. Emmett, his siblings, and his parents, always smiling and laughing whether it be at the beach, on a hike, or in a foreign city in front of some monument or fancy tourist attraction. A real family.

"We do a big summer vacation every year," Emmett says, coming up beside me with the plate of cookies. "Have you been to any of these places?"

"Some." I point at the Grand Canyon, the Rocky Mountains, and Vegas. Only it wasn't because my mom was taking us on a family trip. A bitter laugh spills out of me. "But they weren't really vacations. They were just another one of our moves."

"Oh. Sorry." Emmett immediately looks away, and I feel bad for making him feel bad. "I didn't mean..."

"Don't feel bad," I reassure him. "It's not your fault I've moved around a lot." I pause for a second. "I think La Jolla is actually the longest we've stayed anywhere."

"Do you like it here?" Emmett asks, leading me into the living room.

An upright piano sits against the wall, and the eclectic, mismatched furniture is arranged around a brick fireplace. He sets the cookies on the coffee table and then plops into an overstuffed armchair, gesturing for me to sit wherever. I take the love seat.

"I do," I say, surprised to mean it. "The ocean breeze makes the weather really nice, the traffic's pretty light, and it's big enough without being, you know, gigantic. Which is way better than L.A. because it doesn't take an hour and a half on the bus to get from one side of town to another."

His mom returns with a tray loaded up with our coffee mugs, half-and-half, and two kinds of sugar. I thank her profusely, take a quick sip of my coffee, and then immediately dig into a still-warm cookie because I just can't wait any longer.

They're peanut butter with big chocolate chunks, the

gooey chocolate melting on my tongue. It's chewy perfection, and I almost let out a moan. "Oh my God," I mumble.

Emmett's mom grins at my expression. "Does that mean they're good?"

"They're perfect."

"I'm glad." She musses Emmett's curly hair, making him blush while he tries to maneuver out of her reach. "I'm gonna go get some corporate tax stuff done upstairs. Give a holler if you need anything."

I wait for her to leave the room and then look over at Emmett. "Wow."

He sighs. "I know. She's too much. It's embarrassing."

"Not at all," I tell him. "She's awesome. I mean, I wish my mom would bake cookies for my friends and tell me to call if I needed anything."

Then maybe I could actually invite people over instead of anxiously avoiding the subject at all costs.

"Oh, she *is* awesome," he admits. "But I wish she'd treat me like I'm almost eighteen, and not six."

"Maybe she would if you knew how to make your own coffee."

Emmett bursts into a contagious laugh, and I join in a little. All teasing aside, I can definitely relate to what he's saying, even if our moms treat us like babies for entirely different reasons—his because she clearly loves him, mine because she doesn't pay enough attention to me to realize I'm almost an adult. Except when it's convenient for her, that is.

"Is your dad the same way?" I ask, curious.

"Worse." Emmett rolls his eyes. "Imagine if a big teddy bear became a surgeon and then got a job at the children's hospital in San Diego. That's him. That's my dad."

I laugh because I am imagining it, and it's the cutest thing ever.

We get our laptops out—his silver and sleek, mine ancient and bulky. While his hums to life the second he opens it, mine takes a couple minutes and sounds like it's about to take off from the coffee table and shoot through the roof.

I definitely win at the sticker game though. Emmett's laptop has a single one for the Lakers, whereas mine is absolutely covered in everything, from a "Save the Waves" decal, to a smiling cartoon avocado, to the Deathly Hallows, to a *Six of Crows* quote. They give my computer a bit of flair while also hiding all the scratches on the plastic.

Our World History paper gets done pretty quickly, since Emmett knows his shit and so do I. After Hunter's assholery in debate class all this week, it's a huge relief to be able to do a group project with someone who actually participates.

The cookies definitely help, too, as does the coffee his mom brought. It's all so shockingly different from what I've known and the way I've been raised. How would I have turned out if I'd had parents who cared and didn't have to worry about money all the time? Would I be less guarded with people, more happy-go-lucky like Emmett is?

"By the way," he says, "there's a party on Friday. Wanna come?"

I don't look up from my English assignment. "I don't know. Is this the same party all the popular kids have been talking about?"

"Probably. Why?"

A long breath escapes my nose, and I set my reading aside. "Do you remember that first day? When we left World History and—"

"What, and Hunter and all those girls were laughing?" His brows come together. "I mean, I guess. But I wouldn't worry about them. Beck can be a dick, and those girls will do anything they think he wants, but it's not like you have to hang out with them."

"The thing is, I work for him. For his parents, I mean. I'm their nanny, and my mom is their housekeeper." I don't know why I'm comfortable spilling my secrets, but something about Emmett just makes me feel...safe. "I'm pretty sure he's told the whole school about it already, and if not, then they probably know I'm on a need-based scholarship. Don't pretend you don't know how most richie-rich La Jollans look at poor people like me."

Emmett frowns. "That's bullshit. But yeah, I get it. Last year, Kenny Johnson moved here from East L.A., and they gave him a shitty time until he single-handedly took the basketball team to nationals. Zero to hero in a second."

It's such a rich-person thing to despise those you assume are "below" you until they prove themselves. "Too bad I suck at basketball then," I say drily.

"So that's why you don't want to go to the party? Because Hunter might be there, acting like a dick?"

"Not just him. There was this...thing during debate class, and the girls who were there are going to the party too. They already seem to hate me for some reason," I say.

Emmett knows I'm not as well-off as he is, but he still doesn't know about my alcoholic mother or the Incident. Parties and I don't gel, and I'd rather stay home and read than go out to some rando's house and get wasted. He looks disappointed, though, and it was nice of him to invite me, so I add, "But I don't know. We'll see. And please don't tell anyone I babysit his brother."

"Your secret's safe with me," he tells me, and I don't doubt it.

The conversation switches to colleges, and I find out that a lot of our dream schools are the same—Stanford's number one for me, then Berkeley, UCLA, UC Santa

Barbara (I'll admit, it's for the beaches), CSU Long Beach—
except that Emmett has a lot more viable options than I
do. And not because his family is monetarily comfortable.

"See, Mom tells me *not* to go into accounting, and Dad
tells me *not* to go into medicine, but they'll both support
me even if I want to make bad life choices like choosing a
career that's all work and very little play." He runs a hand
through his hair, shaking his head. "My siblings are even
worse. Carlos is at NYU, Angie's at Harvard in Boston, and
they're both begging me to go to school there and move in
with them."

"Lucky," I say. "It's going to be hard to choose. I'll be in
Cali no matter what."

"I wouldn't mind staying close to my parents," he
muses.

Meanwhile, I've barely talked to my mom about college.
I'm afraid to, I guess, in the same way she's afraid to open
those letters from the property manager. I know she won't
be supportive about it. In fact, if she were here, she'd probably pull me aside and pressure me to make a move on
Emmett—say something about how I need to lock him
down before some college co-ed takes him away.

"So where do you want to end up?" I ask. "Not just for
school, but in the long run. Do you have a plan?"

"That's the thing—I don't know," Emmett says. "And
they want us to be so sure of ourselves for those college
application essays. 'Tell us your story.' 'Talk about your
dreams and how you're going to change the world' and all
that." He picks up one of the surviving cookies and chews
on it. "Wherever I get in, it's not going to be based on my
essay. Everything about me is just so...average. What about
you?"

"I had a hard time too," I admit. "It seemed like we
were supposed to write about some magical life experience

and how it transformed us, but I couldn't think of a single one to talk about because my life is pure shit."

"Camilla..."

"No, really. It's such shit it's embarrassing." I reach for the coffee cup so I have something to do with my hands and then turn to face him. "You want to know the reason we move so much? It's because my mom's first priority is alcohol. I've lost count of the places where we've been evicted, the jobs she's been fired from. Nothing ever feels... stable. It's like I'm always waiting for more bad news to drop."

There's a long pause and then Emmett says, "I'm sorry."

"It's not your fault. It's just hard not to freak out thinking about the future. If I don't get a really good scholarship package, I won't be able to go to college at all. And then I'll end up at some dead-end job that I hate, barely scraping by, just like my mom."

"I bet you'll get tons of scholarships," Emmett says.

I let out a snort. "Yeah, I wish. Most of the scholarships go to students who write about all their community service or their extracurriculars, and I can't compete with that. We've moved around too much for me to join any clubs, and I don't have time for volunteer work when I'm so busy nannying." I take a sip of the coffee, but it's cold now. I feel hopeless.

"I get it." Emmett nods to himself, pursing his lips. "The thing is—I know this might come off wrong—but did you ever think, I don't know, maybe you should try to *use* your shitty life?"

"How so?"

"Well, those scholarship people probably get bored to death reading all the same essays every year. 'I help old ladies cross the street,' 'I knit socks for shelter dogs,' 'football is my life,' blah blah blah. But then they pull yours out of the pile, and they get something...real. Even if it's shit, like you say, I'm sure it'll have an impact. They'll want to help you."

"Right. Or the scholarship committee will just think I'm totally pathetic. Going for the pity vote."

"*Or* they'll see how hardworking you are and how motivated it's made you," Emmett insists, all seriousness. "Don't be ashamed of the hand you were dealt. We don't get to pick where we start, but we do have a say in where we finish. These people will be impressed by that. Anyone would be."

I look at him and take in his earnest expression, the way he doesn't break eye contact. He believes in me. This guy barely even knows me, but he believes in me.

"Maybe you're right."

And just like that, I know I've made a friend.

Chapter Nine

CAMILLA

"Remember the one last year where Shapiro's crappy punk band was playing so loud that someone called the cops? And everyone was like, climbing over the fence trying to run away because we were all drinking underage?" a voice is saying.

Girlish giggles echo off the tiled bathroom walls.

I roll my eyes at the banter that's still going on behind the other stalls as I step out, straighten my blazer, and start to wash my hands.

Apparently, this conversation is far too urgent to be halted by customary human needs like peeing. In fact, it seems like all week, the only thing I've heard *anyone* at school talk about is this stupid party tomorrow night. Emmett is still bugging me to go.

Another girl chimes in, "OMG that was insane! Matt's parties are always *epic*."

"Yeah, except for the part where I had to hide in the neighbor kid's treehouse for two hours because I didn't have any pants on!" a third voice says.

It's Thursday between classes, and after hanging out at

Emmett's last night, I'm actually starting to feel better about myself. Not just because his mom treated me like a princess or because Emmett's the kind of person I can really be myself around. I think it has something to do with our talk about my scholarship essays. Maybe he's right, and my honesty will get me that much closer to being able to live my own life.

Even my reflection looks better in the mirror. My chin is high, my eyes are bright, and the freckles across my nose (the ones I usually try to hide with makeup) appear kind of whimsical and cute today. My long brown hair could definitely use a trim, and it's a bit frizzy, but I can appreciate the way it falls in thick, loose waves, especially since I can't really afford styling products for it. Air dry for the win.

Toilets flush, and I glance up in the mirror to see Hillary and her minions come out of their stalls. Of course it's her. She and her two friends stand in a cluster behind me, inspecting themselves in the mirror like I'm not even here.

Hillary is rolling the waistband of her skirt to make her hem higher and then she turns around to get a view of the back of her thighs. "God, look at this. I have more cellulite than a freaking cow."

Her friend laughs. "I don't think cows have cellulite, Hill."

The other girl dabs on a fresh layer of lip gloss and rolls her eyes. "No guy at this school is going to care once he has you locked in that room for seven minutes."

That gives me pause. Locked in *what room*? And seven minutes...oh. Right.

They must be talking about seven minutes in heaven, the party game where you're supposed to get locked in a dark closet with someone for seven minutes so you can paw at each other and make out. Wow, how fun. I'm clearly missing out.

"But Hillary doesn't want just *any* guy," the second girl says, turning to Hillary. "Did you find out if he's going yet?"

"He'll be there." Hillary shifts to look at herself in profile, probably admiring her perfect little nose. I wish they'd stop blocking the paper towel dispenser so I can get to class before they start talking about Hunter because I'm sure that's who they mean.

I'm not safe from his influence anywhere. Not even the sacred ground of the girls' bathroom.

"I need to do like a thousand crunches before tomorrow night," lip gloss girl is saying. "My pudge is out of control. Too many carbs this week. PMS."

"Mm," Hillary says, all faux sympathy.

Honestly, all three of them are a size nothing. It's hard not to roll my eyes. And harder still to not compare myself to them, even though I know I shouldn't.

I clear my throat and turn off the tap, then shake off my hands. The movement triggers exactly zero reaction from the girls, and they keep on blocking the dispenser while talking about which body parts they'd trade for other, better body parts.

Yeah. Time to get the hell out of here.

"Let's all meet up at my house to get ready and then Uber over together," Hillary says. "So, like—"

"Excuse me," I interrupt politely. "I just need to grab a paper towel."

At once, I'm the center of their collective attention. Like we're tributes in *The Hunger Games* and they've allied against me.

They exchange a look before lip gloss girl steps back, allowing me to reach the paper towels. I pull one out, mutter a quiet thanks, and dry my hands. I pray they'll go back to ignoring me and resuming their chitchat, but that would be too easy.

"Ooh, I have an idea." The girl on Hillary's left claps her hands, her charm bracelet jingling. "*New girl* should come to the party!"

Her comment leaves all of them giggling, and it's obvious the suggestion is a sarcastic one.

"Thanks, but I already have plans," I lie, tossing the wadded up paper towel in the trash. But when I try to leave, they close ranks on me, and I find myself blocked.

"That's probably for the best," lip gloss girl adds with a pitying smile. "Would you even have something nice to wear? I mean, that isn't from the Salvation Army?"

The words hit me like a slap. Like they automatically assume I'm less than them because I can't afford a dumb Chanel bag or five-hundred-dollar Jimmy Choo heels, like I should be ashamed for not being born to rich parents.

"That's easy to solve." Hillary smiles sweetly, and I'm still too stunned to move as she looks me over from head to toe. Between flight or fight, I've frozen in place and am completely at her mercy. "You can borrow one of my dresses," she says.

Charm bracelet girl lets out a huge laugh. I can't even imagine what I'd look like trying to squeeze into one of Hillary's tiny dresses. Probably like a sausage ready to burst from its casing, and it's clear they're envisioning something similarly amusing.

"Parties really aren't my thing," I say, trying to squeeze by them.

The warning bell rings, and I'm thankful for it. We all have to get going.

"That's too bad," lip gloss girl says, glancing back at me as the three of them shuffle toward the door. "But it's probably for the best. You wouldn't fit in anyway."

"Emma's right," Hillary adds gently with her bright white mannequin smile. "We prefer not to associate with *the help*. It's tacky."

With that, she flips her blonde hair over her shoulder and swans out the door.

My cheeks are hot, and my stomach is twisting. It's not just the insult itself—it's that the only way they'd know I'm "the help" is if Hunter had told them.

As I race to my next class, my shock and embarrassment turns into anger. So much for blending in here. Though if it weren't for Hunter Beck's trash talk, these girls wouldn't have it out for me.

This is all Hunter's fault.

Chapter Ten
CAMILLA

*S*crew it.

I'm going to that party.

I've had an entire day to think about it. Rather, an entire day to seethe about it because every time I think of Hillary and her friends demeaning me, my blood starts to boil. How dare they assume I have nothing to wear, that I wouldn't fit in, that I'm less than just because I have a job and I happen to work for the Becks. I'll show them.

It's Friday night, and all my clothes are piled up on the bed as I try to put together an outfit. Skinny jeans and a black top? No, too simple. And all I've got are T-shirts and flowy blouses, neither of which will give me the effect I'm going for. I have two skirts that might be okay, except the pencil skirt kind of screams "middle-aged secretary," and the floral A-line has a two-inch tear in the bottom that I sewed up myself, and I just know Hillary and her minions will see it and say something.

My dresses are worse. The few I own are all too long, too formal, or too small.

Throwing myself on top of the clothes pile, I let out a

huge sigh. Much as I hate to admit it, Hillary and her posse had a valid point. I really don't have anything to wear to a high school party full of rich kids, and I have zero idea what to do with my hair. I know two styles total: up in a ponytail or down in its air-dried mess of waves.

But there is one more option because my mom has exactly the kinds of clothes that will help me fit in with a bunch of trust fund babies and party girls.

Which means I have to ask her for a favor.

I find her sitting on the couch, head tilted back, glass in hand. Though the TV is on, she's not looking at the news on the screen—she's not looking at anything.

"Um, Mom? Would it be okay if I borrowed something to wear?"

She looks over at me, curiosity written all over her face. "What is this for? Do you have an interview, or—"

"There's this party tonight that everyone at school is going to, and I don't have anything that looks right." I inhale, steeling myself for her disapproval.

"*Milla*." Mom grins, setting down her glass and standing up. "Look at you—finally ready to socialize and snatch yourself a rich boy. It's about time!"

With that, she motions me to follow her to her bedroom, and I try to push down the icky feelings I'm having. I hate that she's cheering me on for what she sees as my first step toward gold digging. Especially since that isn't at all what I had in mind.

"Let's find something with spandex in it so you don't stretch out my clothes," she says as she flips through the hangers in her closet. "Can't afford to buy anything new with the rent going up."

I grit my teeth at the jab about stretching out her clothes. It's like she actually can't help herself from poking at me, the way she says it all casually in passing, like it wasn't even on purpose. Guess my weight is just constantly on her mind.

But that's not what really caught my attention—did she just say our rent's going up? When did this happen, and can we even afford it? I have about a million questions, but I can't get into it with her right now. She'll probably just tell me it's none of my business anyway, which is obviously not true when I'm the one paying our power bill.

"This?" she asks, holding up a long black dress. The bottom looks like it's meant to wrap from thigh to mid-calf like a second skin, but the top is loose and blousy.

"Eh. Too adult," I tell her.

She frowns, diving back in. "How about this one?" The dress is actually pretty cute—ice blue with a camisole-style top and a big fluffy ostrich feather skirt on the bottom—but it's *so* not me. "You can wear a denim jacket over it to dress it down."

"I don't think I can pull off feathers," I tell her truthfully. "And honestly, I just want to blend in."

Mom throws a hand on her hip and lets out a huff. "Well, I don't have all night to play personal shopper for you. Just take whatever you want and don't make a mess."

With that, she's (blessedly) gone, and I turn to her closet with trepidation.

I don't know how she can find anything in here. It's crammed full of various types of clothes in no particular order with regard to season or style, though her more formal outfits all hang separately off to the side. I pull out a few things and try on several skirts that are too tight, dresses that won't zip, and blouses that do fit but make me look like I'm forty. At this point, I'm full on sweating with anxiety. If only Mom had deigned to pass the thin genes down to me.

My phone buzzes on the bed, and I see it's a text from Emmett.

You coming tonight? I can pick you up on the way. :)

Ha. Emmett dropped me off after our study session the other night, so he knows where I live, and that means he's well aware that my apartment is hardly "on the way" to this guy Matt's house. Thanks to all the gossip I've overheard this week, I know for a fact that Matt lives up in the hills in one of the rich neighborhoods. Still, it would be nice not to have to take a bus there when I'm all dressed up, get all disheveled from walking, and then have to awkwardly walk into the party all by myself.

What time? I text back. *Still getting ready.*

I agree to be downstairs at 8:30 p.m. and turn back to my mom's closet with fresh determination. Her idea about wearing the denim jacket over a dress was good—plus, if I leave it unbuttoned, it won't matter that it's too small for me.

In the end, I settle on a navy blue dress that's cut low up top and hits me mid-thigh, which is way out of my comfort zone and probably more suited to a date night, but with the casual jacket on top it should be okay. My mom doesn't have much in the way of jewelry, but I find a silver chain with a simple star pendant on it that hangs mid-chest and adds a little bit of flair. Hopefully, I won't draw too much attention. The whole point of this party is to have a good time, not get accosted by the fashion police.

After a quick shower, I bend over and dry my hair upside down, scrunching in a bit of Mom's volumizer to give my waves a bit more oomph. Then I get dressed.

My makeup takes twice as long as usual. In addition to my usual tinted moisturizer and pressed powder, I go to town with the smoky eye effect after watching a YouTube tutorial and then brush the apples of my cheeks with blush.

My lashes feel heavy with mascara, and my lips are sticky with red gloss, but I'm happy with the end result. I look a little older, a little more mysterious, and a lot less like someone you'd call "the help." Take that, Hillary.

My phone buzzes with another text from Emmett, and I realize it's a few minutes after nine. Time to go.

On my way out, Mom gives me a once-over. "Not bad," she says, reaching for her purse and rummaging around in it. "You have money for the bus?"

"I got it, Mom," I tell her. "See you later."

"Have fun. And be home by midnight!" she calls after me, and I give a little wave as I close the door behind me.

On the drive over to Matt's, I notice Emmett side-eyeing me.

"What? Did I pick the wrong outfit?" I ask, suddenly anxious.

"No, not at all," he says. "You look great."

"So do you," I tell him. He's wearing perfectly fitted jeans, a black button-down, and some kind of fancy woodsy cologne that smells so nice it has to be super expensive.

Matt's street is so packed with cars that we have to park a block away. Even if I didn't have Emmett with me, I'd know which house the party was at—every other person we see is heading in the same direction.

"How big is this house?" I ask, sliding out of the SUV. "There must be a hundred people showing up."

"Big enough," Emmett says with a shrug.

We walk side by side, and I'm content feeling the cool ocean-scented breeze against my skin while Emmett tells me about the Richardsons and the Roys and the families he grew up around. How he, Matt, and Steve Roy have been going to the same schools since they were toddlers. Must be nice, having friends that go back for so long. I wonder how Danielle, the friend I had for six months back in Fresno, is doing.

"...what made you change your mind?" Emmett's asking. I've lost half of the question in my reverie about Danielle but assume he's talking about the party.

"I guess I wanted to prove to the bitch brigade that I can fit in just fine."

Emmett glances over. "What if it's better that you don't?"

Shaking my head, I tell him, "The high school game is different for me, Emmett. If I stand out, I make myself a target. Someone to be taken down. Even when I'm not at a private school full of elitists, I still feel like I don't belong."

"You think I'm an elitist?" he asks, sounding amused.

"Never," I tell him, bumping him playfully with my elbow. "You're one of the good ones."

We slow our pace as we come up to the house, a Mediterranean-style mansion that looks the same as all the others in the neighborhood. White stucco, arched windows, wrought iron balconies, and a carved wood front door. The muffled sound of music pounds from within.

I notice a girl sitting on the lawn under a huge palm tree lit up from below, her hair in two pigtails. She's wearing a sleeveless white shirt with a tie and bopping her head to the music as she drinks from a red cup. Once she spots Emmett, her face breaks into a grin.

"Emmie!" She sets her cup down and barrels down the driveway, tackling him in a hug. "Tell me you're here to save me from Steve's bad breath and even worse jokes."

"Consider yourself saved." Emmett returns the hug, lifting her off her feet, and finally they release each other. "Isabel, meet Camilla." He gestures toward me. "Camilla, this is Isabel. We've known each other since, what..."

"Second grade. And nice to meet you, Camilla," Isabel

says with a smile, and before I realize it, she's hugging me too. She's petite and bubbly and just a little bit punk, with various safety pins adorning her plaid skirt, a piercing in her lower lip, and ballerina flats with little spike studs on them.

"I love your shoes," I tell her.

"Thank you!" she says, kicking up one foot behind her like she's modeling them. "Do you go to our school?"

"Sort of. Monday was my first day."

She raises a mischievous eyebrow, her hazel eyes bright underneath. "Has Emmett's mom invited you over for cookies yet?"

I laugh. "Yes, and ten out of ten, would eat again."

"Right? They're gooey perfection and fill your belly with warm hugs!" Isabel very seriously takes a hand to her heart and sighs. "Ah, Mrs. Ortega. I'd marry her if she wasn't married already."

"Ugh. Can we please not?" Emmett groans.

"Pfft, relax." Isabel nudges him with her elbow. "Your mom's cookies are half the reason you're popular." She goes back for her red cup and takes a swig. "And now I need a refill. Shall we?"

"I don't know," Emmett says. "Is the party that bad that you had to come drink outside?"

"Meh. More like people being dicks and Steve not letting up. Seriously, how many times do I have to shoot him down?" She sighs. "Plus, it's seriously hot in there, so I came out for some fresh air. But I'm ready for round two."

We step inside, and I stick close to Emmett while Isabel leads us to the living room. The smell of weed and beer is strong, and I see at least two spilled drinks on the white carpet plus someone sitting by the open window smoking a cigarette. I instantly feel sorry for whoever has to handle the cleanup afterward.

On our way through all the people and furniture, I notice Hunter out of the corner of my eye, talking to some blond guy I don't know. He's got his arm around Hillary's waist—she looks irritatingly chic in a black miniskirt and matching crop top with a light pink, silk boyfriend blazer worn open to finish off the ensemble.

Hunter doesn't seem to notice me. But Hillary does, and flashes me the nastiest smirk before whispering something into his ear and then nuzzling his neck.

The room shrinks, and I immediately avert my eyes, the air too hot and thick in my throat. Isabel's hand tugs mine as she guides me to the kitchen, and I let her.

We come to a halt in front of a huge island piled up with bottles and kegs.

My eyes drift over the many options on display.

"What do you want?" Isabel asks, pouring herself a vodka and red Gatorade.

"Can you make me one of those?" I say, pointing at her drink.

"Coming right up."

Even though I've never touched alcohol before, tonight I'm ready to try it. Because if I've learned anything from my mom, it's that it turns you into someone who's numb from the inside out.

And that's exactly what I need right now.

Chapter Eleven

CAMILLA

hree drinks later, and Isabel and I are having a blast. We've spent the last two hours drinking and talking by ourselves in a corner, and I feel like I've known her my whole life. When I let it slip that I'm embarrassed I had to borrow one of my mom's dresses because I can't afford new clothes, she said I wore it well. And that you don't need a lot of money if you know how and where to shop.

"This entire *ensemblé*," she says, pronouncing it *on-som-blay* and gesturing at herself from head to toe, "cost me twenty bucks. And most of it was for the shoes, which I studded myself."

I gasp. "No way."

"Yes, way." She threads her arm around mine and looks up at me. "We should go shopping together. I will teach you my DIY tricks and bargain bin ways. This tie? Seventy-five cents at Goodwill from the boys' section. My shirt is just last year's uniform with the sleeves cut off, and the skirt is a hand-me-down from my cousin in—"

A hiccup breaks her speech, and she slaps a hand over

her mouth, but not before we both dissolve into drunk giggles.

Our cups are empty again, so we go pour ourselves another round on the other side of the kitchen, where Emmett seems to be playing bartender. "Hey ladies, maybe you should slow down..." he starts, reaching out to stop us, but Isabel slaps his hand away, the laughter gone from her lips.

"If we want to get shit-faced, Emmett, we get shit-faced," she says very seriously.

"Yeah," I pile on, even though a small part of me knows he's right. The room's starting to spin whenever I move, and if it weren't for the solid surface of the island, I'd probably be toppling over. "Let us drink!"

With that, I take a long swig of the vodka-rade. It's really growing on me.

"How are you two already ganging up on me? You literally just met." Emmett sighs and shakes his head but doesn't try to stop us again.

"We're *kindred spirits*," Isabel spits. I realize I've become aware of how her face lights up every time she looks over at him. And now that she's pinching his cheek, she's positively glowing. "Don't be jealous, Emmie. We'll still be your friends so long as your mom keeps baking those crack cookies."

The smartphone connected to the speakers starts sounding an alarm, and someone rushes to stop it. Voices die down in the sudden silence, and a guy stands on the coffee table in the adjoining living room to shout, "Ladies. Gentlemen. It is *time*!"

"Time for what?" I whisper to Emmett, but he doesn't seem to hear me.

The guy—who's really just a blurry figure to me at this

point—gestures to the doorway where Matt Mason grins and yells, "Whoever's playing, follow me upstairs!"

Kids start drifting off with him, though I still have no clue what this is all about. Before I can ask more questions, Isabel's arm goes around my shoulders, and I realize she's herding me along with her toward the stairs.

As we walk, she explains, and it all clicks as I remember Hillary's minions talking about this in the girls' bathroom the other day.

"So it's basically seven minutes in heaven, except instead of just kissing in a closet, you get seven minutes in the kink room."

"Wait, the *what* room?"

"It's not scary," Isabel assures me.

I am not at all assured, but before I can even think about making a run for it, we stumble into what must be Matt's parents' bedroom along with everyone else.

Despite my warm, fuzzy haze, I can see it's tastefully decorated with a four-poster bed, plush carpet, and elegant dark wood furniture. There's a little hallway at one end of the room with three doors, two of which open onto a bathroom and a walk-in closet, and as for the third, which is closed... I assume it must lead to the kink room.

The fifteen or so people in here are busy arranging themselves in a circle on the floor, and Hillary's sitting in the middle with a grin on her face and an empty Ketel One bottle in her hand.

Isabel pulls me down next to her on one side of the circle, Emmett goes off to the other side, and as I tug the too-short hem of my dress over my knees, I take a look around. The copious amounts of alcohol I've consumed must be working. My anxiety seems distant and irrelevant, and instead of being nervous, I feel giddy and unafraid.

As host, Matt has the first turn, which he eagerly takes.

My heart races as the bottle spins and spins on the rug, but I'm fully prepared to accept my fate if it ends up pointing toward me. Besides, I'm sure I can use a whip to defend my integrity if necessary. Or whatever else Mr. and Mrs. Mason have in there.

But then the bottle lands on some other girl, and I'm cheering along with everyone else as someone calls out their names and says, "Here goes round one!"

I have to say, being drunk is not as bad as my mom makes it seem. I feel at ease, I'm not trying to pick any fights, and when I catch Hunter staring at me, I'm totally unselfconscious about it. Hell, I even flash him a smirk.

The minutes must fly because someone's phone alarm goes off and then Matt and the girl I don't know are walking out of the mysterious room with blushing faces. Then the bottle's spinning again.

"You doing okay?" Isabel asks next to me. I nod just as the bottle slows down and stops to point at someone else. Isabel leans to whisper in my ear, her words a little slurred as she explains who's going in next with whom and what their backstory is.

"Who should go next?" Hillary asks, eyeing us all one by one. Her gaze sweeps past me, and I'm sure she's about to pick someone else when she announces, "I know! How about new girl?"

"Drunk people shouldn't play," Hunter says, interrupting Hillary. He turns to me and says, "Just leave, Camilla."

"I'm fine," I insist, indignant. "Besides, everyone here is drunk."

That draws another cheer from the people in the room, and then Isabel is grabbing the bottle from Hillary and putting it in my hand.

Before anyone can stop me, I give it a spin, almost

afraid to see where it lands. *Anyone but Hunter, anyone but Hunter*, I think to myself, my heart pounding so hard I can feel it in my chest. And then, *Please let it be Hunter*.

But it stops on Emmett.

Relief washes over me. At least I got someone I know, someone who won't try to make a move.

I get up so fast it makes my head spin, but I don't let it stop me. Holding out a hand, I bravely profess, "Come on, Emmett. Let's see what floats the Masons' kinky boat."

Emmett's hand is sweaty, and it's a struggle to stay upright while I help him off the floor. Several "Oooooohs" and "Hee-hee-hees" follow us as we enter the kink room and close the door, and for a moment, I'm actually speechless at what I'm seeing.

"Oh. My. God," I let out, looking around at a surprisingly spacious room that has walls covered in padded pink velvet. There's a swing on the far end, a table with leather straps that someone already lowered from the wall, and a shelf filled with all kinds of toys and ticklers and other unidentifiable kinky accoutrements. "Do you think everything's been properly disinfected?"

Emmett bursts into an awkward laugh and pulls me toward him so we're face to face. He looks into my eyes, and even through the alcohol, I can sense a weird tension between us. "So, um. Camilla. I don't know if y—"

"Agh!" I squeal, breaking away from him to grab a pair of red fuzzy handcuffs I've spotted on the shelf. "Wow. These are so soft," I murmur, holding them up to show Emmett. "Put your hands behind your back and spread 'em."

"No way!" he says, reaching for what looks like some kind of flogging device. Holding it up, he lowers his voice and does a spot-on impression of our World History teacher. "Miss Hanson, are you familiar with the leading causes of death among sailors? Answer right or prepare to receive a historically accurate punishment. Ten lashes!"

Grinning, I grab the flogger and lightly slap it against my palm, which hurts more than I expected. "Ow! Do people seriously enjoy being hit with these?"

"I suppose it's all in the touch?" Emmett says, stealing it back and twirling it around in his hand. "And who's doing the flogging."

He's looking at me again, too seriously, and I blurt, "If they don't call this the Chamber of Kinks, they're missing a golden opportunity."

"You mean..." Emmett wags his eyebrows. "The *golden snitch* of opportunities?"

Laughter bursts out of both of us. After it dies, another awkward silence is born where we're both kinda giggling, and I notice he's standing too close. I scramble for another joke, but then gasp because I've found the craziest, purplest thing in the room.

"Holy purple dildo-in-a-harness, Batman." My jaw hangs open, and I let loose a fit of giggles. I no longer know the concept of shame, so I grab the whole thing and wield it like a sword. "*En garde*, Emmett!" I make a wobbly stab toward the flogger he's still holding, laughing so much that tears prick my eyes. Emmett's laughing too, bent over and clutching his stomach.

The door opens, and a voice professes, "Time's up!"

Relieved and still catching my breath, I wipe my eyes and put the harness back. Before we leave, I catch Emmett looking at the floor a little wistfully. Like maybe he's disappointed all we did was joke around.

Or maybe I'm just drunk and reading too much into it.

Putting those thoughts aside, I step outside the Chamber of Kinks, still giggling like a fool, but glad I'd talked myself into coming tonight. It wasn't so bad, this party.

Everyone is cheering, as they did with all the couples before us. I'm not paying much attention as I trail behind Emmett and end up almost colliding with a very broad, very muscular chest as we make our way down the dim hallway. I raise my head, but my gut already knows it's Hunter who's in front of us, whose smell of vetiver cologne is filling my nose. How the hell does he still smell so nice?

Then I see the tight line of his mouth, along with the glint of anger in his blue eyes, and the joy drains out of me like air from a popped balloon.

Chapter Twelve

CAMILLA

My sight is a blur, as is the sequence of events that happens next.

Hunter grabs my wrist and pulls me to his side, and I'm too stunned to resist. Unfortunately, I'm also too drunk to do it gracefully. My foot stomps on his, and I almost trip—the only reason I don't is his arm coming around to steady me.

"The hell you doing, Beck?" Emmett asks him.

"I could ask you the same," Hunter spits back. "What were you thinking, letting her drink this much?" He's growling at Emmett like he's my guard dog, and my wrist is burning under his tight, hot grip. "Look at her, she can't even walk straight."

It's true. Even now, I'm swaying against Hunter's side like a branch in the wind. Heat spreads to my already warm cheeks. Sure, I might be intoxicated, but I was just fine before he came along, and now everyone in the room is craning to listen in.

"I'm not going to let anything happen to her," Emmett

says defensively. "And what do you expect me to do, take the glass right out of her hand?"

"Precisely. But that wouldn't have been in your best interest, now would it, Ortega? Then you couldn't have played knight in shining armor."

"Oh, like you're doing now?" Emmett asks. "How's that working out for you?"

I look up at Hunter, my chest strangely tight. *Is* he trying to rescue me? From *Emmett*? And why? He thinks I'm worthless. It shouldn't matter what I do.

"You let her play the game knowing full well she was trashed and could've ended up in that room with anyone." Hunter lets go of me and takes a step toward Emmett. "I see right through you. Remember that next time you try to act innocent."

Emmett's eyes narrow. "Not everyone is a selfish prick like you, Beck."

Hunter closes in on Emmett at once, and the claustrophobia of this narrow hallway has me panicking. On top of which, the thought of this escalating further—with a bunch of people watching, to boot—completely mortifies me. I throw out a hand and grab Hunter's arm, feeling his taut muscles beneath my grip.

"I'm the one who chose to drink as much as I did!" I blurt out. "It's not Emmett's fault."

Glancing back at me, Hunter's nostrils flare. "Don't try to defend him."

"Hey, lay off!" Isabel appears at the end of the hallway, scowling at both of them. "You're making a scene."

"Do I look like I give a fuck?" Hunter says. "I'm calling her a Lyft and sending her home. Which is what *you* should have done." That last bit he throws at Emmett.

Isabel ignores Hunter and turns to me, brow drawn in concern. "Camilla, is that what you want?"

I glance at Hunter, who already has his phone out, and then nod, the motion making me feel a little seasick. "I'm supposed to be home soon anyway."

"You sure?" she asks.

"Yeah. I'll text you later," I answer.

That's all I get to say before Hunter basically drags me away. People who were supposed to be playing kinky spin the bottle are all staring at us as we leave, and I'm still too baffled by this whole situation to do anything but let Hunter lead me.

Hopefully, the night air will do something about the heat assailing my body because not even the icy daggers Hillary and her posse are throwing at me can keep the little trickles of sweat from rolling down my back.

When we get to the top of the stairs, Hunter wordlessly offers me his arm, and I cling to him as I take each shaky step. Once we're in the foyer, I look up at his tense expression of concern and feel a smile spreading across my face. My hero.

"Hunter Beck is worried about me," I mumble, teasing.

I tilt forward, and his arms tighten around me, keeping me from falling. "Fucking hell, Camilla. How much did you drink?"

My eyes roll up while I count. "I don't know. Four? Ish?"

"Four-ish what?"

"Vodka Gatorade. It tastes like fruit punch," I tell him very seriously. "Isabel made 'em. I never drank before."

"What? How are you even...?" He stops, looks me up and down, and sighs.

Once we're out in the driveway, he spins me to face him and rests his hands on my shoulders. Dazed, I look up at him, but I can't keep my eyes focused.

"What?" I ask when he says nothing.

"Do you have any idea what could have happened to

you in there?" His voice is husky, and I can't help but feel a little ashamed as I drop my gaze to the contour of his square jaw and the curve of his lips. "You're fucking lucky the bottle stopped when it did and you got locked inside with a coward like Emmett. Anyone else, Camilla..."

My eyes snap back up. "What, Emmett being decent makes him a coward? He's my *friend*."

Hunter glares at me. "You're stupid if you haven't realized he's just waiting for his chance to pounce. Did he touch you?"

Maybe I did get a tense vibe from Emmett when we'd been in the kink room, but nothing creepy or pushy. Just a little awkwardness at first. Who cares, though? He's a good guy. Nothing happened. And even if it had...

"How is this any of your business?" I ask, sidestepping the question.

He just laughs bitterly and shakes his head, taking a few steps back.

"Did you know that room is soundproof? That if someone took advantage of you and you screamed, no one would have shown up to help?"

"I'd whack him with the flogger," I answer without hesitation, grinning.

"Do you think this is a game?" he growls.

"God, Hunter, I'm not as defenseless as you think."

"Oh no?" Out of nowhere, Hunter drops his hands to my waist and pushes me back against the garage.

My adrenaline is pumping hard, and my knees feel weak. It's not just the vodka.

"Let me go," I say. I'm not smiling anymore.

"What if it had been me in that room with you, Camilla? Huh? You're wasted."

Didn't I wonder that exact same thing earlier, before he decided to talk to me like I'm a child?

I meet his stare, the alcohol making me bold when I'd normally just walk away. "What would you have done?" I ask, challenging him.

His Adam's apple bobs with a dry swallow. He didn't expect me to talk back. I think this is the first time I've surprised him in any way, and it feels like a triumph.

It's not long-lived.

"I don't take advantage of drunk girls," he says, finally releasing me.

"How can you say that? Every single person here is drunk!"

"Not like you are," he scoffs. "And besides, I've already..."

He trails off, leaving the sentence unfinished, but it's obvious he was going to say that he's already hooked up with pretty much every girl here.

"I'm leaving," I say, starting down the driveway. I'll probably be home late, but hopefully my mom will be passed out and won't even notice that I broke curfew.

Hunter comes up beside me, pulling his phone from his pocket. "Camilla, stop. I'm calling you a Lyft."

"The bus is fine."

"God, why do you have to be so stubborn? Just let me help you," he says, his voice hard. "What's your address?"

"I'm not telling you."

He shakes his head. "Whatever, I already know it." At my glowering silence, he begins to type. "Shawn G. will be here to pick you up in two minutes."

I clench my hands into fists, whirling on him. "How the hell do you know where I live?"

"You're my brother's nanny."

"So?"

"So? My dad did a background check before hiring you."

Oh my God, these rich assholes. "That's an invasion of privacy!"

"And yet it ensures we don't hire sex offenders or ex-cons to take care of my little brother." He puts his phone back in his pocket. "And you're working, aren't you? Obviously, you passed."

I can't dispute the bit about Harrison's safety, or that yes, I still have the job; I'm also not comfortable with people paying to find out about my past. "Regular people make do with interviews and references just fine," I say through clenched teeth.

"Well, we're not regular people."

The look he gives me—a raised eyebrow over an unimpressed stare and a shrug—is so smug I want to slap it off his face.

He takes a step back, lips tightening as he looks at the road. "Your ride's here."

A dry cackle leaves me. "You're so worried about me in my current state, yet you're sending me home alone with a stranger?"

"Don't worry, I'll be tracking the ride." Hunter waves his phone at me.

"What a gentleman," I scoff, stalking toward the Lyft. Every step requires focus and thought, and everything feels a little off-kilter, but I keep my balance, managing to slide into the car and slam the door without any mishaps.

As the driver pulls away, I watch Hunter storm back into the house.

He doesn't look back.

Chapter Thirteen

CAMILLA

The next morning greets me with a massive headache, dry mouth, and intense nausea. I'm lucky my mom's not home to see my frequent trips to the bathroom where I puke my guts out.

I drag myself to the kitchen with a wet washcloth around my neck and pour myself a glass of water. Last night's events flash by in my mind as I pop two slices of bread into the toaster, and my stomach churns at the memories. I'd had so much fun with Isabel and Emmett, and not even the kink room had ruined the evening. Hillary had mostly ignored me, and I never even saw her minions.

But then things started sucking the minute Hunter decided to tear into me for trying to have fun the same way everyone else was: getting drunk and playing games.

I just don't get it.

After my dry toast breakfast, I take a long shower and try to do some schoolwork. With this hangover, however, I find that getting any homework done is a bust. Unfortunately, I need to get it together and fast because I'm due at the Becks' house this afternoon, except instead of babysitting Harry, I'll be there to see Hunter so we can work on our debate project. I'm dreading it. I really wish I hadn't suggested a study date earlier this week, but it's too late now to cancel.

My phone vibrates on the desk with another text from Isabel. She's been blowing up my phone since last night, first to make sure I got home safe, and now, to commiserate over our hangovers. I really love her.

Why is drinking so much fun in the moment until the next day when you always regret it? And then next week you do it again ARGH

Grinning, I text back. *Doubt I'll be doing that again anytime soon.*

Isabel responds, *Smart lady. I think you're gonna be a good influence* ;)

Speaking of which, I'm trying to do homework but kind of failing

Sleep today, homework tomorrow? Isabel suggests.

God, I wish. *Can't. I have a big group project due this week*

Boo, she texts back. *LMK if you need me to drop off a care package. I have plenty of ibuprofen, and FYI Jack in the Box serves breakfast all day.*

After that, we make plans to hang out soon. The texting isn't enough to cure my hangover, but it does make it bearable.

Around noon, I run a brush through my hair, change my shirt, and then take the bus to the Becks', where my mom has been working since this morning. When I walk through the front door, I see her scrubbing the floor in her uniform, so I give a little wave and then head upstairs to say hi to Harrison first. I'm hoping his sweet smile will give me a boost before I have to face his older brother.

I find Harry in his room, lounging in his beanbag chair with a video game controller in his hands. He's so engrossed in his game that he doesn't even look up when I enter.

"Hey, kiddo," I call out.

"Can't talk. On a streak," he says, big blue eyes unwavering while his small fingers press the buttons. The sound that accompanies every jab is unmistakable—he's playing *Super Mario Odyssey*.

Some people might demand that he hit pause right now and offer a proper greeting, but I've played *Odyssey* with him before. If he's about to get the jump-rope Power Moon on Metro Kingdom, I'm not about to interrupt.

So much for stalling.

"Come find me if you need anything, okay?" I tell him, tiptoeing out the door.

Hunter's bedroom is next door, but he doesn't answer when I knock. Crap. Is it possible he's still sleeping off his own hangover? I'd text him, but I actually don't have his number, which is kind of ridiculous since I have Mr. and Mrs. Becks' and even Harry's, though he's always forgetting where he left his phone.

Cracking open the door just a smidge, I see a sunlit but empty room with an unmade king-size bed on the left side and a desk, TV area, and couch to the right. He also has his own walk-in closet—smaller than his parents' but completely unnecessary.

I try the living room next and come into the rare event of a full house. There's Hunter, in shorts and a blue T-shirt, lounging on the sofa while staring at his phone.

His stepmom Karleigh is there too, taking up the armchair while she browses something on her iPad—probably properties her husband can buy on the cheap and flip for exorbitant amounts—or scrolling through Instagram to work on her influencer side gig. I check up on her page every once in a while, and I've noticed that Harrison only shows up when she wants to remind her followers she has "the sweetest son" and to be called "a great mom." Which is about once a month.

That's the only time she pays attention to her kid. And speaking of women who neglect their children, there's my mom, who's currently cleaning the glass panes of the French doors like a Windex mercenary on a mission to annihilate fingerprints.

"Hi, Mrs. Beck," I say. "Hi, Hunter."

"Hi, sweetie," Mrs. Beck says absently, not taking her eyes off her screen. "Are you taking Harry somewhere today?"

"Um, no, actually. Hunter and I have to work on a school project," I tell her.

"How nice. I'm sure he could use the help."

I catch Hunter shooting his stepmom some nasty side-eye, but then he immediately goes back to his phone.

With that, I'm left standing there awkwardly. There's a weird tension in the room, and I'm not entirely sure where it's coming from. My mom seems weirdly focused on scrubbing windows, Mrs. Beck is off in social media la-la land, and Hunter seems to be ignoring me on purpose. Which is infuriating, since the whole reason I came over—hangover and all—is because we have to work on this debate thing.

"Hunter?" I say, but I get nothing. What the hell?

My instincts are telling me to go back upstairs and watch Harry play Mario because that sure beats interrupting whatever's happening here. But I need a good grade in debate to keep my GPA high enough to keep receiving the Oak Academy scholarship, and I can't do it without Hunter.

I step in front of him. He doesn't acknowledge me at all, even though I'm certain he's noticed my approach.

"Hey—"

"Go away," he growls without looking up.

Usually, I'd lean toward being nonconfrontational and walk away. Not today.

"We're supposed to be practicing for our presentation," I say, crossing my arms. "I'm not saving it till the last minute."

He rolls his eyes. "All debate consists of is arguing our points in front of the class. We don't need to write anything up in advance. We can just wing it."

"Wing it? Are you serious?" I whisper, my temper flashing. "I'm not going to stand there and look like a fool because you won't even do the bare minimum. Let's just get this over with."

The sound of Windex spraying against glass, then the cloth wiping it—Mom cleaning the windows—fills the room. Hunter's jaw clenches, and he glances over at my mom as if he's actually annoyed that she's making noise while cleaning his stupid fancy house. I don't know what to do. Maybe I should just figure out the project on my own and tell our teacher that Hunter refused to participate. I obviously can't force him.

But then he's looking up at me with what has to be the most patronizing smirk I've ever seen. "What was the topic again? Is marriage an outdated institution?"

I stiffen, surprised he remembers. "Yes."

"Then what is there to debate? Everyone knows it *is* outdated. People shouldn't legally bind themselves to anyone else when it's common knowledge that men can't stay sane and remain faithful to one partner." He crosses his legs and leans back on the couch. "It's not practical for us."

My eyes narrow. "Oh really?" It's exactly the kind of thing a manwhore like Hunter Beck would say.

"It's biology, Camilla. Our brains are wired differently.

Women are made to nurture, and men are made to screw. It guarantees the survival of our species. And besides, a single woman can't keep up with a man's sex drive forever. Once she gets old and tired out," he says, glancing over at his stepmom, "the man has no choice but to look somewhere else."

"So women just dry up, and all men are basically animals." My voice is cold with sarcasm.

"Yes." His tone is low and menacing.

I recoil. "Well, we can't use any of that. We have to argue our side with facts, not feelings. Unless you can reference actual published research on the topic."

Hunter pointedly looks at his stepmother. "It's obviously a *fact* that men will always move on to the next hot young thing rather than stay with their wives."

Shaking my head, I sigh. "What about people who marry for love and stay in love? There's nothing outdated about that."

"Ha!" Hunter scoffs. "Love like that doesn't exist. It's just not believable. There's lust and the thing people *call* love, which is really just temporary insanity, but it never lasts. It's just chemicals. Dopamine, oxytocin, serotonin.

"But they drop off after a few years, and then you just hate each other. But you can't leave because you're too tied up with kids and bills and your shitty routine."

·Where is all this bitterness coming from? And why is Hunter lashing out at me? "This is for a grade. Can't you take this one thing seriously?" I beg.

"Yeah. I could." He shrugs. "I just don't want to."

I want to throttle him. Too bad there are multiple witnesses in the room.

"Listen to Camilla, Hunter," Mrs. Beck suddenly snaps, scowling at him over her iPad. "You know your dad expects you to get your GPA up this semester."

At once, his head whips in her direction. "The fuck do you care?"

I stiffen, wishing I'd just gone back upstairs to hang out with Harry.

"Watch your mouth." Eyes sharp as daggers, Mrs. Beck lowers the tablet. "You should be ashamed of yourself. The girl who babysits your brother is doing better at school than you are, and she doesn't have half the help you do."

There's a compliment in there, I suppose, though I don't appreciate that it's delivered in such a backhanded way. Even my mom stops cleaning and looks over her shoulder. I just paste a tight smile on my face and hope to disappear.

"Ah. So that's why your panties are in a bunch," Hunter says to her. "If I flunk my classes, then Dad will have to start paying attention to me instead of you." He smiles cruelly. "Newsflash, Karleigh. Dad's already paying attention to someone else."

He pauses, watching his words hit their target.

"You should know it's not befitting to discuss this in front of other people." Mrs. Beck gets up, gathers her notebook and iPad, and says, "Go do your homework."

Her footsteps fade away, but she takes none of the room's tension with her.

"She's still your brother's mom, you know. Hurting her hurts him," I tell Hunter, shocked at how mean he was. "And if your dad's cheating, how is she to blame?"

"Camilla." He lies back, long legs uncrossing, and lets out a sigh. "It's almost cute how clueless you are."

"Well, it's not cute at all that you're such a dick," I hiss.

"Right, because you're just so perfect," he hisses back, leaning forward now to look me in the eye. "Miss Camilla Hanson, who never steps out of line. Just like your mom, right? Perfect on paper, nothing to hide, nothing to see here. Or is there?"

I don't realize I've stepped back until the coffee table hits me behind my knees. Does he know about my mom's drinking? Or the Incident from my last school? Shit.

"You don't know what you're talking about," I say, but there's a wobble in my voice, and I know Hunter noticed it. I can tell by the way he's grinning again.

"Everyone has secrets, Camilla," he says, his voice like poison. "What are you hiding?"

"Nothing. I—I have to go."

Turning on my heel, I make a beeline for the foyer, grab my bag, and rush out the door. I can't get away from this house fast enough.

Chapter Fourteen

CAMILLA

*A*fter that spectacular encounter, any further attempts on my part to practice for the debate are shut down and dismissed. When Hunter and I cross paths at school, we don't even acknowledge each other. It's the same when I'm at his place to babysit Harrison, although sometimes I could swear I feel eyes on me. Except every time I look over my shoulder, there's no one there—but I know Hunter is watching me. He's simply too much of a coward to show his face.

Several times over the past few weeks, I've thought about asking Isabel or Emmett for help with the project, but even though I know they'd say yes in a heartbeat, I also know that neither of them have taken debate. And I'm not exactly in a hurry to explain to them why I'm in a fight with Hunter, so the conversation never happens.

Still, I'm grateful for my new friends. Isabel and Emmett are the only reason I make it through my days at Oak Academy more or less unscathed by the gossip about me. It's just debate class that's a complete nightmare. Half the time, Hunter doesn't bother to show, and Hillary is constantly whispering behind my back. Literally. It's like there's a fly buzzing around me every day, saying things like, "Did you hear *the help* got so drunk at Matt's party that Hunter had to call her a cab?"

"So tacky. But you know, rehab *is* expensive."

"Maybe she can get a scholarship for that too." A round of giggles ensues.

"Of course lesbo dumpster diver Isabel is obsessed with her. Losers do like to stick together."

I wish I could say I've found the secret to tuning them out during class, but I haven't. The best-case scenario is when Ms. Spencer hushes them, though even that is only temporary. Sometimes it takes all my willpower not to just turn around and tell them to get a life. It probably wouldn't help with the whole scholarship thing, though, since Hillary's mom is on the school board. And it would only serve to fuel their gossip even more. I can already hear them: *ooh, look at* the help *getting all feisty today*.

In terms of my project with Hunter, I've long since given up on him and spent my time researching everything I can about marriage, collecting facts and statistics like weapons. I have to prove I deserve to be here, just like everyone else at this school.

And now, today is the day. My turn to present. There's a horrible knot of anxiety in my stomach, and my pulse is pounding in my ears.

The seat next to me is empty. I'm praying it remains that way. Maybe if Hunter isn't here, I'll be graded based on my own work. I'll happily take a few docked points over presenting with him. In fact, I've decided to volunteer to go up first so I can get this out of the way as quickly as possible and so I don't actually throw up at my desk.

But just as Ms. Spencer is saying, "So which group would like to go first?" and my hand is shooting up in the air, the door squeaks open, and in walks Hunter like my very own personal worst nightmare. "Hunter and Camilla! Great," she says, seeming to think this was all planned out. "Go on ahead."

As I walk to the front of the room on shaky legs, my heart's beating so loud I can barely hear anything else. I'm always nervous when it comes to public speaking, but today is especially dire since I'm counting on someone who can't be counted on for anything. I'm not even sure what Hunter plans to say. Guess he's going to "wing it."

Ms. Spencer takes a seat at an empty desk with her notebook open in front of her and gives us an encouraging nod as we take our places behind the podiums.

I neaten the stack of notecards in front of me, take a deep breath, and begin. "The topic we'll be debating is marriage. Is it an outdated institution?" The tutorials online said to begin with a definition, and since Hunter was so adamantly against marriage the one time we talked about this, I chose my side to oppose him. "By definition, marriage is the legal or formal recognition of a union between two people as partners in a personal relationship. I will be arguing why it's *not* outdated."

Stealing a look at Hunter, I give him a chance to say something. The affirmative is supposed to begin, after all, but he's just leaning against the whiteboard, arms crossed, exuding *don't give a shit-ness*. Fine. No surprise there.

I swallow down my nerves and continue. "Some would argue marriage is outdated because people cheat, and divorces happen. But the failure of a marriage isn't the fault of the institution in itself, but rather of the individuals. Just as the court of law isn't to blame when people commit a crime, the institution of marriage isn't to blame when people decide to break the commitment they made to each other."

Again, I stop, giving Hunter room to argue. He lets out an audible sigh. There are giggles somewhere in the back of class, cut short by a silent glare from Ms. Spencer.

"When faced with the argument that marriage isn't legal for all couples, hence it's outdated, we can argue that, as it currently stands in the United States as of a Supreme Court ruling in June of 2015, it *is*. And in other places in the world where it isn't, it's more a matter of updating anti-quated notions about sexuality so that marriage envelops all unions, not just heteronormative ones."

Ms. Spencer is scribbling in the margins of the grading rubric in her notebook. She doesn't look happy. Meanwhile, Hunter's exchanging looks with his fan club at the back of class. Thanks to my comments regarding gay marriage, I'm sure Hillary is having a ball gossiping about the nature of my relationship with Isabel. So childish.

"Furthermore," I push on, "having a personal commit-ment legally recognized offers other advantages, such as hospital visits when one spouse is ill, shared health insur-ance policies, or joint tax filing to reduce financial strain on the home..."

We were given a full ten minutes, but I finish reading through my notecards after about five—though it felt like a hell of a lot longer. Hunter hasn't said a thing the entire time. I can feel my cheeks burning, and since I'm done now, I step out from behind the podium and shift on my feet.

"That's it, I guess," I say awkwardly.

"Where are the arguments on the positive side?" Ms. Spencer asks. Hunter shrugs, checking his watch rudely.

I clear my throat. "I can't force Hunter to speak if he doesn't want to."

"That much is true, but if you can't get your partner to

cooperate, your project is only half complete." Ms. Spencer narrows her eyes. "Which means the best-case scenario is that you both get fifty points out of a hundred, though that won't be possible—this was more of a legal primer on marriage and a list of potential benefits than any kind of debate regarding whether the institution is applicable to modern-day society."

All I can do is nod. "I understand," I say meekly.

"I'm not sure you do since you didn't adequately complete the assignment, Miss Hanson. You were obviously not prepared to tackle the subject as directed. Not at the level we practice in this class. I'm aware this is new territory for you, but I expected more."

All I can do is nod. How was I supposed to know how this all worked? I've never taken a debate class before. And Hunter gave me zero help, not even to tell me I was on the wrong track. This presentation seriously could not have gone any worse.

"And as for you." Ms. Spencer turns to Hunter, already shaking her head. "Well, I guess there's nothing to critique since you didn't participate."

"A flawless performance," Hunter announces, giving a mock bow. The class applauds, eating it up. As for me, I want to die.

"You're obviously mighty pleased with yourself, Mr. Beck," Ms. Spencer says coldly. "Would you like to share what's so amusing about having your partner fail because *you* wouldn't pull your weight?"

Tentatively, I steal a look at him from the corner of my eye. His lips are pursed, a sign that what she said actually bothered him. "No, Ms. Spencer."

She sighs. "I'm signing you both up for after-school homework together." She shoots Hunter a glare. "And you had better not leave your partner to fend for herself again,

Mr. Beck. At least she tried. The same can't be said for you."

The world is a blur as I force myself to walk back to my seat, completely humiliated. It's someone else's turn to present, but I can barely pay attention as I try to process what just happened.

Hunter brushed off Ms. Spencer's scolding like a dog brushes off water. He doesn't care about failing and doesn't feel guilty about dragging me down with him. Not only that, but because of his slacking, I'll have to stay after school, which is going to affect my babysitting shifts. I am not looking forward to explaining to his parents why I'm going to be late showing up for Harry during the week.

When class ends, I bolt from my seat. I can hear Hunter calling my name behind me, but I just walk faster. I'm never speaking to him again.

Chapter Fifteen

CAMILLA

....

*H*arry asks for homemade mac and cheese for dinner, and I'm happy to oblige. It's easy enough, and there are plenty of fancy cheeses in the fridge that I'm kind of excited to experiment with. Mr. and Mrs. Beck are out of town for the weekend, which means my babysitting duties have been broadened for the next two days to include staying until Harry's tucked into bed, which I do half the time anyway, and then coming back first thing in the morning to make him breakfast.

Things Hunter *could* do but can't actually be trusted with.

He can't even be trusted with the house, it seems, because he swaggers into the kitchen while I'm instructing Harry to pour milk into the flour and butter roux that's bubbling in the pot and loudly announces, "I'm throwing a party tonight in the pool house. Just FYI."

This is the first time he's directed any attention my way since our disastrous presentation on Wednesday, and of course it's not to *ask* if he can have a party, but to *tell* us.

Because he's just automatically assuming I won't say a word to his parents.

"You can't do that!" Harry says. "Mom said no friends over."

"Well, 'Mom' isn't here," Hunter tells him. "And if you say anything, I'll hide all your dolls, and you'll never get them back."

"They're action figures!" Harry asserts.

"You gonna keep your mouth shut, squirt?" Hunter asks.

"I did last time," Harry replies. "Does the cheese go in now?" he asks me.

"Just the first two cups," I instruct, whisking all the while. I glance over at Hunter, who's still waiting expectantly nearby. "I don't care what you do," I tell him. "As long as the noise doesn't keep Harry up."

Hunter looks at his brother, who's glued to my side as he watches me stir the sauce. "It's on the other side of the property, Camilla. Harrison won't be bothered."

"Can I go to the party too?" Harry asks, eyes shifting between Hunter and me.

"Not this one, bud," Hunter answers as he musses the kid's hair. "But we'll have our own party at the pool tomorrow, okay? I'll even order us a pizza. Pepperoni."

Harrison nods eagerly. "Deal!"

It's moments like this, when Hunter is kind and attentive toward his younger brother, that I almost believe his usual aloofness and jack-assery are a front, not his real self. His gaze softens, as does his voice, his demeanor, his everything. No one who so obviously loves a kid as much as that can be wholly bad.

As I tip the strainer full of cooked pasta shells into the pot of melty, cheesy goodness, I feel a heat at my back. My body tenses as Hunter leans in over my shoulder. "Looks amazing," he murmurs. "Save me a bite?"

It makes me shiver, his voice right beside my ear, every word a caress. "Sure."

I know it's pure disgust that I should be feeling in such close proximity with Hunter, but instead all I can muster is blinding horniness.

Harry takes over stirring with the big spoon as I look for a glass baking dish.

"Gonna go Postmates some booze," Hunter says, footsteps fading as he exits the kitchen. Like every other rich kid, he uses his parents' account to order in all the alcohol, and I guess the adults either don't notice or don't care enough to stop it.

I don't realize how tense my muscles are until it's just me and Harry in the kitchen again, and I feel my shoulders slump and my neck relax. It's as if Hunter's presence alone is enough to suffocate me.

The delivery guy comes in when Harry and I are watching Nickelodeon after dinner. I can hear a cart rolling onto the tiles in the foyer, and I lean halfway off the couch to look in there and see just how much Hunter has ordered.

I start to panic. Silently praying this night doesn't all go to hell, I take Harrison upstairs, draw him a bath, and then read to him once he's in his pajamas and tucked in. We're almost to the end of the chapter when I hear a car door slam, the doorbell ring, and then the first wave of people who begin arriving.

And keep on arriving. I don't have to go downstairs to know that dozens of Hunter's friends have been invited to what's rapidly turning into a huge party. There's no way Harry's going to be able to fall asleep with all the commotion.

"You want to put on *Iron Man?*" I suggest.

"Yeah!" Harry agrees.

I don't normally let the kid watch TV in bed, but a

superhero movie is just the thing to drown out the noise of music and conversations getting louder and louder.

He's so transfixed by the movie that he doesn't conk out until somewhere around ten, but I'm glad he's out cold because the music coming from the pool house is now loud enough to rival a club. The deep bass echoes off the walls, and someone's turned on a smoke machine and some kind of strobe light out by the pool. What do they think this is, a music video shoot? Ridiculous.

Under the covers, Harry rolls over and buries his face in Roo's belly. At this rate, they're going to wake him up, which is exactly what I was worried about. *Damn you, Hunter*. Peering at Harry one last time, I stalk out of the room and head downstairs.

No one's in the main house, which thank the Lord for small mercies. Once I'm in the backyard, however, the story is different. A few people are smoking weed by the pool, feet in the water, plastic Solo cups at their sides. I watch, dismayed, as someone puts out a blunt directly on the stone tiles and *leaves it there*.

"Seriously?" I hiss, picking it up and tossing the butt into one of their cups.

"Hey!" one of the guys complains. "That's my drink."

"Congrats. Now it's an ashtray," I snap.

I stomp into the pool house, my foot immediately finding an empty cup and sending it rattling into another. Turns out the stoners were marginally more decent than everyone else because they at least weren't throwing their trash all over the place.

EDM is rattling the windows so loud I have to plug my ears. I notice the dining table has been moved to the corner and seems to function as the chips and snacks station. The kitchen-slash-bar area is crowded, and the rest of the place isn't much better. A couple people I recognize from school are here, but mostly it's a sea of strangers that surrounds me, and I wade through the human chaos like it's mud.

Someone's drink spills on the floor. There are laughs. Rage boils inside me.

Nobody here is going to clean this. They're not going to be mopping beer off the floors, scrubbing the sticky tables, washing the stench of marijuana and cigarette smoke from the drapes. My mom is.

They can't even put their empty cups and bottles in the garbage. Or maybe they are, in their minds, because they're treating this house like it's a gigantic trash can.

I walk right to the sound system in the corner and lower the master volume. "Can you all please be quieter?" I scream to the room. "Hunter's brother is asleep."

But they just keep talking, their loudness even more obvious with the music quieter. Then someone slips behind me and turns the volume all the way back up.

"Are you kidding me?" I yell at the guy, someone with thick brows and the same douchebag attitude I've seen countless times in these trust fund babies.

"I'd never kid you, Miss Hottie," he says, looking down at me like I'm a platter of shrimp and cocktail sauce that pairs perfectly with the beer in his hand. "What's your name?"

I roll my eyes, heading for a circle of people standing at the end of the hallway that presumably leads to the bathroom and whatever other rooms are back there.

"Where's Hunter?" I demand, raising my voice to be heard over the music.

Confusion flits between them. Two of them look at each other and shrug, but someone else points down the hall, where all I see are closed doors.

My stomach turns. If he's in one of the bedrooms, he's

definitely not alone. A repeat of the X-rated pool situation isn't something I want to experience, but what else can I do when letting the party blow up out of control like this isn't an option? I can't even imagine how bad it would be if the cops showed up. I'd be out of a job for sure, my mom would blow a gasket, and I'd never get to see Harry again. I can't risk that.

With every step down the darkened hallway, my body becomes heavier with dread. There are a couple people in line for the bathroom, which leaves two other doors to try since the smaller door next to the bathroom opens onto a linen closet.

The room at the end of the hall has a light on and the door ajar, so I peer in there first. About five or six heads swivel my way, and it's obvious there's nothing going on in here but the requisite smoking and drinking, just a bit more quietly. Frankly, I'm surprised no one's hijacked the room to get down and dirty yet. I guess it's still early.

This leaves the other bedroom, the door to which is closed. I knock, though with the music on full blast, I doubt anyone inside heard. Pressing my ear to the door doesn't reveal anything either.

"Hunter?" I yell. Nothing.

Breathing deeply to steel myself, I fling open the door.

It's dark in here, the only illumination coming through the window from the pool lights outside. Still, it's enough for me to make out Hunter sitting in an upholstered chair by the window. A girl sits on his lap, straddling him, breathing hard. They're both clothed, thankfully, but he has one hand flat against her back, the other down between her legs. Her skirt is pulled up so high, I see a flash of her round, bare ass twitching back and forth over his hand before I turn away and throw up a hand to cover my eyes. I could be wrong, but I think he had his fingers inside her.

"What do you want?" he asks, and I hear the girl murmuring something to him.

A combination of embarrassment and anger ripples through me. How do I always end up in these awkward situations? And why does Hunter Beck always have to act like such a Neanderthal?

Refusing to turn in his direction, I say, "You said you were going to keep the noise down. This—," with my other hand, I gesture to the music blaring in the other room, "isn't keeping it down. Your brother's bound to wake up any second."

"You're overreacting. If Harry's asleep, he'll keep on sleeping through it."

My nostrils flare with my sharp inhale, and I snap, "Either you turn the music down, or I will call the cops with a noise complaint myself. Your choice, Hunter."

Without looking back, I stalk out of the room and slam the door behind me.

Chapter Sixteen

CAMILLA

I stampede out of the pool house and go back upstairs to check on Harrison. Although the music does soften behind me, my eyes burn with tears, and my breaths have become desperate gulps for air.

After peeking in at Harry, who is blessedly fine, I ease his door shut and lean against the wall with my head tilted back and my eyes closed. Technically, my shift is done—I can go home now. But I'm too angry and shaken to keep it together, and the last thing I want is to have random people driving down the street all staring at me as I walk to the bus stop crying and alone.

"Camilla," a voice says. I know it's Hunter before I even open my eyes.

"What are you doing up here?" I rage, glaring at him as I try to blink back tears. "Think I can't take care of your brother? I do it almost every day, so I'm pretty sure I can handle it." I spit the words like they're poison. "Go be with your friends."

My chest feels like it's being crushed. I can't stand that he caught me crying.

"I didn't come up here to check on my brother," he says.

Stepping toward me slowly, like I'm a bird about to take flight, he reaches toward my face and brushes a tear away with his thumb. He's so gentle, I gasp. All I can do is go still under his touch, my gaze dropping to his full lips that are slightly parted.

When I look back up, our eyes catch. We're so close I can feel his body heat.

"Were you curious what I was doing to her when you walked in?" he asks, his voice husky, stepping in closer.

I'm already back against the wall, so there's nowhere for me to go. "I mean, I... It was pretty obvious," I say, but I'm whispering.

His torso presses into mine, and lower down, something thick and solid brushes against my hip. *Is that his cock?* A rush of adrenaline courses through me.

My pulse is kicking so hard and fast I can feel it in my throat. I can feel every point of contact between us like it's fire. I want to feel more of his body. I want to press back. I want to touch him. But I don't.

I have no idea what I'm doing, especially when it comes to Hunter Beck.

His hand comes up to cup my cheek, making it impossible for me to look at anything that isn't him. "Did you want it to be you?"

I try to deny it, but my voice lacks conviction. "No."

"I think you're lying." He trails his hand down the curve of my neck, just barely touching the sensitive skin there, a teasing gesture that has me on the tips of my toes. I have to bite my lip to keep myself from gasping again.

Hunter's mouth forms a sinful smile as he leans in, stealing my breath, letting me think he's going to kiss me. I hate myself for being so eager, so desperate. Hate how hot he's making me, how good it feels to have him so close, how it's too damn hard to walk away because all I want is more, more, more. His other hand skims the outside of my thigh. My knee jerks, and I squeeze my legs together and turn my face away.

Touch me, I'm thinking. *Touch me because I'm too scared to touch you first.*

I feel his warm breath on my neck as he says, "Have you ever had someone's fingers inside you?" He may as well have said *open sesame* because the low rumble of his voice in my ear is so good that my legs actually open.

Taking it as an invitation, his fingers trace the seam of my jeans where my legs meet, and my insides go liquid. All of me is heat and longing. I can't say no, but I can't say yes either. I'm afraid of how bad I want this. Want *him*.

I move my legs farther apart, giving him easier access, and Hunter smoothly dips his hand down to cup my center, using the heel of his palm to stroke me through the thin denim. My body instinctively reacts by grinding into his hand, demanding more.

Heart pumping faster, I let out a breath as he unbuttons my pants.

"Camilla," Hunter draws my name out in a whisper as he slides my zipper down.

I know I should be ashamed I'm letting him have his way with me, but everything he's doing feels so good.

He slips his hand down the front of my pants, over my cotton underwear. I'm throbbing under the heat of his touch, trembling at the way his fingers are just a thin shred of fabric away from me.

"Tell me to stop, and I'll stop," he murmurs.

My nails dig into his chest, bunching up his shirt. His pecs are taut and smooth under my hands.

"Tell me," he says again.

I shake my head. No, I don't want him to stop. And now he knows it.

His fingers suddenly hook around the crotch of my panties and tug, so his knuckles are brushing against my pussy lips. My core tightens in pure agony, and all I can do is hold my breath, both wanting and not wanting him to do more.

I hide my face in Hunter's shoulder. He makes little circles with his knuckles, stroking me until I'm buzzing and breathing hard. He's not even inside me yet, and I'm already seeing stars from the lightest of touches. How will it feel when he goes all the way? His fingers are so big, I wonder...

And then he's turning his hand, slowly teasing my lower lips apart and sliding a finger between them, gliding it up and down my slit to gently swirl my own wetness around. My toes lift me up, and I bury a soft moan in his shoulder. *Just do it*, I think. *Put it inside me.*

I can feel his lips against the shell of my ear. "You're so fucking wet."

About ready to die, is what I am. Of shame. Of agony. Of want.

I've still got his shirt in my fists, clinging to him to keep from falling. I lift my head from his shoulder just enough to bite the outline his collarbone makes, for no other reason than it's there, and it's part of him, and it's safer than his mouth.

He gives a sharp intake of breath and then switches to longer strokes, his fingers sliding from my opening up to my clit, back and forth, up and down. I'm tight with antici-pation, dizzy with it. When he finally pushes the pads of his fingers directly against my clit, lightning strikes. And again, and again, as he repeats the pattern, sliding down and then up and then pressing that sweet, aching spot.

My breath turns ragged, and I realize my eyes have squeezed shut. I'm anticipating his circles now, tensing up just before he taps my clit, thrusting just a little every time his finger dips down low, waiting for the delicious moment he'll finally stop teasing and push his finger inside. The pleasure is building, and as it does, so does the need to let myself continue with this indulgence, ride it out to the end.

"Maybe you weren't jealous," he whispers.

And then he's sliding his finger into me, slow and strong and so perfect. I moan, the ecstasy bending my back, and holy shit it feels incredible, more than I'd ever dreamed of.

My hands go to his shoulders, and I press my face into his neck, breathing hard, waiting for more. He pulls his finger out and then slides it slowly back in again, stopping again, drawing pleasure out of my body with expert precision.

He's good. Too good. It's a miracle I'm still holding myself upright. I'm going to come right in his hand any second if he keeps using his fingers like this. I can feel it.

"Maybe you were turned on by what you saw," he goes on, his voice a hot, low murmur as he pumps his finger slowly back and forth. "Or maybe it turned you on because it was me."

And that's when I realize he hasn't even kissed me yet. He has no problem sticking his hand down my pants, but his mouth hasn't touched mine.

The reality of the situation slams into me. I'm not going to be another one of his one-night conquests.

I pull his hand away and then push him back, hard.

"You're so full of yourself," I say, zipping my pants up and buttoning them angrily. Disappointment bubbles inside me, both at myself and at Hunter. Looking at him makes it worse. "Go back to your party. I'm sure there are plenty of other girls for you to choose from."

I run back to the refuge of Harrison's room and close the door behind me. Sinking to the floor, I start shaking, unable to believe I let Hunter do those things to me. Unable to believe I'd enjoyed every minute of it...and that even now, I want him to do it all again.

Chapter Seventeen

CAMILLA

*W*hat kind of girl just stands there and lets some guy she's not even dating do that to them? It's all I can think about later as I toss and turn in bed. Hunter had jumped right to third base with me for his own amusement, or maybe just to take something from me, and I'm still shocked and ashamed at how good it felt to almost give in to him.

What was his motive? Has he been planning something like this all along? Is my lack of experience or my status as "the help" some kind of sick challenge to him, or does he just like toying with me because it's entertaining for him— some story he can laugh about with his friends later?

Or maybe it's pure entitlement. After all, he's used to getting whatever he wants. *Whomever* he wants.

I bury my face in my pillow and let out a deep sigh. It's after midnight, and I'm completely wide awake.

Giving up on sleep, I switch on the nightstand lamp and open up the book I'm reading. It takes me about five minutes too long to realize I've been going over the same page over and over again, not absorbing any of it. I toss the book down in frustration and turn out the light again.

Between my legs, a hot ache throbs, and I curl onto my side and squeeze my thighs together as I try to ignore it. My body still hums with pent-up tension, silently demanding that I finish what Hunter started.

It's a vicious cycle. The more I try to wish it away, the more I remember, and as I recount the details, I can't deny that everything he did to me turned me on.

The way he pressed me into the wall, the way he touched my face, the glide of his hand up my thigh. The stroke of his hot fingers up and down my wet lips. Tapping my clit at just the right intervals, plunging inside me so agonizingly. He knew exactly what he was doing, exactly what would make me feel good—even though I didn't.

I try to dissect it, think about it scientifically. This isn't about Hunter. It can't be. It's just the result of perfectly natural, raging teenage hormones. They're the sole reason I'm attracted to him at all, the reason I couldn't push him away right at the beginning. Why I let him go as far as he did. He could have been anyone.

God, I'm a bad liar.

The truth is, I only stopped him because I realized he was treating me like another one of his toys. But what's worse than the way he played with me is how quickly I lost all sense of myself. That's what scares me most. That even though I knew full well there was no intimacy to him touching me, I'd still wanted it to go on. And on.

I'd almost lost control.

Thankfully, I pulled his hand away before I had an orgasm. There's some kind of bonding chemical that gets released in your brain when you come with a guy, and I don't need any more reasons to get attached to that asshole. At the same time, part of me does regret running off, just a little. Hunter's fingers felt so good. I was so close.

Even though I've read about orgasms before, I've never actually had one. What I've put together from my research is that it's usually a series of muscular contractions, a flood of endorphins, and a release of sexual tension that's sort of like a warm explosion. Which makes it sound more like a science experiment having to do with combustibles than the sublime experience I always assumed it would be.

Either way, it's hard to get in the mood to touch yourself when you live in tiny crappy apartments with paperthin walls, and when you're usually so exhausted at night that you just collapse into bed and fall into a dreamless sleep.

But tonight's not one of those nights.

Plus, it's not like I'll ever know what I enjoy if I don't try it myself first.

I've already wedged one of my stuffed animals between my legs by the time I realize I'm trying to convince myself it's okay to finish myself off. I squeeze my legs together around the plushie, and the pressure feels good. I take a deep breath.

My door's locked, I'm alone, and I can't sleep with Hunter on my mind. There's no way I'll be able to relax if I don't take care of this.

I press harder on the stuffed toy, grinding gently against it.

Behind my closed eyelids, I see Hunter gazing down at me intently, our bodies pressed against each other, the wall at my back, his fingers sliding up and down my pussy. His cock digging into my hip as he breathes into my ear. Now that I'm replaying it all in my mind, I realize something. Although I'd been too caught up in the moment to think about it at the time, I'm pretty sure he was as turned on as

I was. I heard it when his breath caught, and more importantly, I felt it.

I should've grabbed him, seen how he liked it. Traced the shape of him with my finger, stroked him through the fabric. Maybe I should have pushed *him* into the wall, rubbed myself against the bulge in his pants.

Under the sheets, massaging myself with the toy, my imagination takes flight. Hunter's voice, telling me the reason he dragged me away from Matt's party is that he didn't want anyone else touching me. His lips on mine, his fingers pumping inside me, harder, deeper, the friction driving me to a pleasure close to madness.

"You like that?" I imagine him saying.

"Yeah," I'd say back.

"Tell me to stop, and I'll stop," he'd say, just like he did earlier.

"Don't stop, Hunter. Go harder."

Something's happening, and my hips move on their own, thrusting faster against the plushie as I lose myself in the pursuit of this. I feel little electric sparks in my core, a sweet twisting feeling, and all the while my fantasies about Hunter get more intense.

That time when I heard him jerking himself off in his room—had that been to me after all? Was he imagining me on his bed, legs spread wide? Looking up at him all innocent and hungry at the same time, ready and waiting for him?

And what about the way he'd whispered my name? "Camilla." Like he was begging me for something. Begging me for *me*.

What if I was the girl in the pool, bouncing up and down on his cock, letting him drive himself into me with harsh little gasps?

"Fuck me, Hunter," I'd say. And he would. Harder and

faster, both of us breathless and moaning, his lips crashing onto mine—

A wave slams into me from inside, hot and tingling, so strong my back arches and my hips buck. I hold my breath, riding out the aftershocks squeezing my core, a shudder going through me as I realize that I just came while fantasizing about Hunter.

My face meets the pillow. The last thing I think about as I drift off is him.

Chapter Eighteen

CAMILLA

*M*andatory homework sessions are held in the library, so that's where I go on Wednesday after my classes are over. Predictably, Hunter hasn't shown —he's been avoiding me all week, in fact, both during and after school—and Ms. Spencer sighs as she comes over to the table where I've spread out my work.

"Flying solo again, Miss Hanson?"

I look up from my notebook with a tight smile. "Seems so."

She shakes her head. "Honestly, I don't know what to do anymore. Hunter was great first quarter, but then out of nowhere he just...stopped caring." Giving our immediate area a cursory glance, she lowers her voice and confides, "I've had serious talks with him, left messages at home, had a one-on-one conference with his mother—"

"Stepmother," I interrupt.

"Right, of course," Ms. Spencer says, dropping into the seat next to me and massaging her temples.

"Are you feeling okay?" I ask.

"To be honest, Hunter's been a tough nut to crack." She

quietly goes on, "I was hoping he'd bounce back with this project, knowing his work ethic would affect his partner... but it doesn't seem to have made a difference. I'm at a loss here. When students don't perform well, parents call administrators and principals looking for answers. And then the blame falls on me."

With her frustration clear, Ms. Spencer seems so human that for a second I'm too stunned to reply. I'm not used to teachers treating me as an equal or letting their guard down like this. I suddenly realize her harshness during my debate presentation with Hunter might have had nothing to do with me and everything to do with her. And I also realize how young she actually is, probably early twenties. Her career is on the line.

"I'm sorry," I say, feeling sympathetic and a little guilty. Damn you, Hunter.

"Don't be," she says. "I shouldn't be telling you any of this. It's just...Oak Academy is a private school. Parents have expectations, things they demand because of what they're paying. I'm already on thin ice thanks to a few complaints last year."

"What happened?" I whisper, not sure she'll even answer.

She smiles wryly. "I refused to bump up the grades of some football players who weren't maintaining their GPAs. I guess debate has traditionally been a 'cruise class' for jocks, but that's not how I run my ship. So."

"That sucks," I blurt. "I mean, it's really unfair. You're just doing your job."

"Not everybody sees it that way."

For a few moments we just sit here, lost in our thoughts. It's hard not to be even more annoyed with Hunter, knowing his dad is probably going to be yet another parent lodging a complaint against Ms. Spencer—even though it's on Hunter to do the work.

"Listen," she says, "this after-school work was really more for him than for you, but I do think you'd benefit from it. And I'm more than happy to help get you up to speed with your classmates, okay? Let's just think of this as extra credit." She smiles.

"Will it be enough extra credit to balance out the F we got on our project?" I can't help asking.

"I'll make sure it is," Ms. Spencer says. "Come get me if you need anything."

With that, she heads over to a corner table where she's set up a pile of papers to grade. I feel better about debate now that we've talked, but I'm still pissed at Hunter.

My notebook is open in front of me, but after about fifteen minutes of zoning out, I have to admit to myself that I can't focus on my notes at all.

I still can't believe I let him touch me on Saturday. That I thought I might even like him. This is *Hunter Beck* we're talking about. God, what is wrong with my brain lately? And what makes it all even worse is how he's just flat-out avoiding me now. Maybe he's as upset about getting to third base with me as I am.

That doesn't ring true though. Putting his hands up a girl's skirt is par for the course. Unless he's ashamed (or worried his friends will tease him) about screwing around with "the help." But that seems incredibly unlikely. Even if he thinks I'm white trash, he's not the type to care about the socioeconomic status of the notches on his bedpost.

So what the hell is going on?

I'm an idiot for letting myself think he cared. That he was being protective and honorable when I was drunk at Matt's party rather than just disgusted with my behavior.

There's no way in hell Hunter would ever go for someone like me. It was delusion, all of it. Plain and simple.

And besides, I can't let myself be the girl who falls for the walking bad boy cliché, thinking he's secretly good underneath it all. Because he's not.

I spot a girl with a familiar set of pigtails by the windows to my left. Isabel. She usually doesn't tutor on Wednesdays, so I'm glad today is an exception. Talking to her always distracts me from whatever I've got going on. Plus, she seems to be the only other girl at this school who realizes Hunter isn't all sunshine and roses.

After packing up my things, I go over to where she sits with three underclassmen who have their geometry texts splayed open on the library table. "Hey, girl."

"Milla!" Isabel squeals, loud enough to get a few "shh!"s and glares from the other students.

Rolling her eyes at the shade, Isabel turns in her seat to hug my side. Her expression quickly shifts to one of irritation once she looks over my shoulder. "Wait, why are you all by yourself? Isn't today..."

"Debate practice. Yeah." I shrug, a poor attempt to downplay it. "Hunter didn't show."

She frowns. "Milla..."

"It's whatever. I talked to Ms. Spencer and we're cool. Hunter on the other hand..."

Isabel gives me a long look before she turns back to her study group, who have their eyes glued to us. With a hand-wave in their direction, she says, "Work on those triangle problems. I'll be back in a few." She gets up and points me toward the elevator. "I need a snack. Let's go see what the vending machines have to offer."

Mouthing a "be right back" to Ms. Spencer over my shoulder, I let Isabel lead me upstairs to the Snack Nook. It consists of two couches arranged in an L shape, a coffee table covered with magazines, and a few vending machines against the wall.

We agree to split a bag of peanut M&Ms and a granola bar and get two mochas from the instant coffee machine. Drinks in hand, we plop onto the couch.

"So what's up with that boy?" she asks. "Is he trying to get you flunked?"

"I wish I knew," I say.

Isabel taps her cup with a finger before taking it to her lips for a sip. "I will say he's been weird this year. Not the entitled, aloof, wannabe frat boy part—he's always been that way—but like, not being on the swim team? That's not Hunter Beck."

Now, I'll admit, I've seen Hunter's naked torso several times because babysitter. Even before I caught him in the pool with that random girl, I've been there when Harrison wants to join his big brother for a swim. But somehow, I never connected his lean, muscled build to a swimmer's. Which, let's be real, makes sense.

"Swim team?" is my entire contribution to get Isabel to keep talking. I can't manage anything more because I'm trying not to remember how that very toned physique felt pressed against me and the way his fingers played with my pussy.

I can't mention any of it though. That I let him finger me up against a wall even though Isabel and I both know he's nothing but a massive jerk is my deepest shame.

"Yeah," she muses. "He was a CIF state champion. Makes no sense he'd quit senior year when he already had college recruits circling. Wonder what happened there. I never heard about him getting an injury or anything like that." She wrinkles her nose.

The cloud over my head darkens. "Maybe he just got

too caught up in his *other* extracurriculars," I say sarcastically. I pop a blue M&M into my mouth.

"Spill the tea," Isabel prods, leaning forward.

Shrugging, I say, "It's not my place to gossip."

And what a load of gossip it would be. Gossip about all the girls I've seen sneaking in and out of the Becks' house, or the one I watched him with in the pool, or how I overheard him masturbating in his room. Or how he took advantage of me outside his brother's room—no, how I let him take advantage of me—and I liked it.

"Anyway, I don't actually think that's it," I deflect. "I mean, when I went over to practice for the debate assignment, his stepmom was in the room, and watching them snipe at each other was super awkward. But I don't think it's a secret that he hates her."

Isabel shakes her head. "Yeah, no. He's been very vocal about that since his dad married her." She pauses to sip her mocha, tilting her head as she thinks. "So maybe this is all a product of neglect on his dad's part, and he's just self-sabotaging to get a rise out of the old man. Tale as old as time. Hunter's just a typical jackass, I guess."

We eat our snacks in silence. "He's sweet with his younger brother though," I finally find myself saying, much to my own puzzlement.

"Aha." Isabel smirks. "I thought you were crushing on him because of his looks, which, fine. I get it. But *this* explains your Hunter-itis. You found his soft spot."

"I'm not crushing on him!" I deny.

Isabel waves me off. "Please, Camilla. You're not the first case of Hunter-itis I've come across. I'm not judging you. However, I must urge caution. He's left plenty of shattered hearts in his wake, and I'm not going to let you become another casualty."

"Are you saying... Do you have history with him?" I ask,

more curious than jealous. I just can't see Isabel going for someone like him.

"Ew, no. All those muscles, and that chiseled jaw? Please. My type is someone else entirely." She blushes and clears her throat. "Anyway, just know I'm here for moral support if you need a shoulder to cry on." Leaning even closer, she squeezes my shoulder. "And like I said, be careful. I don't want to see you get sucked into that Hunter Beck quicksand. That boy is pure sin."

"Don't I know it." That's the whole problem.

I laugh along with her, but I wish I could tell her more. Then again, I don't even know what I really think or feel about him. Every time I make up my mind, Hunter does a total one-eighty, and I start questioning myself again.

And what could I say to Isabel, anyway? Hey, you know all the times Hunter was a complete jerk to me? How he picked a fight with Emmett and then dragged me out of the party where I met you? How he made me fail my debate project? Yeah, after all that, I let him finger me.

It'd sound insane when Isabel knows he's such a dick to me.

So I don't tell her any of that, and I don't insist she spill who she's crushing on either (although I suspect it's Emmett). I just thank her for the talk and tell her she can always count on me too.

*I*t's four o'clock on the dot and I'm bolting out the door, backpack half zipped, already calculating how many hours of babysitting I'm going to have left if I can make the 4:05 bus at the corner. Having extra homework time wasn't exactly torture, but that still had to be one of the longest hours of my life.

Talking to Isabel *did* make me feel better, but only temporarily. Now that I'm rushing to the bus stop, my thoughts immediately go back to Hunter. I still can't believe he didn't show. I mean, I can believe it—I should have expected it, actually—but some part of me was still holding out hope. Hope which has now been crushed.

Maybe I should drop debate. I kinda love Ms. Spencer, and I'm sure she won't pair me with Hunter again anytime soon, but I'm tired of that sick feeling I get every time I walk into class and see Hunter's chair empty. Or worse, when he does show up and then ignores me. It's still early enough in the semester to sign up for another class and catch up. At the same time, I hate the idea of letting Hunter win. It's not fair.

As I pass the parking lot, a familiar laugh reaches my ears.

Pivoting automatically toward the sound, I spot Hunter leaning casually against his car with his blazer off and his tie undone, joking around with his friends, all of them looking like they have absolutely nowhere else to be right now. Except that Hunter does. Or *did*.

A flash of anger jolts through me. I seriously cannot believe he's been out here this whole time shooting the shit with his lackeys, not a care in the world, just nonchalantly blowing off the mandatory study session we had together.

Rage fuels my every step as I storm toward him. I recognize two of his friends—Steve Howard, the one who keeps hounding Isabel, and Matt Mason, of kink closet party fame. One of the two douchebros I don't know spots me and nods in my direction while looking at Hunter. "Heads-up, Beck. 'The help' has arrived."

There it is, that word again. More proof that Hunter and all his friends see me as subhuman. Livid doesn't even begin to describe how I'm feeling. The pent-up anger inside me screams to be unleashed, but I hold it in tight, setting myself to simmer.

Hunter turns to look at me, raising an eyebrow lazily. "What up, Hanson?"

"*What up?*" I echo, fuming, my voice gone low and icy. "Did you somehow forget about the mandatory homework sessions you got us dragged into? Because that was today. Every Wednesday for the rest of the semester, actually, if we want to pass."

"Chill out, Camilla," he says. Behind him, his boys are chuckling to themselves. "It's just a grade."

Something in me boils over, and now I'm inches away, jabbing a finger at him.

"You entitled. Little. Shit. You might not care about

grades, but some of us depend on them! Because unlike you, I don't have a rich daddy at home to pay my way into an Ivy League. I have to work for it!"

The guys instantly quiet. Throats are cleared. Gazes are avoided.

"Catch you later, bro," one of them says, and then they all shuffle off, leaving me alone and seething with Hunter still slouched in front of me.

"You've made your point, okay?" he says, eyes shifting around the parking lot. "And I get it. So you can stop freaking out now."

Ha. He doesn't want me making a scene in front of his little friends.

But it's too late to stop "freaking out." Because I've just made a few decisions for myself. As far as I'm concerned, securing my future is the only thing that matters, and Hunter Beck is nothing but a cockroach in my path. He thinks he can just ignore me? Pretend I don't exist? I'll do him one better.

"I'm done with you," I say flatly. "And I'm going to transfer out of debate so I never have to see you again."

There. I said it out loud. And it felt like a huge weight just lifted from my shoulders, proving that it was the right thing to do.

Hunter has the nerve to scoff and roll his eyes. "Sorry to break it to you, but you still work for me."

"I work for your *parents*!" I spit, raising my voice again, any coolness I'd managed to summon evaporating under my still very present, still very hot anger.

My self-control has shattered. All I see is red red red, and I'm breathing hard, my feet restless as I stand there. Now that I think about it, I realize that dropping debate isn't enough—it will never be enough to get him out of my life.

I need to burn every bridge that leads back to Hunter Beck.

"You know what? I'm not going to babysit your brother, either. So you can tell all your friends to stop making fun of me. I'm not 'the help' anymore."

Genuine shock slackens his jaw for a brief moment. "I call bullshit."

"Call it whatever you want." I straighten my shoulders. "The fact is, I resign. Starting today."

I don't stay to see his reaction, just turn on my heel, go to the bus stop, and jam my earbuds in place. The tension won't leave my muscles though, and in my head, the events that have just transpired play over and over. I feel good about standing up to Hunter but positively sick to my stomach over losing Harry. It's for the best, I tell myself. I just wish my eyes would stop tearing up.

My ride home is packed, sweaty bodies pressed together like we're sardines in a can. Arm up and hand in the strap, I close my eyes, trying to will the tears away. I'll cry when I get home because dear Lord, I could use a good cry after torpedoing my life.

I can't believe I just impulsively quit my only source of income. But I had to. As much as I care for Harrison, the shadow Hunter casts over me is much bigger than any brightness I get out of my time with Harry. Which really and truly sucks.

God, I'm going to miss that kid more than anything. Miss helping him with his math, reading books together, playing games, building with Legos. I'll miss his sweet, happy face when I make him a snack he likes, and his delight when I give him fruit arranged in the shape of a face, a cat, or a dinosaur. What's worse than my own sadness, though, is thinking about how he'll feel when someone tells him I'm not coming back. What if he thinks I abandoned him? That I didn't love him enough?

Shoulders heavy, I trudge up the steps of our apartment building, sighing as I dig around in my bag for my keys. As soon as I walk through the door, my mom calls out.

"Camilla! Come in here a sec," she says from her bedroom.

I swallow the lump in my throat, dreading having to tell her I'm quitting my cozy after-school job. A job she supposedly pleaded with the Becks to give me, a job I've managed to hold on to in spite of the Incident That Shall Not Be Named.

The state of her bedroom stops me short.

My brain immediately spins into panic mode as I take in the open drawers and closet, the half-packed suitcases on the bed. A scene I've witnessed far too often, a scene I've been a part of enough times not to immediately realize how it'll play out.

It figures.

"Where are we going?" I ask, my voice defeated.

"We're moving," Mom says, stating the obvious as she rolls up a dress and shoves it into the suitcase, not even bothering to look at me when she delivers this latest batch of life-changing news.

It's a good thing I'm close to the doorframe because right now I need support, and it's right there for me to lean against as my world is completely torn off its hinges. For the first time in years, I've made two real friends I want to stay close to, so of course it's the perfect time for her to decide we need to up and leave.

My voice is small and choked as I repeat, "Okay, but where are we going?"

She keeps packing, as if what she's about to say is trivial. "The Becks' house."

And that is the moment my entire body just stops. I stand there, jaw unhinged, my mind blank. There's no freaking way. This is a joke.

"Mom, for real," I say with a thin smile.

She pauses to look at me finally. "I am being real. Mr. Beck's been asking if I want to transition to live-in house-keeping, and with all our bills piling up lately, I decided to go for it." Going to the closet, she pulls out another armload of clothes.

My mouth moves, but for a moment I have no words.

This can't be happening.

"You're telling me I have to move in with *Hunter Beck?*" I blurt. "Seriously?"

Mom huffs out a sigh of annoyance. Her voice is all barbs and sarcasm as she says, "It's a pool house, Camilla. I'm not asking you to share a room with anyone."

Scrambling for a plan B, I draw a blank. We don't have relatives or friends who'd be able to take us in on such short notice, if at all, and we sure as hell don't have the money to move into a new place. Not when we'd need a security deposit and first and last months' rent. And besides all that, I doubt we'd get approved now that we're breaking our current lease. Maybe a homeless shelter? She'd never go for it.

FML.

"What are you standing there waiting for?" Mom snaps. "We're supposed to move our stuff in tonight. Chop chop."

I'm in zombie mode on my way to my room, listlessly dragging my suitcase out from under the bed. For a moment, I sit on the mattress, head in my hands.

What the hell did I do to deserve this?

Chapter Twenty

HUNTER

The last few days have not been pleasant.

And then, this afternoon, I had to contend with the fallout from Camilla's little hissy fit and my friends being total dicks about it.

"The fuck was that all about, dude?" Matt had said after Camilla stormed off.

"Nothing," I told him. "She just quit as Harry's nanny. Whatever."

"Maybe it's a good thing," he said. "I wouldn't want that psycho babysitting my siblings."

Steve had cracked up. "No wonder Ortega's all over her. The crazy ones are always the hottest in bed, am I right?"

Hearing them laugh and make asshole comments had set my teeth on edge, but I didn't correct them or even object. I hadn't felt like getting into any more fights.

But when I got home, I just sat in my car in the drive-way, zoning out. I couldn't stop thinking about how pissed off Camilla had been at me, and how she'd wanted me to tell my friends to stop calling her "the help." Hillary was the one who started using the term when I mentioned that

Camilla was our babysitter—I hadn't meant anything by it. Even still, I feel like shit for starting the whole thing. I've known Hillary for years; she smack-talks every girl that crosses my path. Camilla is no exception. It's like Hillary actually thinks she owns me just because we made out at a party once.

But me? I never called Camilla "the help." Servant girl? Sure, I said that once, in a very heated moment when I'd wanted to send her running and decided an insult would work fastest. Humiliation was simply payback for Camilla making my brain short-circuit on the regular. And when I'd seen her staring at me, dick-deep in another girl (who I haven't spoken to since), it had been worse than a short-circuit.

It was a complete blackout.

Looking at her, I was struck dumb, and then I was imagining she was under me and not several feet away, and suddenly it was too late to hold back, and I was over the edge. It was embarrassing, to be honest. So I reacted like I always do when I'm thrown off my game: I make whoever's responsible run away with their tail between their legs.

I realize that sounds bad, and yeah, I might act like a jerk sometimes, but just for the record, Camilla Hanson is no better than I am, walking around with her holier-than-thou attitude. An attitude that I know for a *fact* to be hypocritical.

And then, just to put a cherry on top of my shit sundae of a week so far, I get to walk in the front door to the sound of yelling coming from my dad's office.

Harrison's sitting on the living room couch, eyes glued to the TV and Roo snuggled at his side. He's hugging his knees, and I can tell right away that he's fully aware of the fact that his parents are fighting and is trying to block it out with cartoons turned up too loud. I went through this same thing plenty of times myself when I was his age. As soon as he spots me, he looks up, big eyes red-rimmed, and I realize he's been crying. Probably upset that he can't do anything to make it all stop.

"Hey, man," I say, plopping onto the couch next to him and pulling him against me for a side hug. "You watching *The Last Airbender?*"

Harry sniffles and nods, still too shook up to talk.

I know exactly how he must feel. My mom and dad were at each other's throats twenty-four seven for years before Mom finally left. I can't blame her. After that, I just got numb to all the bullshit and reached a point where I became completely desensitized when my dad would fight with whoever he was dating, especially so when it comes to my stepmom. Dad might be able to ignore the blatant gold digging and social climbing, but I can't. The only worthy thing Karleigh's done with her life is give birth to Harrison. My brother is a total sweetheart, and I'm not too proud to say I love him like crazy.

"Don't pay attention to them," I say, giving him another squeeze. "It's not your fault, and it isn't anything about you. It's their own shit. Okay?"

"'kay," he manages, his voice soft.

I sit there on the couch with him for a few minutes, pretending to watch TV, straining my ears all the while to eavesdrop. What the hell are they at each other's throats for again? Part of me feels bad for wishing it'll be the last straw, the fight that finally leads to a divorce, because obviously Karleigh *is* Harrison's mom, and I don't wish a broken home on anyone, least of all my little brother. But his mom is so terrible that the positives of her leaving far outweigh the negatives.

"The girl's good with Harrison," Dad is saying. "It'd be a shame to lose her. And a hassle to look for a new sitter."

Ah. Camilla must've called already to officially quit. I wonder if she told them I'm the reason she doesn't want to come over anymore. The thought of it turns my stomach a little. I mean, Harry didn't deserve to lose Camilla on my account.

"I'm not denying that, but..." Karleigh concedes, her voice dropping away.

"The alternative is you spending more time with your son. Is that something you want?" Dad asks, his tone even and patronizing.

That calculated voice of reason is why everyone thinks he's a level-headed man. I know better though. It's just another mask he puts on to hide the hideousness inside.

"What about my *me time*?" she snaps back, getting louder. "I already spend all day doing work for your business. You do what you want in the evenings. So do I!"

Hearing her talk like that makes my blood boil. A good mom would be spending as much time with her son as humanly possible. She would *occasionally* hire a nanny, not insist on having one around for most of the week. Same goes for Dad, who never really spent time with me and is exactly the same way with Harrison.

Some parents learn from the mistakes they make with their eldest children. As twisted as it is, I wish that had been the case with my dad. That he'd used his failures with me to course correct. But no.

I ruffle Harrison's hair and then get up off the couch to go upstairs when I hear Karleigh shout, "Why didn't you tell me sooner they were coming to *live with us* then? And why do you keep insisting we need a live-in housekeeper?"

With that, I freeze in place.

Is she fucking serious? *Live* with us?

"I wanted to surprise you," Dad says patronizingly.

"You've always wanted a live-in nanny and maid. Now you have both."

Immediately, I barrel down the hall and explode through the office door, and before I can stop myself I blurt, "Are you shitting me? They can't come live here."

"Hunter! Language!" Karleigh shrieks in her obnoxious Valley girl tone.

Dad glances at me from the other side of the mahogany desk. "Last time I checked, this was *my* house. *My* money." He gets up from the leather chair and leans menacingly toward me, knuckles on the surface of the desk. "So you will mind your manners while you're living under *my* roof and out of *my* pockets. And while you're here, your principal emailed me to let me know that once again you..."

I stare at his tie and block him out after that. I know whatever he's saying will just be a variant of the only conversation he ever has with me, about how we have a name and a reputation to uphold, and I'm ruining it all by being needlessly difficult.

I'm pretty sure he's never actually cared about me, only about what I can do to make him look good and shine more light on the family name. Because La Jolla's favorite real estate legend has a "reputation" to uphold, so he can't have people realizing his eldest son is an abject failure. Things were so much easier when I was just the cute toddler in his arms for his real estate headshots. He also had this brilliant campaign where he'd stick an extra sign on the front lawns of his properties, right next to the Beck Properties sign with his name and face and contact info. It was a photo of me as a smiling baby, waving a chubby little hand, and it said in big letters "Hunter approves!"

Well, times have changed. Hunter definitely does not approve of this.

It still burns me up that when I made CIF state champion last year for swim, the first words out of his mouth were, "It's nothing less than what I expect from you."

No congratulations.

No I'm proud of you.

Just "what's expected."

"Whatever," I say when his mouth finally stops moving. On my way out I add, "By the way, next time, try to keep your voices down. Harrison doesn't need this crap."

My chest feels like it's being crushed by a pile of bricks as I make my way back out to the living room.

"What were they fighting about?" Harry murmurs.

"They're just excited," I lie. "Your babysitter's moving in."

"Milla's coming to live with us?"

The kid is beaming with happiness at the prospect. An enthusiasm I don't share in but can understand. Dad had been telling the truth when he said Camilla's good with Harrison. Not once have I seen her angry with him, not even when he's being stubborn and won't do something he's supposed to. And I've seen how happy she is when she serves him a snack or helps him build Lego castles. It's adorable.

"Yeah," I tell him. "I'm sure it'll be great."

Not long after, I hear the front door open, a cacophony of footsteps and the unmistakable glide of suitcase wheels on the tiles, and Karleigh saying, "Helena! Camilla! Welcome. Thomas just filled me in—I've been trying to get us a live-in housekeeper, so it all works out perfectly. We're so happy to have you."

I know it's the excuse Dad gave her, but still...Karleigh can't actually be this oblivious, can she? Does she truly think he did this as a favor to her? That it came from the kindness of his heart and not as a mandate from his dick?

There's more faux-enthusiastic conversation from my

stepmom, and then they all file into the living room since the patio doors are the quickest way to the pool house. Camilla's red-faced as she walks by, suitcase rolling behind her. Harrison immediately runs to her, hugging her waist. "Milla, you're moving in with me?"

"I guess so, for a little while," she says, cracking a smile for his benefit.

"Awesome!" Harrison looks at the luggage in her hand. "Do you need help? I can carry something!"

Camilla laughs, a light, free, genuine sound. "That's fine, kiddo. I'll manage."

She ignores me. I ignore her, keeping quiet, though inside I'm nothing but pissed off. So she makes a huge scene in front of my friends and then has the balls to show up at my house and freaking move in on the same day?

However.

Judging by the permanent pinch in her face and the fact that she basically won't even look at me, I can tell Camilla's as unhappy about this entire situation as I am. I want to blame her, but I know it's not her fault. Our parents are the ones at fault, both of them, but if I'm not my dad, then I can't treat her like she's her mom.

And she wasn't, and isn't, entirely wrong to be upset with me.

I *have* been a jerk to her, and without good reason. The truth is, I don't have one. It's just that every time I see her, all shy and clueless, I have the urge to bend her, to see how far I can push until she breaks. And she *did* break, at least a little, earlier today.

From the living room couch, I take a long slug from my Coke can and pretend not to watch her move in, going back and forth from the car to the pool house over and over. Pretend not to notice how her jeans hug her ass, how a bead of sweat runs down the back of her neck. She's got her hair up in a ponytail, leaving that perfect slope uncovered, as if asking me to lick it off her.

Harrison flits around her, and I see she's caved in to his offer to help since he's happily carrying small items— books, mostly, old and worn out, and a couple shoe boxes that I assume belong to Camilla's mother since I've only ever seen Camilla in her school shoes or her sneakers.

Shit, I guess I could go help too. I probably should. But I don't trust myself around her, not after what happened the last time we were alone.

It hits me that I can't stay sitting here any longer, or I will say or do something that will make things worse. Normally, I wouldn't care, but Harrison's here. And he's so happy, how can I take that away from him?

Camilla shouldn't be living here. I shouldn't have to deal with her living here.

I take off to my room, and that's where I stay for the rest of the evening.

The days pass, full of awkward tension every time I walk into a room and see Camilla or her mom, until finally it's Sunday afternoon. I'm having my late morning swim with Harrison when Camilla shows up, telling him it's lunchtime. Guess she didn't quit, after all.

As Harrison gets out of the pool and lets Camilla wrap him in a dry towel, I don't say anything to her. She doesn't say anything to me either. But I can tell what she's thinking because she's as open as the books she's always reading.

She's thinking about how she failed our debate assignment because of me. About how I avoided her afterward because I didn't want to deal with the consequences.

Even when I tried to be nice that night I had a party and she walked in on me and some girl at the pool house, the worst of me had come out. All I meant was to wipe away her tears. Until she looked at me, her long eyelashes still wet, her parted lips trembling, and I knew it was because of what I'd done.

I don't know why I didn't kiss her. I wanted to. Camilla looked like she wanted it too.

The way she'd felt when I pushed her against the wall— warm and breathless and curvy in all the right places. The way she'd bitten my collarbone, as if she'd been as hungry as I was.

No one had ever pushed me away like that before, though, not when they were right on the edge. I could feel it, the way she was about to come in my hand.

She must really hate me.

She has no idea that the reason I didn't go to the mandatory homework sessions Spencer assigned us was because I knew Camilla would be there. Now I can't even relax in my own home because she's here all the time too.

It was hard enough avoiding her when she was just a babysitter. Now that she's living here, it's going to be impossible.

And I'm afraid of what I might try to do the next time we're alone.

Chapter Twenty-One

CAMILLA

*A*fter a few weeks, we're all settled in at the Becks' pool house. My mom has the big bedroom where I walked in on Hunter and that girl he had on his lap, and I have the small one, thank the Lord. I don't think I'd be able to sleep in a room where I'd witnessed something so blatantly X-rated happening.

It's funny. I'd always thought this place looked big enough for a family to live in. That I'd actually end up here myself is not something I ever imagined. I still can't believe my mom made us move in. I've never been so angry (or humiliated) in my life.

Our living situation is perfectly fine, to be fair. It's much nicer here than any other place we've rented, and we've got luxury accommodations in comparison. Gleaming hard-wood floors, brand new Restoration Hardware furniture, crisp white linens, huge flatscreen TV, state-of-the-art kitchen appliances, reliable Wi-Fi... But if anyone at the academy finds out my mom and I are such a charity case that we had to move into our employers' pool house? I will be raked over the coals of shame.

It hasn't escaped me that no one at school seems to know about it though. Which can only mean that Hunter hasn't spilled my secret. Yet. And I still can't figure out why. He had no problem telling his little cronies that I was his brother's nanny; I would have expected him to leap at the chance to embarrass me further. But he hasn't.

All I can figure is that he's holding back because it would be as embarrassing for him as it is for me. Or maybe he's just biding his time so he can use it against me as blackmail or something. Who knows? Hunter Beck is an enigma.

I'm currently sitting on a floor cushion in the living room, my homework spread out on the coffee table in front of me, but I can't concentrate. The space has recovered nicely from the catastrophe that was Hunter's last party. The floors are shining, the couch spotless and draped in a thick knit throw, the coffee table sporting a few cute succulents and fancy photography books instead of beer bottles and red plastic cups. Mom spent an entire day (and I an entire afternoon) getting this place back in shape after Hunter's friends were through with it, and we've kept it immaculate ever since.

Even still, the knowledge that my mother is passed out in her room next to an empty bottle of booze is ruining my concentration. It was one thing to drink at home, but now that we're here, she's technically drinking on the job. Sort of. And I guess some small part of me was holding out hope that this move might be an opportunity for her to quit drinking entirely. Or at least cut back. But no. She's as bad as ever.

We might fight, and she might be hard to live with sometimes, but she's my mom, and I love her and hate seeing her like this. I don't want her to die. I want her to get better. And there's nothing I can do. Which is why I'm having such a hard time outlining my research paper, which I've titled "The Consequences of Colonialism."

Next to my history book, my phone buzzes. I quickly snap it up and unlock it, glad to see Isabel's name on the screen.

Before I can even say hello, Isabel's mouth is going a mile a minute. "Hey, you wanna hit up The Sweet Spot? I got a two-for-one deal on Groupon. I'm dying for a shake. Say yes. They have salted caramel, your favorite."

I laugh. "How could I possibly say no to that?"

"Cool. Meet you there in like twenty? I'm calling a Lyft now."

"Ish. I'll text you an ETA once I'm on the bus. See you soon."

After leaving a note out for my mom, I practically run out the door. The past few weeks have been nothing but stress and agony, and that milkshake is calling my name. It won't be enough to erase everything I've been through with the move and Hunter and school—that'd require an entire bakery and half a library—but I'll take what I can get.

When I get to the parking lot at The Sweet Spot, Isabel immediately sweeps me into a hug before we head inside. She's in a cute red polka-dot dress that resembles a vintage apron, with ruby red sandals and a headband to match. It's almost like she jumped out of an episode of *I Love Lucy*.

"You look adorable," I tell her. It boggles my mind how Hillary & Co. use the way Isabel dresses outside the academy against her. The girl has flair.

"Thanks! And I knew that sweater was totally made for you," she says.

It's a V-neck she gave me, saying it wasn't her style—sky blue, featherweight cashmere with three-quarter sleeves. It feels like a dream, but this is the first time I've had a chance to wear it in public. Admittedly, the neckline dips a little low.

"Not too much cleavage?" I ask, suddenly self-conscious. My mom told me I could keep the silver star necklace I borrowed for Matt's party, and I've been wearing it lately. Unfortunately, with this sweater, it seems to draw attention directly to my boobs.

"Hells no," she assures me. "Just the right amount."

With that, she links arms with me and half drags me through the glass doors.

It's gotta be jealousy on Hillary's part. Not only is Isabel friendly and kind and cute as a button, she's also *smart*, like straight-A, genius-level smart. She's won every science fair she's entered since second grade, she's on track for valedictorian, and she's so fluent in Spanish and French that she's taking Latin at school for her foreign language. The other day she showed me her sketchbook, and even at that, she excels.

The Sweet Spot is busy, but there are still a few U-shaped booths open, so Isabel asks the host to seat us in one. The place has that classic diner aesthetic with a stainless-steel counter along one wall, little jukeboxes at every table, and red vinyl seats.

"God, I love it here," Isabel sighs, dropping a few quarters into the jukebox and punching the code for a Chuck Berry song. "Want to pick one?"

"Are The Archies on there?" I ask. "I love that one song."

"All they have is 'Sugar Sugar,'" she says after flicking through the tabs.

I grin. "That's it. My mom used to play that on Sundays and make us banana pancakes." A wave of sadness hits. "I guess it was forever ago, but I still remember."

Isabel pushes the buttons on the jukebox and then gets settled across from me.

"So, life at Douche HQ still treating you rough? You look peaked."

Okay, so I told Isabel about my living arrangements. I had to talk to someone, and she always offers open ears and zero judgment.

I shrug. "Meh. Same old."

"It's not forever," she offers. "And besides, if Hunter keeps acting up, maybe his dad will ship him off to a military school. Then you'll be footloose and fancy-free."

"I wish," I say, but I'm not totally sure I mean it.

A peppy waitress in a checkered apron with her hair in a topknot comes over and introduces herself as Brenda. She takes our drink orders and tells us about the special of the day—chicken fried steak—before leaving us to peruse the laminated menus.

"Okay, I've chosen." Isabel fans herself with the menu and stretches her legs. "What are you gonna have?"

"Not sure." My eyebrows knit as I look over the plethora of offerings.

"Don't come here much?"

"Maybe twice in the last four years, but all I need is my caramel shake, and I'm happy." My eye catches on the burger section. "Actually, a veggie burger sounds good."

"I usually get that! It's super yum," she says. "But not today. Today I want to taste grill marks and feel meat juice dripping down my chin—sorry, is that gross?"

"You're fine," I tell her. "As long as you use a napkin. Or five."

The waitress comes back to take our order and drop off our shakes. Isabel got a strawberry banana, and mine is a perfectly sweet and salty caramel confection with a huge tower of whipped cream and little flakes of sea salt on top.

"Mmm," is all I can manage as I suck down the first cold strawful.

"Sounds orgasmic. Can I try it?" Isabel asks.

"Of course." I slide the shake over to her and watch her face as she shovels a few spoons of it into her mouth.

"This is like a religious experience," she tells me, her eyes gone dreamy.

"Told you."

Our burgers come out, along with two sides of extra well-done fries. I dip one into the lake of ketchup I've squeezed onto my plate and take a big bite. Perfectly crunchy. Isabel and I talk about nothing and everything, and it's so comfortable that I can't help bemoaning the fact that I can't live with her instead of the Becks'.

"You probably could," she says. "I mean, I can ask my mom if you want. We could even get bunk beds!"

"That sounds amazing, but my mom would never go for it," I tell her. "Plus, I'm at the Becks' so often already, it'd just make my bus scheduling even more complicated. But thank you. For real. Maybe one day we can have our own apartment."

We're happily eating and chatting, and I can physically feel myself relaxing, my shoulders loosening up.

When I'm with Isabel, I feel like there's nothing I can say that'll be wrong or stupid or awkward. We love a lot of the same things—like Jenny Han and beach days and (secretly) Disneyland—and whatever we don't agree on isn't a deal-breaker. Her penchant for classical music isn't something I share, but I'd never hold it against her, just like she doesn't hold my very passionate defense of *Twilight* against me.

Look, I know most people hate it, and that its popularity is long past. But it was the easiest YA series to get my hands on at the public library, and it basically normalized stories where girls my age find themselves inexplicably attracted to a guy who won't give them the time of day. If that isn't true to almost every teenage girl's lived experience, then I don't know what is.

We're giggling, halfway into our meal, when the little bell on the front door jingles, and I look up to see a familiar and completely unwelcome set of kids come into the restaurant.

My heart sinks. Figures that out of all the burger places in La Jolla, Hunter ends up crashing the one where I'm actually having fun.

"Ugh. My God," I mutter under my breath as I shift in my seat. "Hunter and his entourage just walked in."

Isabel leans forward to whisper, "I'm not turning around, but is Steve there?"

I steal a glance at the group and unfortunately recognize Steve's black hair, all gelled-up into spiky ends, like he thinks it's the 90s or something. "Affirmative."

"Ugh," she echoes, slouching down. "Hopefully they won't look this way."

As soon as those words leave her lips, Hunter's eyes fall on me, and here they stay. I immediately turn my head, directing my gaze out the window, readying myself for the inevitable sounds of derision aimed my way.

My spine is straight, my limbs tense as the group passes our booth. Meanwhile, Isabel animatedly tells a long and pointless story about a missing sock, just so she can pretend to not see them.

"What's the deal with Steve anyway?" I ask her once it's safe to assume the boys are seated.

Isabel fiddles with her straw, and after several seconds, she sighs. "Okay, don't judge me for this—it was super long ago, and I had yet to develop standards." She takes a long sip of her shake.

"Do tell," I say, rubbing my hands together like a greedy villain.

"So I sort of drunkenly made out with him once? Because I was sixteen, and I wanted to get my first kiss over with?" Her cheeks go pink. "I mean, it wasn't even a thing! It felt like nothing. But he hasn't let up since."

"That doesn't sound like the worst thing ever," I tell her.

"It kind of was. We were in the kink closet, and everybody whistled when we came out." She sighs and shakes her head. "I don't know what I was thinking."

"Desperate times, desperate measures," I tell her. "My first kiss wasn't all that great either."

"Now you have to share!" she insists.

"I promise I will tell you, but not right now," I say. "I need to work up to it."

"Oh, fine. You're no fun. But don't think you're getting out of it."

That's the other thing I love about Isabel. She knows when not to push.

"I'm glad Emmett isn't in Hunter's group though," she goes on. "I couldn't bear it if I had to stop dropping by his house because I might run into those a-holes."

Isabel claims she's constantly dropping by his place to score cookies, but I suspect the reason is something else entirely.

The check comes, and we decide to split the bill and head out. As we wait by the cash register, Isabel informs me that Hunter is looking at me, but he doesn't make a move. Aside from that first moment of eye contact, he's completely ignored me.

I tell myself I'm glad and not at all disappointed.

Chapter Twenty-Two

CAMILLA

*W*hen the cashier rings us up, Isabel begrudgingly accepts my crumpled dollars, then does something I'd never thought I'd witness from a girl who knows all the best consignment shops in town. She saunters back to our booth and leaves a hundred-dollar bill under the salt shaker as a tip.

As we walk out the door, I'm still wide-eyed and stunned.

"Why'd you leave such a big tip?" I ask.

Isabel shrugs. "Waiters only make minimum wage, and ours was really nice. Besides, my dad's an arbitration lawyer, and my mom's architecture firm designs houses for celebrities. I'm happy to spread their money around to people who work just as hard as they do but get paid way less."

I wish everyone was more like Isabel.

See, there are rich people like Hunter and his friends who act like assholes about their money and make sure everyone knows they're loaded. And then there are rich people like Isabel and her family who are even more obscenely wealthy, and yet they never give any indication of it until you witness moments like this.

Isabel's Lyft arrives, and she tries to get me to share it with her, but I tell her I'd rather walk. There's a slight chill in the air, but I'm looking forward to having some time and space to shake off the aggravation that I'm feeling thanks to seeing Hunter.

"You sure you don't want a ride to the bus stop, at least?" she offers. "I don't like you walking by yourself at night."

"I'm fine," I assure her. "I've walked this way by myself plenty of times. And plus, I need some time to think."

She bites her lip. "Okay. But text me the second you get home, or I'm calling the cops. I mean it."

I wait for her ride to pull out of the parking lot and then heave a big sigh as I make my way toward the sidewalk. The streets *are* pretty dark, and this isn't exactly the nicest part of town. But I'll be fine. I'm sure of it. Besides, this isn't anything new. I've walked alone at night in La Jolla plenty of times before.

But just as I start down the street, I hear footsteps behind me. I start walking faster, and the steps speed up to keep pace with me. Heart pounding, I pull out my phone and dial 9-1-1, my finger hovering over the call button.

"Camilla, stop!" Hunter's voice calls from over my shoulder.

I whip around with a gasp. He's just a few feet away, hands casually in his pockets. In the parking lot of The Sweet Spot, his friends are nowhere in sight.

"What do you want?" I ask, breathing hard. I'm doubly annoyed at him for not only chasing me down and commanding me to stop, but also scaring me half to death.

Hunter tilts his head toward his BMW. "Come on. I'm taking you home."

"Not a chance." I cross my arms in front of my chest. "So why don't you run back to your friends now, before they notice you're out here with 'the help'?"

Under the yellow street lights, his expression hardens. "We're going. Now."

The rudeness in his tone is unbearable, and I can't help but laugh at how he expects me to follow his orders. "Are we? Okay. You planning to throw me over your shoulder or just drag me by my hair like a Neanderthal?"

His chest puffs out, and he shakes his head. "Cut the shit, Milla. You aren't walking alone at night. It's non-negotiable."

Wait a second... Did he just call me Milla? No one but my friends and Harrison call me that; Hunter certainly has made a point of never using my nickname before. But no. I'm reading too much into it. It was probably a slip of the tongue.

I regard him in silence, considering my options.

"Do you *want* me to carry you?" he asks, moving closer.

My mouth goes dry, my stomach doing a little tumble. "Fine. Let's go."

Stalking past him, I make my way back to the lot, where his stupid BMW gleams under the harsh sodium lights. The thing looks like a spaceship with its clean, curved lines and tinted windows. I've never been inside it before.

Without a word, Hunter unlocks the car with his key fob and slides into the driver's seat. I get in on the passenger side and make sure to slam the door extra hard before buckling my seatbelt. It smells like new leather in here. And, faintly, Hunter's cologne. He must get his car detailed every week for it to be so clean. Or maybe he's just a neat freak, and I never realized it.

"Music?" is all he says.

"Whatever," I answer.

He punches a button to start the car, and the sound of Tamino fills the cabin.

"Is this 'Indigo Night' live?" I blurt. "I love this song."

"Yeah."

Ah. So he's back to monosyllables. Fine. Why do I even bother?

And yet I have to admit, I'm kind of impressed. Hunter Beck does *not* strike me as the indie rock type. I suppose it's possible he has more depth than I give him credit for. That doesn't mean he's not still a total jackass though.

We pull out of the lot, and as I relax into my seat, I realize it has a seat warmer that's heating up my back and my ass. God, this is heaven. I could fall asleep right here.

Glancing at Hunter from the corner of my eye, I see how tensely his jaw is set. I bet he's hating this. Well, good then. He's the one who insisted on driving me out of some sense of obligatory chivalry. Next time maybe he'll just let me walk.

He is entirely too close though. The space between our seats isn't nearly enough to diminish the taut energy radiating off of him. I cross my legs and turn toward the window, keeping my eyes on the road so I won't have to look at him.

So far, I've recognized all the streets he's taken. But when we get to the intersection where we'd turn right to get to his neighborhood, he goes straight instead.

"That's not the right way," I say, looking over at him in confusion.

"Yeah, it is," he says, which does nothing to reassure me.

Sinking back into the seat, I tell myself everything is fine. Maybe he just wants to drive around until he calms down. I don't have a car, and getting my driver's license made me all kinds of anxious, but I know that some people find driving very relaxing.

But a few minutes later, he still hasn't given any indication of where we're going, and we keep moving farther and farther away from our intended destination and closer and closer to the beach. He also seems focused, not like he's just taking random turns. What the hell?

I'm about to tell him to turn around and drop me off like he said he would when he finally turns into an unlit dirt lot beside an old lighthouse. Then he turns the car off.

"Why are we here?" I ask, my voice quiet, more curious than angry now.

"You'll see," he says.

To the left, city lights flash in the distance; to my right, I can see the black expanse of the ocean softly crashing against the cliffs. Before us is the lighthouse, which is small and white and box-shaped with windows along the front and a tall tower rising from the center of the roof with a glass observatory on top of it.

Well, okay then. Here we are.

Hunter gets out of the car, so I do the same. The ocean breeze hits me as soon as I step out, chilly and salt-scented, raising goose bumps on my arms. I barely notice. It's deserted and beautiful out here, magical almost, the lighthouse seeming to glow in the dark. When I look up at the sky, the stars are the brightest I've ever seen.

It's obvious that the lighthouse is no longer functional, probably serving as a museum nowadays. Which means we probably shouldn't be here after hours...

I turn toward Hunter, but he's already opening the gate in the white fence surrounding the property.

"Um, Hunter?" I start. I have no idea what he's up to, and yet I can't believe he's taken me somewhere so nice. That said, it's obvious we're trespassing.

"Come on," he says. "This way."

As I follow after him, I wonder: aren't we breaking and entering?

And if we are, do I even care?

Not that I can afford to get arrested, but some part of me is giddy at the idea of this adventure, this secret something that Hunter is wordlessly sharing with me.

I come up beside him at the door and whisper, "Is this legal?"

"Jesus, Camilla." He turns to me, pinching the bridge of his nose. "Why do you always have to overthink everything?"

"Because people like me can't afford to take risks," I answer.

"People like you? What's that supposed to mean?"

"It means not everyone gets to have everything handed to them on a silver platter, and some of us can't just weasel our way out of an arrest record."

"You assume my life's been easy because I have money," he says with a smirk.

"No. I just assume it's been easier for you than it has been for those of us who *don't* have money." I fold my arms over my chest. "So is this your brilliant evil plan? Getting me to commit a felony crime on a school night so your dad kicks me and my mom out?"

"Fucking hell," he says, shaking his head. "Just relax. And by the way, it's not a felony, it's a misdemeanor, at least until you steal or break something."

"Of course you'd know that," I shoot back.

"I guess I would."

With that, he digs into one of his pockets and pulls out a key.

Chapter Twenty-Three

HUNTER

*E*ver since Camilla moved in, I've been spending less and less time at home. Which is stupid—it's *my* house, and if anything, she should be the one avoiding it as much as possible. But when we aren't at school together, she's either babysitting Harrison or she's "home" at the pool house, and when she's not there, she's in my head.

I can't even go for a swim without wondering if she's watching.

That's why I let the guys convince me to go out to The Sweet Spot tonight, even though I wasn't in the mood for greasy diner food. Getting space to just breathe and clear my mind sounded fucking great. But of course she was there, laughing with her friend as my posse walked in. I heard her all the way across the restaurant, and I knew it was Camilla before I even turned to look.

At this point, it's like fate keeps throwing us together just to torture me. Like some bastard god is enjoying watching us clash every time we get near each other.

I tried to keep my friends distracted as we passed her table, hoping the others wouldn't notice her. If they did, the conversation would've inevitably shifted to what's up with her and me and whether I've put her back in her place or just fucked her yet. The distraction was for Steve, too, since he always zeroes in on Isabel as soon as he sees her, and I couldn't risk him trying to get us all together at one big table or something.

Luckily, we got seated far from her booth, and we were almost done eating when I noticed Camilla and Isabel getting up to leave. I figured they'd ride home together, but a few minutes later, through the huge front windows of the restaurant, I saw Isabel duck into a car and Camilla stay behind. Steve made a joke then, and the guys dragged me into their loud-ass camaraderie. The next time I looked up, Camilla was gone.

That's when I caught a flash of the light blue sweater she was wearing and realized she was making her way up the darkened street. Alone.

There was no way in hell I was letting her walk home by herself.

It took an entire split second for me to open my wallet and drop two twenties on the table while telling the guys I had to leave early. The fuck was she thinking? How could she not know this part of town is dangerous, that it's the place people come to hold up corner stores or score random opioids and cheap coke?

It was like Matt's kink closet party all over again, with Camilla completely oblivious to the danger surrounding her. There are a lot of shitty things I can live with, but risking my brother's nanny apparently isn't one of them.

My brother's nanny. Right. That's all she is.

So I chased after her. Of course she fought me at first, but she finally gave in, got in the car, and let me drive. But every time I looked over, it was obvious how miserable she was. It's not just that she's as easy to read as an open book, it's like she's a freaking kid's book. It was almost too easy to see she was uncomfortable, to see she was counting the seconds until we got home.

And then I noticed how clear the sky was, and I started wondering if she'd appreciate the view from the lighthouse. So I didn't turn toward home and then didn't answer any of her questions. I wanted to see what her face looks like when she's surprised with something good. At least, I hoped it would be good.

What is it about Camilla that I can't shake? I've had plenty of other hot girls. Girls who don't argue with me, who don't constantly call me out. The kind who do exactly what I say, when I say it, and don't make me work hard to get what I want. It makes zero sense for me to be hung up on her.

Yet even right now, when I'm trying to do something nice, she's looking at me like I'm some sort of rogue. Accusing me of breaking and entering without a care because being rich supposedly guarantees you a free pass on misdemeanors.

I'm holding the door open, waiting for Camilla to come inside. But she won't budge. She's looking right at me and saying, "I know you have connections and whatever, but how'd you get a key to this place?"

I shrug. "Fine, I'll admit it. I stole it."

Her whole body tenses, and she hisses, "Hunter, seriously. Let's just *go*."

"I'm joking, Camilla," I say, holding up my hands defensively. "My dad's real estate company owns the property, and he sometimes brings people to see the place."

I don't mention that the people are generally his side-pieces, not prospective buyers, or that I've overheard him bragging about how many women he's screwed here.

"But you're not a licensed real estate agent," Camilla

points out.

That forces me to crack a smile. "Maybe not, but clearly I'm within my legal rights to be here. More or less. And you're my guest. So come on in."

I gesture for her to follow me, and finally she does, shuffling in small steps.

"It's so dark. Can't you turn on a light?" she asks, keeping her voice low even though there's no way anyone would hear us over the sound of the ocean anyway.

"Someone might realize we're here," I tell her.

"But you said—"

"Just because it's not illegal to be here doesn't mean my dad wouldn't be pissed, yeah? And you don't have to whisper."

"Okay," she whispers.

Using my phone's flashlight app, I lead her across the room to the tower stairs.

"So does your dad ever throw the occasional real estate party up here?" she asks as she climbs the spiral steps behind me. "That might be kind of cool."

"Depends on what kind of party you're talking about," I say, moving extra slowly to make sure she keeps her footing. "But I assume the guest list stays at two."

I let the words hover in the air as we pass the service room, still climbing.

"You mean..."

"It's not like he can bring his girlfriends to the house," I clarify.

She clears her throat, and I can tell she's not sure what to say. "Oh."

"You can say it. He's an asshole."

"*You* can say it," she says, voice small. "It's different for me."

Right, because he signs her and her mom's paychecks

and now puts a roof over their heads to boot. I know all too well what that feels like.

At this point, we're both breathless from the climb, but we finally reach the last turn of the stairs.

"This is it. The lantern room." I step into the room and turn to wait for her. Once she's beside me, she exhales deeply, like she's letting herself go. A little bit, at least.

"Wow."

A chuckle leaves me. "See? It was worth it."

The glassed-in space offers 360-degree views; from this high up, it's almost like we're floating in the night sky. Camilla walks to the center of the room where the light sits, surrounded by panes of curving, carved glass. If the lamp was on, she'd be blinded.

"This is gorgeous," she breathes.

"That's the lens for the lamp. It focuses the light into a beacon so ships can see it from really far away. Approximately twenty miles, give or take."

"You're a nerd, Hunter Beck," she says, looking at me and smiling. My chest goes tight hearing her say my full name, but I just shrug. "I think I like this side of you."

"It gets better," I tell her. I don't elaborate on whether I mean the lighthouse gets better or my personality does. I'll let her interpret it however she likes.

Taking her hand, I lead her across the room and outside onto the platform, which is enclosed by a metal railing. There's a light breeze up here, and it's a little cold, so I take off my jacket and drape it over her shoulders. I can hear the sound of waves thundering against the rocks below, and something inside me feels like waves too.

"And this is called the lantern gallery," I tell her. "The lookout, basically."

"I—I love it," she says, her eyes big and beautiful, reflecting the stars.

Her loose hair is whipping all around her face, to the point she has to hold it back, and the sight of her bare neck makes my pulse kick higher. I try to shake it off as she moves toward the railing.

"The view is amazing," she says, her smile lighting up her entire face. I step closer until I'm at her side. Closing her eyes, she breathes in. "I can smell the beach."

The waves continue to churn and crack, and next to me, Camilla is a beacon of warmth, begging to be held and kissed. But I don't want to scare her into leaving again.

I brace myself on my forearms as I lean against the metal railing beside her. "I like coming here when everything else is too much. It's loud but also...quiet, I guess."

Milla looks over, her slight frown speaking volumes. I know she must be wondering why I brought her here, why I'm standing so close. But she doesn't say it. Instead, she looks back to the ocean. "I get it. It *is* nice up here, listening to the waves."

"Yeah. It's kind of like being in the water without being in it," I murmur.

"Is that why you swim so much?" she asks. "You love the water?"

"Yeah, I do," I answer automatically. "It reminds me of my mom."

Camilla's fingers tighten on the railing as she softly says, "Your mom?"

I nod, appreciating the careful way she frames it, giving me room to decide whether or not to elaborate. Maybe that's why I tell her more.

"I only have one memory of her, from before she walked out on us. We were swimming at the beach, me and her. The waves were rolling in all around us, rough, but she was holding me in her arms. I was safe, and the sun was warm on my back. I was happy." My voice cracks a little, much to my embarrassment, and I breathe in slowly, letting the waves echo in my ears.

"It sounds like a good memory. How old were you?" Camilla asks softly.

"Little. Maybe four." I stay quiet for a minute, reliving it all in my head. I can almost taste the salt water in my mouth again, smell the coconut sunscreen my mom wore. "The thing is, even now, whenever I'm in the water, it feels like the world isn't so loud anymore. Like there's something good, and...better. I don't know."

I turn to her, and she's looking back at me, her lips parted like an invitation.

The next thing I know, my mouth is on hers, fleeting but firm. Softly, she gasps, one of her hands coming up to rest on my chest, but she's not pushing me away. Instead, she leans in for more, standing on her tiptoes. I kiss her again, deeper this time, tilting her chin up for a better angle.

She lets out a little moan, and it's game on.

My tongue slips against hers, and she opens wider, matching my pace. I can feel her nails digging into my shirt, and all I can think of is that we should've been kissing all along. But tasting her is not enough. My free hand circles her waist, finding the small of her back, and I pull her tight against me and let myself get lost.

"Why?" she asks when we come up for air.

I know what she's asking. Why did I kiss her? Why am I so cruel to her face most of the time but then can't keep my hands off her when we're alone together?

Part of me wants to be honest and tell it to her straight. Right now, I want to be comforted, and kissing her distracts me, takes my mind off of everything else. But that sounds dickish, and lying feels wrong, so I go for half the truth instead.

"The same reason you do," I tell her. "Because this," I kiss her again, slowly but persistently, and pull away just after my tongue strokes hers, "feels good."

She lets out a sharp exhale. "Maybe."

I don't like *maybe*.

Dropping my lips to her neck, I kiss her there too. Camilla's breathing gets faster, like she can't help the effect I have on her, and now I want more. I need more.

"Isn't it better than what you were feeling before?" I ask, biting her collarbone softly, then taking my mouth lower.

One of her hands comes to rest on my shoulder and squeezes. "I just..."

"Milla," I say. "Stop overthinking it. If you don't want to—"

"I want you," she interrupts fiercely.

My arms tighten around her, crushing her to me, and I kiss all her doubts away. It's desperate, and borderline clumsy, but my head's full of her and the desire to hold on to her warmth and never let it go. I shift my grip to hold her ass, and I feel the satisfaction of knowing I was right about how it would fit perfectly in my hands.

There's still more of her I haven't taken, and all I can think about is how badly I want it.

Turning us around, I press her back against the cold glass window and grind my hips into hers. When she lets out a desperate whimper, I do it again.

Her hands slide up the back of my neck, weaving into my hair, her nails dragging deliciously across my scalp. I attack every inch of exposed skin; her neck, her chest, the top of her soft cleavage. Her sweet moans urge me on, urging me to keep going, to use my lips and tongue to unravel every inch of her.

In this moment, she's everything I want.

Chapter Twenty-Four

CAMILLA

*B*eing with Hunter at the lighthouse is like some kind of fever dream. It isn't just the kissing, or his warm, strong hands all over my body, or the way I completely lose my mind whenever I do anything physical with him.

It's so much more than that.

It's how he let his guard down with me and spoke honestly about his mom and his swimming, right from the heart, proving my theory that there's a mask he wears all the time, and that for some reason, he trusts me enough to lower it when we're alone. There's something real between us, whether we're ready to admit it or not.

With his tongue on mine, the waves crashing hard below us, and the purple night sky spread out over our heads, I feel like we're connected. Like there's more to our hookups than just raging hormones or (in his case) the appeal of a new fling.

It's hard to describe, but this isn't something I've ever felt before.

When I say his name as he's kissing the soft spot behind my ear, it sounds like a magic spell.

We kiss for a while longer, and because he moved so fast last time, I'm completely on edge. Whenever his hand shifts, I tighten with expectation, thinking he's going to do what he did before. Then he cups my ass in both hands, and I can actually feel myself getting wet. *Oh, Hunter. How are you doing this to me?*

I'm scared at how hungry his touch makes me. How I forget myself so easily when he presses his body against mine. It's like my brain short-circuits, and all I can think about is getting more and more and more. Also, his tongue should be illegal. The way it's moving against my neck... Even when he bites, it feels good.

Though he told me not to overthink things, I can't help myself. There's too much unsaid between us for my brain to not chase answers to those questions.

For his part—and despite how cold he's acted for the last few weeks—Hunter seems as desperate as I feel. He kisses me like I'm air, and he's out of breath. His hands and lips move over my skin like I'm something to be savored. But as nice as this feels, I can't let it go on when I'm so confused about what all of this is. What I mean to him.

Why can't boys just make sense for once?

And how do I even bring this up without scaring him off?

He acts like he cares about me and then proceeds to be a total ass in front of his friends.

He wipes my tears away, only to slip his hand down my pants and almost give me an orgasm.

He ignores me at home, at school, and when I'm doing homework not ten feet away from him swimming laps in his pool but then offers me—no, *insists on* giving me—a ride home. Taking a detour to bring me to this special place. Kissing me senseless.

I don't want to think he's anything like his dad, but what if he is? What if Hunter hates him not because they're so different but because they're exactly the same? What if he brings all the girls he can't screw on the first try to this place, just so he can wax poetic about being in the water and missing his mom? Even if he's being genuine right now, things are still complicated. For instance, there's the fact that I basically live with him. If things go sour, it'll be even worse cohabitating than it already has been.

And regardless of whether Hunter sees me as more than just his little brother's nanny, screwing "the help" is never a good look from an outsider's perspective. I doubt his parents would approve. I'm not exactly country-club-date material.

Hunter must sense that my mind is elsewhere because he pulls back gently and tucks my hair behind my ear.

"We should go. You're shivering."

He's right. Even with his jacket on, my shoulders are hunched against the cold.

"Okay," I say, even though I'd be happy to stand out here all night with him.

He dips his head down for one last kiss, his tongue tasting every corner of my mouth. Then he breaks away, stroking my soft, swollen bottom lip with his thumb and making me want to suck on it. But I stop myself.

"We should head back," he says.

"You just said that," I point out with a smile.

He nods and ushers me inside first.

Once we're down the stairs and on the ground floor again, he asks, "So, how was your first B and E? You think you'll be ready to upgrade to a felony next time?"

"Shut your face," I say, punching his arm lightly.

"Ow!" he yelps, pretending my little kitten punch felt like anything at all. "I think that's gonna bruise. You're a real tigress under that goody-two-shoes persona."

"I am *not* a goody two-shoes," I shoot back, my cheeks gone warm. I like dorky Hunter way more than I've ever liked smooth Hunter.

"Could've fooled me," he says with a shrug. "But really. Did you like it?"

Even with his casual tone, I can tell he's being vulnerable right now. It cracks my heart right in half. "I loved it," I say. "Really."

"Cool."

He locks up the lighthouse, and we walk back to the car. The drive back is mostly silent, with only Tamino singing between us. I can't believe how late it is, and I find myself leaning back into the warmth of the heated seat and closing my eyes. I know this wasn't a date or anything, but it was kind of completely perfect.

I still wonder what exactly happened with Hunter's mom though. Why she left. Hunter probably wonders the same thing. I can't even imagine what it was like to grow up after being abandoned like that. I might not know who my dad is, but I can at least appreciate the fact that I don't miss him. You can't miss someone you've never met.

It's kind of weird. In all the months I've worked for the Becks, I haven't heard Hunter's mom mentioned once. I guess I just assumed she had passed or that a messy divorce had gone down ages ago. Now I know the real reason she's a sore spot and why getting Hunter to talk about anything meaningful is like pulling teeth.

Still, part of me is a little bit jealous. It's not fair that I know literally nothing about the man responsible for putting me in this world. My mom refuses to speak of him, and although I used to pester her with questions whenever

I could—trying to glean at least one solid fact that I could use to maybe, I don't know, google him or something—I eventually gave up. Sometimes I think she doesn't even know who he was either. Like he was some rando from a bar, or she was super wasted at a party.

Or maybe he was a real asshole, the kind who yelled and beat her. Maybe her getting pregnant is what made him ditch her and take off, or maybe she's the one who ran away from him. Who knows?

Either way, the fact is in all these years, he's never reached out to either one of us. So I guess that's answer enough. I don't have a father. Just an anonymous sperm donor. Maybe I'm better off not knowing.

Which is the same reason I don't push Hunter about what all those kisses meant, if they meant anything. I don't want to hear him laugh or tell me I'm just a rebound or a joke or a dare. Just another piece of ass for him to lay his hands on.

My heart doesn't truly believe that though. We have... something. Something real. I can feel it.

As we turn onto increasingly familiar streets, it dawns on me that each mile gets us farther from the dreamy lighthouse and closer to the real world. And that after tonight, ignoring him will no longer be possible. Once we pull into the Becks' driveway, I have no idea how to act.

I can feel myself tensing up as we go through the front door, and through sheer practiced instinct, I move to disable the alarm before the thirty seconds are up and it wakes up the entire house. Hunter moves to do the same, and our hands accidentally brush over the keypad.

"Sorry," I whisper, punching in the code.

"No worries," he whispers back, his warm breath caressing my ear.

Contrary to my expectations, he doesn't immediately go

up to his room. Instead, he walks with me all the way to the pool house.

Behind us, the pool water is calm and dark, moonlight reflecting on its surface. I pull out my keys and reach for the doorknob, but the silence between us now is so deafening that I break it in a rush of awkward chatter before I can help myself.

"Thanks for bringing me up to the lighthouse," I say, turning to him with a smile. "It was really great."

He smiles back, and not in that superior, I-know-you-want-this kind of way he has. "I'm glad you had a good time."

It feels awkward all over again, with us staring at each other, not speaking, probably both replaying the last few hours in our minds. I have no idea how things have changed between us, or if they've actually changed at all. I can never be sure when it comes to Hunter.

"Well, then..." I clear my throat. "See you tomorrow."

"Sweet dreams, Milla," he whispers and walks away.

I tiptoe into the pool house, lock the door behind me, and then hover by the window, watching Hunter's light go on and then off in his bedroom upstairs.

My lips are still puffy and swollen from Hunter's mouth, and I'm too pumped with adrenaline to go to bed right away. After checking on my mom—who's passed out in bed, and yes, still breathing—I take a quick hot shower to relax my muscles and then climb into bed with a sigh. My thoughts are still racing, and so is my heart.

Why didn't he kiss me good night? Are we back to pretending we hate each other? Or am I reading too much into this?

The confusion doesn't ease up, and I fall asleep with a stomach full of butterflies and a head full of questions.

Chapter Twenty-Five

CAMILLA

*N*ot shockingly, I end up oversleeping, meaning I have barely enough time to put on my uniform and brush my teeth before grabbing an apple, my hairbrush, and a face cleaning wipe (to make use of during my walk to the bus). As I head down the Becks' driveway, I notice Hunter's car is gone—if he already left then I'm really, *really* late.

Disappointment slows me down. I was kind of hoping we'd bump into each other this morning and he'd offer me a ride. Which is stupid. He probably assumed I'd already left. After all, most mornings I'm gone before he's even up for the day.

I cross the academy's front door right as the first bell rings and run to World History, sliding into my seat just before Mr. Robertson walks through the door. Emmett's already there, and we exchange a quick greeting as I catch my breath.

For the duration of class, I take notes on autopilot. All I can think about is whether Hunter is going to start acting differently now or if we'll go back to the usual.

After we're out, Emmett and I are walking down the hall when he says, "Hey, wanna grab lunch off-campus today? Already texted Isabel, and she's in."

I consider the invitation, which isn't exactly a rarity, since the three of us usually grab lunch together on Fridays. But something today keeps me from saying yes.

"Maybe?" I answer. "Not sure I wanna go off-campus today. I might just stick to the library to hit the books. I'm a little behind on homework this week." Which, true.

"Cool cool," Emmett says, unperturbed. "Just don't study too hard. And lemme know if you want us to bring you back some real food."

"You guys are the best," I say.

My homework isn't the only reason for bailing on the invite. The real reason pops up farther down the hall, where I see Hunter hanging with his group of dudebro friends, leaning against a locker and staring right at me.

A smile begins to tug at my lips, my heart beating faster, heat spreading from my cheeks to my toes. Memories of last night race through my mind. The leather scent of his car, the lighthouse gallery, the way he kissed me until I was weak and breathless.

Should I wave? Should I ask *him* to go out for lunch?

But as Emmett and I get closer, I realize that Hunter's not moving. He's not even really acknowledging me. His gaze sweeps over me, a blank expression on his face, and then he's back to joking around with his friends. As if he didn't see me.

As if I don't even exist.

My mouth flattens into a hard line, and I loop my arm through Emmett's as we pass Hunter and his cronies, just to prove that I'm totally unconcerned with them. Hunter wants to ignore me? Fine. Two can play that game.

Emmett and I part at the door to my AP Bio class, and

I mindlessly wander to my seat. I've never known someone who could make me feel so freaking good and so completely shitty, all in the space of twelve hours.

What am I even doing? There's no reason for me to plan my day around what Hunter might do. Why should I waste my time waiting around for something that will never happen?

Under my desk, I tap out a quick group text to Emmett and Isabel, telling them I'll meet them in the parking lot at noon. I feel dumb for not saying yes immediately in the first place. After that, I let myself get lost in the wonders of cell-to-cell communication within the human immune system.

I'm on my way to Emmett's car later when I get a reply from Isabel.

Held up after AP Calc. FML. Go ahead without me. I'll meet you there asap!

I reply with a heart emoji and then return Emmett's friendly high five before sliding into his car, a grey Mercedes he was handed down from his dad.

"Where to?" I ask. "Isabel's meeting us."

"Taco truck at the park?" he suggests. "We can eat under the trees."

"Love it," I say, shooting Isabel one last text so she knows where we're at.

"Windows or AC?" he asks.

"Windows, always. It's gorgeous out."

Emmett drives us the few blocks to the park and lets me blast Halsey the whole way there, my arm hanging out the window to feel the breeze and the sunshine. I'm already feeling a little bit better. Hunter, schmunter.

It's a school day, obviously, so that means the playground area is mostly devoid of screaming children, except for a few toddlers in the sandbox. Nice. I plop into a swing and tell Emmett to leave his backpack with me while he stands in line at the taco truck.

"Ha! Why don't *you* go stand in line while I play on the jungle gym?" he says.

"Okay," I say, laughing. "I'll go."

"I'm kidding, Milla! Just relax. Be right back."

My stomach rumbles as I swing, impatient for my tacos topped with the hottest salsa I can stand. Luckily Emmett is back lightning quick, and soon we're sitting across from each other at a picnic table under the cool shade of a huge ficus, eating out of thin cardboard boxes. Isabel's food rests between us on the table, covered with a napkin.

I pop the lid off my iced tea, gulping it down to fight the fire in my mouth.

"Did I fuck up?" Emmett asks. "You said to get the hottest salsa they had!"

"It's perfect," I tell him, sniffling a bit. "I just need to blow my nose."

"Let me try that," he says, pulling my box over and scooping up a blob of salsa, white sauce, and cabbage with a tortilla chip. I move over to his side of the picnic table so I'm sitting next to him.

"Fine, but consider yourself warned," I caution, watching him closely. "It's not for amateurs."

"I can handle it," he scoffs.

A second later, he's coughing and sputtering, sucking down his soda while blinking back tears.

I shake my head. "Shoulda got an horchata."

"That isn't salsa," he pants, "it's lava."

"Delicious, delicious lava," I say, taking another huge bite of my taco.

I'm midway through chewing when I see a flash of blonde in my periphery and then hear a high-pitched giggle to accompany it.

"Hillary. Fantastic," I say sarcastically.

Glancing to my left, I confirm what I already knew and see that she's here with a bunch of Hunter's friends—but no Hunter. They're all lining up at the taco truck, except for two who break off to play hacky sack in the lot. Of course, at that exact moment, Hillary looks over and sees me staring. The daggers she's throwing me with her eyes might actually kill me if they were real.

"Steve's over there too," Emmett says. "You better give Isabel a heads-up."

"Smart."

She answers with a puke emoji but says she just parked anyway and she'll see us in a second.

Taking a swig of my tea, my sight flits back over to the group.

Hunter saunters over out of nowhere, and Hillary wastes no time wrapping an arm around his waist, tugging him to her. He doesn't pull away.

My stomach knots.

I turn back to my food, but it doesn't taste the same now.

Emmett touches my shoulder. "Hey. Everything okay, Milla?"

Funny, he's been calling me by my nickname for weeks now, but it never once made my heart leap like it did when Hunter said it yesterday. God, it would be so much easier if I liked Emmett instead.

"Yeah, I'm fine. Just...school stuff." I give him a smile. Tight but genuine.

Brow furrowing, Emmett glances up and says, "Beck's got his eye on you, and he looks pissed. Something going on with you guys?"

"Eh, just the usual crap."

Without even thinking about it, I make the mistake of

turning to look. Emmett wasn't exaggerating—over by the taco truck, Hunter's staring at me.

His arms are crossed, and he's blatantly ignoring Hillary, even though she's trying to get his attention by yapping a mile a minute and doing the fingers-through-the-hair thing that my tangled waves would never allow. Murmuring something to his friends, Hunter breaks away from the line and starts walking toward Emmett and me, his gaze narrowing, stride measured and heavy with purpose.

"What's that D-bag want?" Emmett asks when we exchange a look between us.

My chest tightens, and so does my throat. "No idea."

If he's coming over here to cop an attitude, he's in for one unpleasant surprise.

"Ortega," Hunter says by way of greeting when he reaches our table.

"Beck," Emmett replies coolly.

"Camilla," Hunter says next.

"Beck," I say as coolly as I can, mimicking Emmett.

Hunter's eyes shift between us, like he's trying to figure out what exactly is going on. Which is idiotic at best because it's no secret to anyone that Emmett and I are good friends—have been since my first day at Oak Academy. But clearly Hunter thinks there might be more to it than that.

The things he said the night of Matt's party come back to me. About Emmett pretending to be nice; about how Emmett let me get wasted so he could make a move. None of it's true, but I'm happy to lean into Hunter's suspicions.

"Beautiful day, isn't it?" I say, putting my head on Emmett's shoulder.

Jaw clenching, Hunter just says, "It was until now."

"You got a problem, man?" Emmett asks. His voice is

light, but those are fighting words, and I can feel a slight hum of tension in the air.

"I don't know, *man*. Do you?" Hunter responds, moving closer.

Are they seriously going to fight right now? Over me? When I'm dating neither of them? I might expect that kind of caveman behavior from Hunter, but not Emmett. Then again, he's probably just trying to protect me from whatever this is.

Hunter's friends are looking over now, spectators of their favorite soap opera. Meanwhile, Hillary's holding on to her friend's arm, the two of them furiously trading whispers and scowling our way.

"Milla! Emmett!"

We all turn our heads to see Isabel practically skipping toward us, a huge smile on her face. There's no doubt in my mind that she took one look at the body language over here and decided it was her job to intervene. Bless her.

"Sorry I'm late. Ms. Kragen is a beast," Isabel says brightly, plopping onto the bench across from us. "Guess that's why they call her 'Ms, Kraken.' Hey, Hunter!"

"Hey," he says, but I notice he looks more at ease now that Isabel is here, and he's backed off a few steps.

"Did you get me my..." Isabel's voice trails off into a squeal of delight as she lifts the napkin off her food and finds two seitan tacos and two lime wedges, her go-to.

At his sides, I see Hunter's hands clench into fists. "Finish your lunch. I'm driving you back to school."

An incredulous laugh bursts out of me. "Excuse me?"

"Milla," he says. Just that, just my nickname. Then he walks off.

"What's his deal?" Emmett asks. "Does he think he owns you or something?"

"You're not going anywhere with him," Isabel says.

Getting a look at my face, which I can only imagine is bright red, she adds, "Unless...you want to?"

"I don't know," I say.

My chest is tight, and it's not the only thing about me that's tightening right now. I'm remembering all the good parts from last night and wondering if he's ready to talk about it. Or do those things again.

I should say no. And yet... I'm intrigued.

"As stupid as this sounds, I'm going," I tell my friends, taking one last bite of taco and slurping the rest of my iced tea. "Because I want to. Not because he said so."

Emmett and Isabel look at me, and I can tell they're about to argue.

I grab my backpack before they can say anything else.

"Text you guys later," I say, forcing a smile, even though I feel super lame for ditching them to chase after Hunter.

The thing is, he and I are way overdue for a talk because I need some answers. And I can't help thinking this could be my chance.

Chapter Twenty-Six

CAMILLA

I've ridden in cars my whole life, and it's never been anything special. But when a boy who makes your heart race is driving you around and you're in the passenger seat just inches away, feeling the electricity humming between you and him, his hand on the gearshift so close that his fingers could brush your bare knee at any moment...that's something completely different. My whole body is tingling.

And despite the tension between us right now, I can't help daydreaming about us speeding past Oak Academy and hitting the open road, heading for some other secret place Hunter has up his sleeve so we can have more adventures like we did last night.

Unfortunately, it's the middle of a school day, so I'm pretty sure the only adventures we're likely to have are the rest of our scheduled classes.

Once we've turned out of the parking lot at the park, I work up my nerve and finally say, "You have to stop doing this."

He keeps his eyes on the road. "Doing what?"

"Are you serious?" I ask, experiencing a flash of annoyance. "This is the second time I've been having fun with my friends and you've felt the need to interrupt us and drag me away. I'm obviously not drunk today, so what's your excuse?"

"Excuse?" He cracks a smile, but it's not a happy one. "You know, you should be thanking me. One of these days, I won't be around to bail you out."

I blink, even more annoyed now. "Bail me out of what? Lunch with friends?"

Shooting me the side-eye, he says, "That's not what it looked like to me."

"What did it look like then? Like I was in peril? A damsel in distress? Or maybe you were valiantly rescuing me from my spicy chicken tacos?"

Hunter changes lanes, and I cross my arms, irritated, still waiting for a response.

"I'm just saying, the lady doth protest too much," he says.

"What are you talking about?"

"It's Shakespeare."

"I know it's Shakespeare, and I know what the quote means. But what do *you* mean?"

"You keep saying the word *friends*," he scoffs as he pulls into the line of cars waiting to turn into the school parking lot. "But all I saw was you and Ortega cuddled up close. Alone. I told you, Milla, that guy is angling for an in with you."

"News flash, Hunter: he's already got one! As my *friend*. I'm not explaining it again, and you have a lot of nerve even acting like you care when it's obvious you have no interest in—" I stop myself before I say something embarrassing about Hunter not being interested in me, or dating me, or seeing me as anything other than a no-strings-attached hookup whenever he has no other options at his disposal.

"Interest in what?"

I turn my head and look out the window. "Nothing."

"Come on, say it," he goads me. "What am I not interested in?"

He's trying to humiliate me, I know it. But I won't make myself vulnerable in front of him just for his personal amusement.

"You're acting really self-righteous right now, and it's ridiculous," I say, my voice dropping lower with anger. "Why are you pushing so hard, anyway? It's none of your business who I choose to spend my time with or what I decide to do with them."

Hunter's fingers open and close on the steering wheel. His broad chest expands with a deep breath. "So then what, are you dating him?"

A laugh spills from my mouth at how ridiculous that is. "Of course not! What, are you jealous?"

It's finally our turn to pull into the lot, and Hunter drives straight to the far corner where there are still plenty of spots left in the shade. Then he just sits there, silently stewing, the soft whoosh of the AC the only sound in the car.

"Say something," I say quietly. "Anything."

But he won't even look at me. Instead, he just stares silently out the windshield, and I find that I'm all out of patience.

With a frustrated sigh, I unbuckle my seatbelt and grab the door handle, ready to get the hell out of this car and away from Mr. Enigma. But as soon as I open the door, there's the click of another seatbelt, and suddenly Hunter's leaning over me, pulling my door closed and then dragging my face to his for a kiss.

I don't even have to think about it. I'm already kissing him back, open-mouthed, hungrily, frantically. There's no point in lying; I've been waiting for this moment since we separated at my door last night. I love the way Hunter's tongue is dominating mine, like he's channeling all his pent-up emotions into making out with me as hard and fast as he can, at once blanking out my thoughts.

And this. This right here is *exactly* the problem.

Being on the receiving end of his attention has a way of making the rest of the world slip away so that nothing else gets through to me and nothing else matters. I can't let this keep happening.

We come apart with a breath, and I turn my head to the side. "Hunter, wait."

"What's wrong?"

"This," I say, gesturing in the small space that still exists between us. "You never talk to me. You just kiss me."

"And you kiss me back," he says. "That's the way it works."

He starts to lean forward, but I place a hand on his chest to stop him.

"Hunter, seriously."

"I am serious."

His eyes are intense on mine, and it's obvious I'm getting nowhere.

"Let's just get to class," I say, giving up.

I don't have the willpower to keep pushing him away, and it seems better to cut my losses and forget about getting any real answers right now.

Glancing at the dashboard, he says, "But we still have twenty minutes."

There's a massive battle going on between my libido and my logical brain, resulting in a complete inability to force myself out of the car. My body's strung tight, not with anxiety, but anticipation.

"Twenty minutes for what?" I say, my mouth already watering.

Hunger dark in his eyes, he says, "For you to live in this moment with me."

And then he attacks me with his mouth again. Hard, demanding. This time I kiss him back just as hard. He bites my lower lip, and I let out a soft moan.

I should get out, I should say no, but I can't pretend I'm not addicted to how good he feels against me.

So I don't.

Chapter Twenty-Seven

CAMILLA

*I*t's impossible to keep track of time when we're making out, which is why I don't crack any jokes watching Hunter set an actual alarm on his phone. As soon as he sets it down on the dash, I clamber over to his side of the car, yelping when my knee knocks into the gearshift.

His hands come up to help me straddle him, and then I'm in his lap, my mouth on his, immediately forgetting the pain still radiating from my patella.

Eyes closed, I feel the hot weight of his palms on my hips, sliding down the back of my skirt to grip my ass and pull me closer, so I'm right on top of the bulge in his pants. I *like* this. His hands on me, so confident, so dominant. The faint scent of his cologne, the firm expanse of his chest through the crisp cotton of his shirt under my fingers. His lips, his tongue. The sound of us breathing, his quiet groans. All of this.

Slowly, Hunter begins to tug my shirt free of my skirt's waistband. When I don't stop him, he slides his hand underneath, directly onto my bare skin. His thumb brushes my ribcage, the small caress stealing my breath right before he steals my lips again.

Hunter pulls away. We lock eyes, just taking each other in, and then he starts undoing the buttons of my shirt. He moves slowly, popping them open one by one, once again giving me a chance to say no. Except that I know I want this, him touching me everywhere, so I just lean back and let him undress me, watching his eyes drop when he loosens my tie and pulls open my shirt to expose my plain white bra.

I don't even have time to be embarrassed at how basic my underwear is before he's moaning softly, tugging me toward him, pushing the soft cups up over my breasts and wrapping his hot, wet mouth around my nipples, first one and then the other, sucking and biting and making me lose my mind.

My eyes are shut tight again, and all I can do is whimper "Oh my God" over and over again. This is all new territory for me, and I'm panting for air, my heart ready to beat out of my chest.

"You are driving me absolutely. Fucking. Crazy," Hunter murmurs in between sucks, finally kissing the space between my breasts and then nuzzling the side of my neck, sending a jolt of pleasure down my spine. "Is it too hot for you? You're sweating."

I nod, suddenly realizing how tingly and achy my pussy is, wondering if he can feel my wetness through the fabric of his pants. The memory of his fingers inside me is weeks old but still fresh. I want him to do it again.

"Well, then..." Hunter slides my blazer down my shoulders, taking my shirt along with it. My arms are pinned at my sides, and my breasts are thrust out at him, my nipples hard and glistening with his saliva. His cheeks are flushed pink, and I wonder if he's as turned on as I am. My tie still hangs loosely around my neck, and Hunter grabs it and pulls me close for another kiss.

There's no doubt about it now—his dick feels like a rock between my legs, pushing against me through my tights.

"Mm-hmm," I moan.

He tweaks my nipples with his fingers, rolling and squeezing as his tongue strokes aggressively against mine. The ache between my legs grows, and before I know it, I'm leaning harder against him, spreading my knees farther apart, seeking more stimulation.

I could almost come right now, I'm sure of it. My hands are on his shoulders, holding tight. I start to grind on his lap, soft and slow at first, then faster. I want him so bad I'm dizzy.

One thing about the academy's uniform pants: they do not restrain hard-ons the way jeans do.

"Jesus, Milla," he moans, hips thrusting upward to meet my movement.

His hands drop down to slide up the back of my thighs, squeezing as he rocks beneath me. The black tights I'm wearing are so thin, it's almost like he's touching me directly. I should put a stop to this and not overindulge, but I can't help myself. That electric, twisting sensation is happening, and I remember his fingers on me again, how I went home and made myself come while thinking of him.

He's practically fucking my mouth with his tongue now, and my nipples are crushed against his shirt, tingling against the cotton. It's not just me who's disheveled and panting—Hunter is too, and I realize he's as desperate for this as I am.

I like that I have the power to do this to him. That he wants me too.

With an expert movement, he reaches around the seat,

and suddenly we're reclining until we're horizontal. It's the kind of smoothness that can only come from doing this a lot, and the more I let myself think about it, the harder it is to ignore. I wonder why he's doing this with me when he could have anyone else. Girls with more experience. Girls who'd give him anything he wanted, without asking questions.

Then his hand slips down the back of my underwear, palming my bare ass cheeks before moving lower, until his thick middle finger is penetrating me from behind. I gasp in his mouth and then start rocking back and forth so the tip of his finger is slipping in and out of me, exactly as deep as I want it. I can feel myself getting even wetter, plummeting toward the edge. Never in my life have I ever dreamed I'd be doing something like this with Hunter Beck.

But why am I letting him when I still haven't gotten any answers? Why do I get so stupid with just a kiss, and then we go further and I get stupider still? Is any of this even real?

I feel Hunter start to peel my tights down, my underwear rolling along with them, and that's when I snap out of it. I pull back with a jolt, panting hard. "Stop."

His hands go up immediately, as if a cop told him to freeze.

"What'd I do wrong?" he says. "Tell me, and I won't do it again."

"It's not that. I just..." I pause, shaking my head. "We can't keep doing this without ever having real conversations. It doesn't work."

I tug my bra back down and climb back into the passenger seat, buttoning up my shirt and checking the clock as I tuck it in. We have less than three minutes left.

"Come on, Milla. We don't have to talk," he whispers,

and everything about him is so hot—his mouth, his hands, his body—that when he leans over and kisses me again, I almost let myself forget what's bothering me.

Almost.

But I manage to (regretfully) push him back. "I need to know what I am to you."

Hunter's brows knit together. "What does that mean?"

"It means... I don't know. Are we something special? Are you going to walk me to class and sit with me at lunch? I don't understand what this is."

He straightens his seat back up, avoiding my gaze now. "Why does it matter?"

"Because I want to know what to expect. And how to act."

Hunter sighs. "You don't have to act. Let's just take it day by day. Don't make this a bigger deal than it is."

Ah. Of course. He's back in selfish jerk mode. How could I possibly think it would be otherwise?

I can't believe I let him play me like this. *Again*.

"Okay. Here's the day-to-day: I'm leaving right now," I say as I grab my backpack and open the door.

"Milla—"

I get out and then whip around. "*Don't*. I'm not like you, Hunter. I don't just stick it in anything that walks and then move on to someone new the next day."

"That's not what this is," he says.

"Then what is it? Is this a long-term thing? What happens when we go to college next year? I'm not just going to follow you around wherever you go."

His hands go over his face, and his shoulders shake, and then I realize with a flash of rage that he's actually laughing at me.

"What the hell is so funny?" I spit.

He shakes his head, still smiling. "Look, it's just...

What's wrong with living in the moment? You're trying to plan our whole lives here, when all I want to do is make out with you in a car."

"Well, you aren't making out with me anymore. So glad you're amused."

With that, I slam the car door as hard as I can and stalk back toward school just in time to hear the bell signaling the end of lunch period.

Hunter doesn't follow.

Chapter Twenty-Eight

CAMILLA

I may not have a lot of experience with boyfriends, but I do have experience being disappointed by people. Mainly my mom. So you'd think, after all these years, I'd be an expert at just rolling with letdowns. But apparently not.

The entire rest of the school day I'm in a bad mood, and then the bus ride is straight out of hell. All I can think about is Hunter, alternating between being intensely horny and intensely pissed off. It's a good thing he doesn't come home after school because I'm not sure I'd be able to keep calm and carry on during my shift with Harrison if his older brother walked through the door trying to act like nothing had happened with us in the car earlier.

Mom's not around when I retreat to the pool house around dinnertime, face-planting on the couch with sheer physical and emotional exhaustion. She still kept one of her other part-time housekeeping clients despite now being full-time with the Becks, so she's probably out for the rest of the evening. Which is good for me.

What would she even say if she knew about all the

Hunter stuff? Would she be angry I'm messing around with her boss's son? Or would she congratulate me on manipulating my position as the Becks' nanny to get into Hunter's pants? Maybe she'd just be disappointed that I put a stop to it today, instead of milking the relationship—or whatever it is/was—for all its worth.

A grimace pinches my face when I remember the we'll go day by day line. And worse, the "all I want to do is make out with you in a car" line. It was so dumb to think that him randomly opening up to me at the lighthouse actually changed anything.

Isabel and I have exchanged countless texts about what happened at the park, and I've relayed a non-explicit version of what happened in the car. Meaning, I mentioned that we've made out a few times, but not exactly how far he's gotten. It's one thing to tell Isabel about kissing, but I'd rather not share that Hunter and I were basically dry humping in the school parking lot, especially when anyone could have walked over to that corner and seen us through the car windows. I feel trashy. Used.

Isabel is nothing but supportive, of course, and I'm so adamant that this thing with Hunter is really no big deal that she immediately intuits that I like him a lot more than I care to admit. Which, busted.

You sure you don't want me to come over with a bucket of caramel corn and my Netflix password? she texts. *We can binge something. Anything. It'll take your mind off it. Ooh, or* Wonder Woman?

I text back and tell her I'd love to, but we'll have to raincheck because I have a crapton of homework. I don't tell her that I'm also worried my mom will be home soon, and I don't want anyone witnessing her typical booze-fueled debauchery.

But it's Fri-yay! Isabel replies.

Yup, and that means tomorrow is Satur-yay, followed by Sun-yay, I text.

My phone buzzes. *LOL okay but we are hanging out tomorrow deffff*

I smile. *You got it.*

But the second I look back at my textbooks, my mind turns to mush, replaying the scene in the car earlier like it's on a playlist set to repeat.

This is ridiculous.

Even though I'm not hungry, I make myself a grilled cheese and a can of tomato soup for dinner. Then I eat in between taking notes from my history text. I'm barely absorbing the info, though, and I know I'm going to have to put in double studying time before our test on the indigenous peoples of North America next week. Boys suck.

My ear keeps straining for the sound of footsteps or a knock, even though I know there's no way Hunter is going to come over here to apologize. Still, I can't help wishing for it. It's pathetic how I can't shake the ache for him.

I never want to become the kind of girl who lets a guy walk all over her, but Hunter has a way of infiltrating my every thought. All I have to do is close my eyes, and I'm back in that car, Hunter's hands all over me. Why does everything feel so good with him?

The heat rushes through my body again, and I feel that twist in my stomach, my thigh muscles going tense. This is so annoying.

I need to do something. Need to cool down.

Going to the window, I look out at the pool. The water is still and black in the dark without the pool lights turning it a glowing turquoise. Maybe I can do laps. Exhaust myself to the point that I can crash into bed afterward into a dreamless sleep. Besides that, I haven't gone swimming once since we moved in here. Now that I have access to a freaking lagoon, I might as well use it.

My bathing suit is old and a little small for me, but it's all I've got. It's a dark blue one-piece with a cut-out under the chest where two pieces of fabric tie into a center bow. It was cute when I was fourteen, but I'm practically popping out of the top now. Oh well. Not like anyone's going to see me in it, thank God.

While I'm changing, I look down at my chest for the first time since this afternoon and notice the red suck marks along the swell of my breasts. Hickeys. Evidence of Hunter's mouth on my body. Dismay washes through me, but it's short-lived as I remember how it felt to have Hunter bite me. How his tongue tasted my skin as he sucked on it.

It's too hot. Time to swim it off.

I tuck a clean towel under my arm and slip outside, leaving the porch light off and guiding myself by moonlight. Once I set the towel on a lounge chair and then dip a toe in, I almost change my mind. It's a heated pool, but it's not exactly cozy and warm. Then again, cold water is exactly what I need, so without ceremony, I dive in.

The cold burns through me, and I come up gasping, feeling goosebumps break out all over me in tiny prickles. I go under a few more times, and soon enough I'm acclimated to the temperature, ready for my laps.

My technique is sloppy as I try to recall the few handfuls of swimming lessons I had years ago. I do a lap, then another. The weight of the water all around me feels good, soothing, and I like the fact that while I'm exercising, I'm existing completely in the moment. Thinking about the water and my breath and the sound of splashing, the motion of my arms and legs, the number of times I go back and forth.

I count ten laps before I stop to catch my breath. Leaning on my forearms at the pool's edge, I listen to the silence around me. I look up at the moon and stars and try to pick out constellations. They're not as bright as they were at the lighthouse, but they're beautiful still.

I see a shadow move in the corner of my eye and look over. There's a silhouette in one of the lounge chairs. A Hunter-shaped silhouette.

"Jesus!" I shriek, my palm going over my chest. I can feel my heart pounding.

"That's what they call me," he jokes, deadpan.

"How long have you been sitting there?"

"A while."

"And it didn't occur to you to say anything?" I angrily splash water in his direction. "You scared me half to death."

"I didn't mean to." Hunter mumbles something else, too low for me to discern.

"What'd you just say?"

"I'm sorry," he repeats, enunciating this time. It sounds sarcastic to me.

I scoff. "I don't think you are. I think you like to watch. And now you can watch me leave."

194

Chapter Twenty-Nine

HUNTER

I'm lounging in the dark, debating whether to go to the pool house to talk to Camilla, when I see her come out in a bathing suit, towel tucked under her arm. My body tenses at the sight of her, and though I want to say something, I can't.

Her dark suit hugs her curves like it was painted on, her tits almost spilling out the top, and after dipping a toe in the pool, I'm impressed to see her dive right in.

I guess that's a good metaphor for Camilla as a person. She's the type who jumps into things full stop, regardless of consequences. Not because she's impulsive, but because she's determined and headstrong. When she knows what she wants, she goes after it. Whether it's school or confronting me about...whatever we are.

Watching her swim, I can't help but take notice of her form. She's a bit sloppy until she eventually settles in, maybe because of the temperature. Or maybe she just hasn't been swimming in a long time—not like I'm judging, even if it sounds that way. Obviously, most people aren't competitive swimmers like I am.

But seeing her stroke through the water, lap after lap, I have to give her credit for how strong she is. She's clearly tired, but she keeps on pushing, falling into a rhythm. I like that. I also like seeing her body move. I've caught some of the random comments she gets from her mom about the food she sees Camilla eating or how she needs more exercise—such bullshit. Camilla's perfect the way she is.

And I know for a fact that ass is made for grabbing.

Every new lap she finishes, I tell myself now's the time to say something. But I can't make myself do it. It's easier to just stay silent, breathing in and out, watching her splash her way back and forth across the pool. Finally, Milla comes to a halt, leaning over the ledge, breathing hard as she looks up at the sky. *Now. Do it. Say hello. Say her name, say* something.

Suddenly, her head turns, and she jumps, hand over her heart. "Jesus." She sinks to her neck and stabs me with her eyes. "How long have you been there?"

I shrug. "A while."

She splashes water at me, but from this far away I only catch a few drops. "You scared me half to death."

"I didn't mean to," I tell her. "I'm sorry."

"What'd you just say?" she asks. I can't tell if she just wants to hear me say the words again or if she actually didn't hear me over the sound of the water.

"I'm sorry," I say again, slower and louder this time.

Her eyes narrow. "I don't think you are. I think you like to watch. And now you can watch me leave."

Storming as fast as she can through the water toward the pool stairs, she manages to look both incredibly pissed off and also like she's moving in slow motion. I'd probably laugh at the incongruity if she weren't so mad at me right now.

I go pick up Camilla's towel from the chair where she

left it and then head to the pool stairs, holding it open for her to step into, just like I do for my little brother. As she reaches the steps and starts climbing out, all I get for my efforts is a glare.

Say something productive. "Just so you know," I say, forcing myself to look away from her dripping wet body, "you shouldn't be closing your hands when you swim. Contrary to popular belief, relaxed fingers have less drag."

She grabs the towel from me and wraps it around herself. "I don't recall asking for your advice."

If I dove head first into the pool right now, the thermal shock would be less than the ice bucket she just dumped over me.

"Can we talk?" I ask.

She opens her mouth, but then closes it. I can see it in her eyes, that guarded look she gets, like she's expecting someone to come out of nowhere and yank the world out from under her. Like she's preparing for the worst. "Fine."

"I just..." Trailing off, I shake my head. Now I'm the one who's tongue-tied.

I know it's my fault that we're in this mess and that if I let her walk away, someone else will swoop in. Ortega's already in the wings, waiting for his chance, and even though Milla denies it, his odds aren't zero.

"You know what? Don't torture yourself. If you have nothing to say, I think we're done here." She lets her voice trail off, and soon her feet begin to follow.

"Wait! Look, I was jealous. At the park," I blurt out because it's the easiest thing to admit. It gets me what I want, which is for Camilla to turn around. "You looked happy. You were smiling. You never smile like that when you're with me, and it sucked. And I was pissed that I couldn't just...brush it off. Like I normally would."

She straightens her shoulders. "That doesn't excuse

what you did. You don't get to treat me like I'm your property." I'm nodding, and she takes a deep breath. "I'm allowed to go places and have fun and be with my friends, and they're allowed to make me smile. None of that has anything to do with you."

"I know. I never thought otherwise. I just acted like I did, and I know that's not okay," I say.

Her lips purse. "Good."

"Milla, this is all new territory for me," I push on. "Everything in my life has always been...superficial. Stuff with my dad. Friendships. Hookups. One-night stands, whatever. I do better when I compartmentalize. Everything stays in its own box. I deal with it when it's right in front of me, and then afterward I walk away. You know what I mean? But with you, it's like...I don't want that. I want to be...close."

Stepping toward her, I catch her gaze, hoping she sees the sincerity in my eyes.

"You keep plenty of girls close." Her words are bitter. "I've seen it, right here in this pool. And again, at the pool house where I now live. The laundry room. Your car."

The memories come back, all too fresh. I feel ashamed now, but I don't even remember half those girls' names.

"Please, stop," I say, cutting her off. "None of that matters."

"Ha! Of course it doesn't matter. None of it *ever* matters to you. You do realize that makes you look even worse, don't you?" she says. "Why should I think I'm any different?"

"I mean—that's not what I meant."

"Then what did you mean?"

"None of them were you!" I finally grind out, emotion almost cracking my voice. "None of it mattered until you."

That catches her off guard.

"Why?" comes her quiet question. Like she's afraid of what I might say but wants to know nonetheless. "Why am I different?"

I've asked that question enough times myself, and I still don't have a clear answer. But I have something that's close, and I hope it's enough.

I hold my hand out to her, and she takes it. Then I lead her over to the grass so we can sit across from each other, our knees just barely touching.

Leaning forward, I tuck a wet strand of hair behind her ear and say, "This is lame, but...out of all the babysitters we've had for Harrison, you are the first one who really cares. You could be doing the bare minimum, just going through the motions to collect your paycheck, but you don't. You're always going the extra mile to see him happy. You have a smile ready for him no matter what."

Her shoulders relax a little bit, and she places a hand on my knee. I can feel the heat of it through my shorts, but I try to stay focused.

"The more I paid attention to you when you were over, the more I started to learn about you. The more of a puzzle you became, the more I had to figure you out. I know your life hasn't been easy, and I know stuff has happened that hurt you."

She pulls her hand away, looking me in the eye. "I don't want to talk about that."

"Okay. We don't have to." My lips slam shut at her sudden defensiveness. I take in the warmth of her body, the freckles across the bridge of her nose, her deep brown eyes, and make myself speak. "All this is to say...I feel...things. For you. But I don't know what this is. Or what I'm doing."

"This is all new to me too." Camilla shivers, whether from the cold or something else, I'm not sure. I'm overcome with the urge to drag her into my lap and hold her, to still her the way she stills me. But I don't. The last thing I want is to scare her off.

"So what should we do?" I whisper.

Camilla lets out a long breath. "I don't know. I don't know if this can work. What I'm even ready for, if us together makes sense at all—"

"Then let's find out," I say. "Do you want that?"

"Yes." She doesn't even hesitate. The smile I've been waiting for lights up her face, and she reaches a hand up to touch the line of my jaw. "I want that. I want you."

Her breath is hot on my lips.

"I want you," I tell her. "Just you."

This time, it's Camilla who kisses first. And I kiss her back.

Chapter Thirty

CAMILLA

*M*onday morning, there's a knock on the door while I'm brushing my teeth. Still half-asleep, I don't think much of it, toothbrush in hand as I open up to find Hunter standing outside the pool house.

"Uh. Hey," I say around a mouth full of suds, embarrassed at my ratty sleep shorts and tank top.

Aaand of course he looks perfect. The morning sun emphasizes the lines of his cheekbones and strong jaw, his hair tousled in that sexy, rebellious, just-out-of-bed way.

"Hey. You still want that ride to school?" he asks.

All I can do is nod, my pulse kicking at the thought of Hunter Beck driving me to school in his BMW, in full view of the entire student body. Half of me wants to scream from the rooftops (or his sunroof) that I'm in a "let's-try-this"-ship with Hunter, that he said he wants *just me* and me alone, while the other half is completely anxious at the thought of people knowing we're...entangled.

"Cool. I'll be in the car."

His gaze shifts behind me, and I turn around to see a

mostly drunk bottle of Evan Williams on the floor by the couch. Shit. Thanks, Mom. Classy.

"See you in a few," I say, practically slamming the door in his face.

I have ten minutes to get dressed.

Rushing to the bathroom, I spit, rinse, and then run a brush through my hair. After a detour to my bedroom to put on my uniform and zip up my school bag, I'm out the door.

When I slide into Hunter's passenger seat, I turn and realize he's holding out a freshly toasted Pop-Tart wrapped in a paper towel.

"For me? You shouldn't have," I say, grabbing it and batting my eyes.

"Harry said they were your favorite. You don't have to eat it—"

But I've already taken a huge bite, my mouth full as I mumble, "Mmm. Breakfast of champions."

"Glad to be of service then." He laughs, and we're off.

The radio is on, but I can't keep my mind on the show hosts or whatever music they choose to play. Friday night's conversation has changed things between us.

And the weekend...the weekend was *something*. I still haven't quite recovered from the stolen kisses and intense make-out sessions. Like on Saturday, when his parents were out and he invited me over to watch a movie with him and Harrison, then spent the entire two hours with his hand on my thigh. Just sitting there, leaving me to wonder if and when he was going to move it. I can't even remember what we watched.

Sunday I had my girls' date with Isabel, but when I got back home, I saw I had a text from Hunter asking me to meet him by the huge oak tree that grows along the side of the house. When I got there, I realized he was in the branches—in his old treehouse.

"Come up!" he said. "I haven't been up here since I was ten years old, and it's too dangerous for Harrison."

"But it's safe enough for us?" I said skeptically.

"We're barely six feet off the ground," he pointed out. "Unless you're scared of heights?"

"I'm not scared." With that, I'd climbed up the rickety ladder and found myself on a shady platform where Hunter had laid out a blanket and set up a mini picnic of sliced apples, peanut butter, cheese, and spicy pumpkin seeds.

"Did Harry help you with the picnic?" I teased.

"Nope, did it all myself," he said.

After we ate he leaned back, put his head on my lap, and closed his eyes. Leaning down to kiss him was my natural reaction—I swear, it's like he has his own center of gravity, and I can't help being pulled in. We'd spent all afternoon kissing in a tree, just like the schoolyard song, and then I'd snuck back home to finish up my homework, still dazed and with my lips feeling swollen and bruised.

Now I look over at Hunter from the corner of my eye. With him focused on the road, it's easier to get away with staring. The straight slope of his nose. Those cheekbones that seem like they could cut glass. His shapely lips and how they so perfectly fit against mine.

"You're blushing," Hunter observes, glancing over. "What are you thinking about?"

"Nothing," I say, quickly looking out the window.

"Bet I know," he teases, his hand coming over to trace a line from my knee up my thigh.

I swat him away, and he laughs, pulling into the school parking lot. Which is, of course, packed full of cars and students and roving eyes.

"Do you think you should just drop me off?" I ask, suddenly nervous.

Hunter's been decent this weekend, but there's still part of me that expects him to turn back into a jerk at any moment. This car and his house are Switzerland, and for all I know, the territory outside of it could change everything.

"Not a chance, Hanson," he says. "You're stuck with me."

I force a smile, but my stomach is full of butterflies, and once we've parked, I don't make a move to get out. "I can't do this," I say.

He leans over, dropping his hand to my chin and turning me to face him. "What do you say we skip first period then?"

That's when he bites my neck, softly, just below the corner of my jaw. That's another thing he's learned over the weekend: various ways of making me melt without actually diving under my clothes. He's wickedly good at it.

I may be instantly distracted, but not enough to forget that my scholarship is at risk. "I'm not skipping class to make out with you. But thank you."

"Shame." Hunter pouts. "Let's go then."

He gives me one last kiss and deepens it, making me question my decision to tell him I wouldn't skip first period. Mercifully, he pulls away.

"School," I mumble weakly.

"Yup. Let's go." Hunter gets out of the car and races around to my side to open the door for me on the passenger side.

"Playing the gentleman?" I say. "We'll see how long that lasts."

I'm only half kidding, but as we start toward Oak Academy, he makes a point of matching me step for step, his arm brushing mine as we walk. There's no way anyone could mistake us for simply heading to school side by side. My mouth is dry. This is it.

"What's your first class?" he asks.

"World History. Second floor."

"Cool," he says. "I'll walk you."

Here's the thing about Hunter Beck. When it's me crossing the front lawn of the school and heading up the steps, I have to constantly dodge to keep out of people's way. But with Hunter at my side, the crowd just...parts. Students are gawking at us, and they're noticing me, and they're whispering. This amount of attention isn't something I'm used to at all. I'm not even sure if I like it or if I just want to be invisible again.

I don't realize I've subconsciously scooted closer and closer to Hunter until my hand brushes his. When I step away, trying to shrug it off as the accident it was, I feel his fingers wrap around mine.

My surprise is so strong I have to bite down a smile as I squeeze his hand in return. This is good. Holding hands with him feels solid, and being with him like this, like we don't care what anybody else thinks, makes me happy. It's a subtle message: what happens between us is our business, and no one is going to ruin it.

"Are you used to people staring at you wherever you go?" I ask as we make a quick stop at my locker so I can switch my books out and grab everything I need for my pre-lunch classes.

"Downside of being over six feet tall," he says breezily, like it's no big deal. He has a point with the height, but it's not just that, and we both know it.

Conversations stop dead in their tracks when we walk by. Jaws literally drop. Eyes follow us for as long as they can, and so do the whispers. It's making me paranoid, gluing my gaze to the floor like I always do whenever I can tell people are staring at me.

We finally come to a halt outside my classroom door. Hunter steps in front of me, and I can tell he wants to kiss me. But the academy has strict rules on student conduct, and sucking face in the hallways is verboten. Not that students don't hook up on campus, they just do it out of sight. Or try to. I learned the hard way never to walk into one of the private study rooms on the library's second floor without knocking—even if the lights are off. *Especially* if the lights are off.

"Catch up with you later?" he says.

I'm already smiling when I answer, "Yeah."

With that, he gives my hair a little tug that sends tingles from my scalp to my toes and then saunters away. I head into World History floating on a cloud.

Chapter Thirty-One

CAMILLA

$\mathcal{I}$'m on my way to second period with Emmett when my phone buzzes from my blazer pocket. I slip it out and see a handful of unread texts from Isabel.

Heard some very intéressantes rumors about you and Hunty walking into school together...such as might potentially indicate coupledom?? Gasp!

T/F?

Then, right after, *text me baaaack, I am DYING (insert dead emoji with Xs for eyes). Don't let me be the last to knowww*

The third text was sent just minutes ago, presumably when she got out of class. *Someone just asked me to verify if you guys were holding hands in the hall this AM. wtf*

And lastly, *MILLA! You get a pass bc I know your phone is off for class (fair), but if you think I'm waiting all the way until lunchtime for answers, prepare to be called into the main office to take an "emergency" phone call from your "Auntie Isa."*

After that, it's a slew of GIFs depicting tea being spilled or poured. I shake my head with a grin. Always with the drama, that girl.

"What is it?" Emmett asks, kindly making an effort to not look at my screen.

"Just Isabel being Isabel," I tell him.

I don't want to gossip with Emmett about whatever is going on with me and Hunter, and the only reason I haven't mentioned it to Isabel yet is because I wanted to see what would happen after the weekend was over and we had to be out in public.

But something *is* happening. There's no denying it now.

Quickly, I tap out a response. *We're sort of trying to be together? Or something. But we don't have a name for it.*

HA! she responds immediately. *Neither does the rest of the school, but that hasn't kept them from speculating...*

Which btw you're gonna have some nasty gossip coming your way.

That worry, in the back of my mind for the last couple of days, rushes to the forefront. I know Isabel shares first period with one of Hillary's friends. As Isabel has put it before, Minion Emma is quite capable of using her brain academically, but when it comes to everything else, she's incapable of independent thought. Either that, or she's terrified of what Hillary will do if they have a difference of opinion.

But that's just too bad. I'm not going to let anyone shit-talk me out of this. If things with Hunter fall apart, it will be because of us, not them.

"Everything okay?" Emmett asks after grabbing my bag and using it to steer me around a group of students I was just about to plow into.

"Yeah. Just girl stuff," I tell him, sliding my phone back in my pocket. "Tell me about your weekend."

"Meh, same old. Mom's been on my ass about committing to a college even though my acceptance letters haven't all come in yet. I mean, seriously. Like rushing my decision is going to help her cause. I know she just wants me to stay close. You?"

"I got into Cal Lutheran, which was a safety school anyway. Still waiting on my UCs and CSUs," I gripe. "Lemme know when you want to study-buddy again."

"Oh, please. We all know you're just after my cookies," he jokes.

"Guilty as charged."

We pull up to the glass-walled walkway where I go straight and Emmett has to hang a right.

"Enjoy statistics. See you in a bit," I tell him with a wave goodbye.

"Cool cool," he says, and then we part ways.

Luckily, AP Bio is so hard that I don't have time to think about my personal life, lest I spill a vial of methanol on my shoes. When my lab partner drops her voice to whisper, "Are you dating Hunter Beck?" midway through our experiment, I just laugh.

"I'm not sure that's the right word," I tell her, which seems pretty accurate. "But I mean, he's not dating anyone else."

She nods and smiles, but something tells me I've just confirmed all the gossip despite my careful response.

When the bell rings, I pack my things and steel myself for whatever's waiting outside the door. I try not to listen to the voices around me as I walk to the next class.

I try, and I fail.

Come lunchtime, I stop at my locker so I can drop off my stuff. I have no idea what's up with Hunter. Do I wait for him? Find him out in the quad once I have my food? I'm anxious at the thought that he won't be there, and I'll be left awkwardly lurking around his group of friends (who I'm sure will have something to say to me).

"Hanson!"

Glancing over, I spot Hunter heading my way from the other end of the hall, aloof to everyone else who walks by, their eyes glued to him—I mean, how can you not, he's over six feet and looking like *that*—but when he comes up to me, he's all smiles.

"Lunch?" he asks.

"Yeah," I say. And just like that, all my fears evaporate.

My heart skips a beat when he holds out his arm. I try to keep myself from seeming too eager, but the truth is, I take it like it's a lifeline. Walking to class with him was already a nightmare, and I'll need this support if I'm going to last through lunch.

After we grab our food from the lunch line—sushi for Hunter, and a veggie sandwich with fries for me—we head out to the quad. He leads the way to an empty table on the far side of the fountain that features a knight, the school's mascot, and I let out a relieved sigh when we set our things down. Maybe it'll just be the two of us today.

We make small talk about our classes, and soon enough, my nerves are the furthest thing from my mind.

"Hey, is it cool if Isabel joins us?" I ask, realizing I should invite her.

Hunter shrugs. "Whatever you want. She's cool."

"What about Emmett?" I challenge.

"Is this a test?" Hunter asks.

"No. It's just me making sure that my friends are also welcome wherever I am," I say honestly. "Otherwise, I'll have to split all my lunches between you guys fifty-fifty."

"Sure. Ortega too, then," he says.

I smile. But when I text Isabel, she tells me she's already heading off campus with Emmett. Still, I'm glad this talk is out of the way. Hunter's making an effort to be civil, and I'm sure once he sees how Emmett and I act when we're together, he'll relax.

From the corner of my eye, I notice Hunter handling his chopsticks with the efficiency of someone who's been using them since the day they were born. Not surprising in the least. Meanwhile, I've never even had sushi—it's expensive, and besides that, I've never been convinced that raw fish can actually taste good.

Suddenly there's a piece of salmon and rice in front of my face. "Wanna try?" Hunter asks. "It's salmon nigiri."

Any hesitation I might have is negated by the fact that he's actually *feeding me*. Something I find strangely endearing but which also activates those butterflies in my stomach. I open my mouth, and he gently places the piece on my tongue.

He watches me chew, tilting my head as I do. The hint of soy sauce and wasabi goes perfectly with the salmon, which has so much more flavor than when it's cooked.

"So?" he asks.

I shrug. "Not bad for my first sushi."

"That was your first sushi *ever*?" When I nod, he laughs. "And you're already a connoisseur. I should take you to my favorite spot. It's this place in La Jolla Village that is insane. If you think this stuff is good, wait until you try *actual* good sushi."

"Sounds good to me," I answer, assuming it's one of those "someday" things.

"How about Wednesday? We can go after our session with Spencer."

Record scratch. "Does that mean you're actually planning to show up for our mandatory debate tutoring?" I'm dubious.

"It means I'd be waiting for you to get out anyway, so I might as well be there."

An evil idea hits me.

"You know, if you wanted to study together more often, we could probably manage a lot more alone time..."

"That's blackmail, Milla."

"It's an incentive," I quip.

"Is it?" His blue eyes narrow, and his free hand finds my knee under the table. "I don't think you realize the promise you're making."

I'm trying to come up with something smart to say, but his fingers being where they are, I find myself unable to think past it.

Suddenly, there's a hubbub around us, and I look up to see Hunter's group of friends looming over us. Steve Howard, Matt Mason, and another guy who's either a Tom or a Tim. Their faces are full of judgment.

"Huh. We were about to send out a search party for you," Steve says with a smirk. "Only to find you out here, hiding in the corner with your maid. What happened, did she forget to clean your room?"

They all laugh.

My fingers tighten around my iced tea.

I'm about ready to just get up and walk away when beside me, Hunter says, "Camilla's not my maid."

It's the first time I've heard him correct any of his friends. Following his lead, I make myself seem as unbothered as I can, and add, "Technically, I'm the sitter."

"Right." The corner of Hunter's lips rises for a second. "And if that's all you came over here to say, you can fuck directly off."

Steve blinks. "Beck, you serious?" He gives me a pointed look. "Her?"

A single word that encapsulates everything they think about me. I'm not a person, I'm a creature that's beneath them, someone that registers so barely on their radar, I'm just *her?* with a question mark.

Hunter covers the hand I have on top of the table with his own. "Yes, her."

There's a loud snort from Steve. "Fine. But she better be the best pussy you've ever had because—"

Hunter stands, towering over Steve. "I'd be real careful if I were you."

They look at each other for a moment, and I realize the entire quad has gone silent, all of them staring in our direction.

"C'mon, man," Matt says, tugging at Steve's arm. "Let's go."

With a loud laugh that can only be for show, Steve shakes his head and walks away, Matt in tow. Hunter's other friend holds out his hand to me.

"I'm Tom."

I take his hand and shake it, firm but gentle. "Camilla."

"Nice to officially meet you," he says, sliding into the seat across from me and Hunter and throwing down his backpack. "Hey man, you see the Lakers play the Clippers last night?"

"Dominated," Hunter says, and I get the impression that this conversation is about more than basketball.

They fall into sports talk, and in between bites of my sandwich, I chime in where I'm able to follow. When Tom gets up to throw out his trash, he says to me, "Sorry the other guys were shitty to you before."

I shrug. "They'll get over it."

Hunter wraps his arm around me. "And if not, it's their loss. Nobody tells me what to do. I'm a big boy."

"Right on," Tom says. "Though that's not what your last girl told me. Oh!!"

Dick jokes aside, Tom seems like a pretty good guy. However, I can't help noticing that people in the quad are still watching us. Hunter takes it in.

"Glad you're all enjoying the show," he shouts, "but I hope you have actual lives to return to!"

Immediately, I feel the weight of their attention dropping, and my heart, which had been racing, falls into a steady beat. Although I'm no damsel in need of rescuing, having him step up for us feels nice.

"You want to get out of here?" he says.

"I thought you'd never ask."

*H*unter's fingers interlace with mine as we leave the quad together. My steps feel lighter somehow, but imagining all the reasons why he might want to be alone together has me a bit jittery. We walk from one end of the school to the other and then head up the stairs.

"Where are we going?" I whisper as we reach the second floor.

"Somewhere quieter."

"Yes, but where?"

He looks over his shoulder and then pulls up short outside an unmarked door. "May I present..." He gives the knob a jiggle, and the door pops open. "The janitor's closet."

I can't help but laugh. "Are you serious? This is the most cliché thing I've ever heard of."

He leads me inside and shuts the door behind us. We're in a glorified cubicle with shelves stacked against opposite walls, dusty and bare, though I see a few ladders and mops and other odds and ends. At the other end of the room, a

215

small window looks out onto leafy tree branches, so we're not completely in the dark.

We barely have room to move. I suppose that's exactly the point.

"Why's it empty?"

Hunter shrugs. "Nobody uses it anymore. Which is why we won't be bothered."

As he pulls me close, a dark thought crosses my mind. I can only think of one reason why Hunter would know all the hidden corners of the school, and it sends jealousy pulsing through me. "I'm not sure I want to know how you know that."

Cupping my face, he says, "Shh. You're so red right now."

I scowl. "I had to basically sprint to keep up with you. Your long-legged pace is the equivalent of running for a woman of average height."

"I wanted to get here ASAP," he says with a hint of humor in his tone, but it's gone when he speaks next. "So we could have more time to do this."

Our lips touch. Softly, and then harder, more desperate.

I've lost count of how many times we've kissed by now, but it's to the point where I should be used to it. Yet every time still feels like the first: my heart is racing, my stomach doing somersaults, my insides turning to liquid. I can't get enough. I wrap my arms around his neck, bringing him closer.

I can't believe I'm making out in a closet at school. It's a rite of passage, I guess.

Though I have to admit, it's seriously hot. And Hunter is...handsy. And really fond of groping my ass under my skirt.

His kisses turn hard and bruising, like he's starved and

I'm a morsel to be eaten. And being the center of his attention is like being swept up in a hurricane.

I decide to stop being shy and do some touching of my own. But he's wearing a vest, and his shirt is tight-fitting, unlike mine, so I can't just slip my hands under to touch his skin. I growl in frustration, and Hunter pulls away, snickering.

"What are you trying to do?" he asks.

"Touch you," I say, reaching to unbutton his vest, but he stops my hand.

"Tell me what you want," he says hoarsely.

The way we are, all wrapped up in each other, I don't even feel embarrassed when I answer. "I want to feel your skin against mine."

I get no warning before his lips and tongue are on mine again. Our teeth click, and as I unbutton Hunter's vest, he loosens my tie and begins to work on my shirt until it's halfway open. His handiwork from Friday and the weekend is revealed, and he spends a long moment surveying the red marks all over my cleavage.

I trail my palm down his hard stomach, relishing the taut muscles under my fingertips and the way Hunter's breath catches before he starts kissing my neck. My collarbone. My chest.

"Please don't give me any more hickeys," I say before he gets any more ideas. "At least not in places people will see if I wear basically any summer clothes."

Hunter traces the lace edging the soft cups of my bra. "Meaning I can do it here." He tugs the edge down a little and plants his lips over the exposed skin there.

A jolt runs through me when he sucks, and I arch my back. He kisses every stray freckle on my chest, and every time his tongue comes out, I feel myself tighten. He's so good at this, every one of his movements adding to the hot wetness between my legs.

I'm on my tiptoes, my arms around his neck, trying to climb him like a tree. Hunter seems to realize it and lifts up my thigh to pull me closer still. That's when I find irrefutable proof that I'm not the only one who's turned on.

"How are you already hard?"

"You make me lose control. It's like every time I see you, I just want to—" He stops to shake his head and smiles at me. "Look at me, telling you how I feel."

"Admitting to being turned on isn't what I'd classify as a vulnerable moment."

His grin widens. "So, are you?"

"Vulnerable?"

"Turned on," he clarifies.

I look down, embarrassed, but I know that if I want him to be honest with me, I owe him the same in return. "Yes," I whisper, so low I barely hear it myself.

A glint brightens Hunter's eye while his hand moves down my thigh. "Do you want me to take care of it?"

Something in me keeps holding back. What if I let him do more, go further, and then the novelty is over? He says I'm different, but still I can't quite grasp why. My doubts gnaw at me, souring what would otherwise be the hottest lunch hour of my life.

"We're at school, so no. Also." I take my hand out from under his shirt and place it over his chest. "The physical stuff might be no big deal to you, but it is to me."

He has the decency to look chagrined. "I honestly thought you liked it last time I did it. I wasn't trying to push."

"It's not that I didn't, but..." I chew on the inside of my cheek, and then say, "I couldn't understand *why* you were doing it, other than to mess with me."

"I did—I *do* want to mess with you—but not in the way you're implying." Hunter pulls away a little, both hands coming to rest on my waist. "When I saw you crying, I knew it was my fault. And when you reacted the way you did to my brushing away your tears, I don't know what happened. I couldn't help myself." He takes a long breath, eyes straying to the ceiling before coming back to hold mine. "You felt bad. I wanted to make you feel good, and that was the only way I knew how." His gaze narrows. "I told you to stop me if you wanted to. Why didn't you?"

"Because I was really confused at first, and then..." God, this is so embarrassing. "Then it felt good. And I was even more confused."

"That's why you pushed me away?"

I shrug. "It was all too much, too soon. And you wouldn't even kiss me properly. It didn't feel right."

"I'm kissing you properly now." Hunter brings our lips together to prove the point, curling his tongue around mine while he strokes my thigh. "So...does this feel right?"

I grab his wrist. "Slowly, Hunter."

He looks down, and huffs out a sigh. "I'm trying, but I don't know how to take it slow. So just tell me when to stop, or whatever you think will keep me in line. I'll respect that. Also." His hand goes around to grab my butt. "You have a really nice ass."

He presses himself harder against me for a second, and then he's suddenly lifting me, so I do what comes naturally: wrap my legs around his waist. His other hand comes up to massage my breasts through the fabric of my bra. "All of you is really nice."

I know I'm blushing. "Even though I'm a chub?"

"Who told you that?"

"Nobody," I lie, not wanting to bring my mother into this moment.

Hunter gives me the side-eye. "That's bullshit. You're fucking perfect, Milla," he says, kissing the space between my breasts, and in that moment, I believe him.

"You can touch me above the waist. Whenever you want. But." I pause for dramatic effect. "Everything else, you have to ask first. Okay?"

"Deal," he says and brings our lips together. It's slow and measured, and I feel myself sink into it. Into him. Hunter's solid, and he's warm, and he's steady, and I don't want to let go.

But when the bell rings, I make myself pull away. "Come on. We have to go."

He buries his face in my neck. "I don't want to. Let's cut fifth period."

I laugh. "As much as I'd love to do that, I have priorities. And it's not like we won't be with each other later."

"Here I thought you didn't like hooking up at the house," Hunter says as he lets me down gently.

Once my feet touch the floor, I begin to button my shirt back up, and he does the same. "That's because you're as shameless as you are tireless and seem to lack common sense." I fix the knot on my tie and smooth my hair down. "Or have you forgotten your brother almost walked in on us yesterday?"

"You were the one who started it." Hunter finishes closing his vest.

"And you kept it going!" I argue back, but then we're looking at each other, and this is such a silly argument to have I can't help but giggle. As if it's contagious, Hunter laughs too, and then he's pressing me against the door again to kiss me one last time.

Finally, I place a hand on the doorknob and ask, "You ready?"

With an awkward smile, Hunter waves to the tent in his

pants, which I'd been politely trying to ignore. "I think I'll stay here a few more minutes. Think about baseball. Icebergs. Other cold things."

I have to laugh again. "Well, get it under control. I'll see you later."

It's weirdly flattering to know I have this power. That the effect I have on him isn't something he can control, just like the way he affects me isn't something *I* can control.

Hunter nods. "Looking forward to it."

Chapter Thirty-Three

CAMILLA

idterms are coming up, so to combat my anxiety, I've come up with a strict schedule to maximize studying time. Ravenclaw, remember?

Beyond my usual homework hours, I have a bunch of notes saved to my phone for when I'm babysitting and Harrison is otherwise entertained. Isabel and I made flashcards, too, and I go through them every day during meals. It's not just my Oak Academy scholarship that's on the line. My college acceptance(s) are contingent on my final grades senior year, and if my GPA is high enough, I'll be eligible for much-needed scholarships to cover some of my tuition. Or all of it. A girl can dream.

As hard as I study, though, it feels like there's no end to what I need to memorize. Dates, names, major historical events, the scientific method, Spanish words... They all blur together in an endless sea of information. Shockingly, AP Calculus is where I'm doing the best, and it's all thanks to Isabel. She has a way of explaining math that makes it feel logical, breaking it down into bite-size steps. Unlike my teacher, who spends class trying to get us to wrap our heads around big abstract concepts that don't seem to apply to anything in real life.

Unsurprisingly, her parents are pushing her to dedicate her life to numbers and formulas; Isabel being Isabel, all she wants to do is study art and fashion.

"Don't get me wrong, STEM is great, and it'd be awesome if that were my passion, but it's just not," she explained. "I want to get into costume design."

At first, I sided with her parents—I feel like she could be better than Zuckerberg and Bezos put together or go into research and find a cure for cancer. Yet she's so happy when she talks about all the different eras in fashion, or when she finishes a particularly elaborate costume in her sketchbook. There's no way I'd want her to pursue anything that didn't bring her joy. Whatever she chooses to do, I'm sure she'll nail it.

There is a downside to my master schedule though. Because I have to stay away from Hunter whenever it's cramming time or else I don't get anything done. The handful of times we tried studying together rapidly devolved into steamy make-out sessions, leaving me no choice but to draw a line in the sand and enforce it. Whether I like it or not.

As great as Hunter is, I'm not going to let him become the center of my world. My independence comes first, and for that, I need to go to college. Not just any college, but a *good* one, with a degree program that will both challenge me and set me up to secure a solid job after I graduate. The kind of school with a name that makes people pause when they see it on your resume, that gets you job offers on sight.

So, yeah. No pressure.

There is one plus side though. My mom and I haven't been arguing much. Not just because I always have my nose in a book but because she's been making herself scarce as well. I'm not sure if she's just working overtime or if she's trying to respect my studying, but either way, it's led to things being more or less harmonious at home.

I adjust my position in my desk chair and try to go back to my Spanish workbook, but these conjugations are mind-numbing, and as for the vocab, nothing is sticking. I think I'm getting a little burned out from my marathon of Español today. With a sigh, I massage my temples. My chest feels like it's being crushed. I never used to get panic attacks like this. Once in a while, sure, but ever since I started going to Oak Academy, it's been almost constant.

The only time I don't feel that edge of panic creeping up on me is when I'm with Hunter. It's been a few weeks since we started dating, or seeing each other, or whatever this is, and slowly but surely, he's made himself a permanent fixture in my heart. It's not exactly a relaxing time when he's coming at me with all his intensity, but at least that tension is welcome and wanted.

Going to the kitchen, I pour myself a glass of juice. I wish he were here right now. If I'm not going to be thinking about Spanish, then at least it should be because I'm having a good time, not because I'm too tired and miserable to study properly.

A knock on the window in the living room breaks my daydreaming. Even though this has happened countless times, every time I look up and see Hunter on the other side of the glass, my heart jumps. He's wearing a T-shirt and jeans, and as always, looks like he stepped right off the page of an Abercrombie & Fitch catalog.

It's like he's the devil, and my dirty thoughts have summoned him.

After I open the door for him, I grumpily comment, "You should be studying too, you know."

"I have been."

"Mm-hmm."

"During the times you so very cruelly force me away," he finishes.

Without missing a beat, he scoops me up in his arms and walks us over to the couch, where he sits down with me in his lap.

"And while I was cramming, I ran across this study..."

"You ran across a study," I deadpan.

"I did. Read it too. And it said that breaks are necessary when you're working hard. If you give your brain time to relax, it will absorb the information better when you resume studying."

"So you came over here to make me *stop* studying, so that I can actually study better later?"

"Precisely. It's in your best interest," he replies, very seriously. "Otherwise I'm afraid your brain will melt from all the work and no fun."

I narrow my eyes. "And let me guess, you want to melt my brain in a different way."

"You said it, not me."

We haven't pushed things any further since that janitor's closet talk. Yet I know that he wants to. I can feel it in how he looks at me, in how his hands linger on my waist, in how he kisses me, in how he marks me all over with those goddamned hickeys.

What Hunter doesn't know is that lately, I've started to want more too. I fantasize about him constantly, and truth be told, I find myself dwelling on that time he fingered me up against a wall and wondering if it'd feel different to me now.

He draws an arm around my shoulders, and I automatically sink forward, resting my chin on his shoulder. I shouldn't be doing this. I should be cramming harder, not cuddling. "I still have one more unit left to go," I say, but it comes out a tired whine.

"If you *really* want to keep studying, I suppose I could indulge you." Hunter trails his hands down my back, squeezing as he goes, making me moan at the massage. The boy is good with his hands, I can't deny that. I can feel his smile against my scalp as he kisses the top of my head. "We could have some fun with those flashcards of yours." His hands fall to my hips, and there it is, that *weight* that tells me he wants more. "You get a question right, you get to take one item of clothing off me."

I laugh against his neck, smelling soap and cedar on his skin. "And let me guess, if you get a question right, you get to take one item of clothing off me."

"Correct."

Ha. I see where this is going, and while it would distract me, I wouldn't get any studying done. "Playing strip study with you would be an exercise in futility."

"Oh? I think that depends on what your goals are."

I walked right into that, didn't I? A sigh bursts out of me, and I take another breath of him. He must've taken a shower right before coming over, he smells so clean. "I need to concentrate," I murmur drowsily.

"Okay. Think of it this way..." He shifts me so he can hold my face and force me to look at him. "If you can keep your concentration through a game of strip study, then you can keep your concentration through any midterm."

Sure. Or I'd start thinking about him during the exam, and my mind would go completely blank. "Some other day. Right now my brain just needs a quick rest. So..."

I lean forward and brush my lips against his. When I lick his lower lip, turning more aggressive, he shivers. When I bite it, he groans. Our mouths fuse together, and now my body acts on instinct, as if it's developed a will of its own. I want to be closer, to feel his heat against mine, but I don't have Hunter's boldness or his experience.

"Milla, you keep grinding on me like that, I..." Hunter's breath catches, and it sends a thrilling chill down my spine.

I'm already playing, not with a small fire, but with a full-on blaze. But there's something to seeing him as out of breath as I am, as desperate as I am, that has me pushing for more, asking, "You'll what?"

All of a sudden, Hunter flips me over so I'm horizontal on the couch, back against a throw pillow with him on top of me.

His kiss is hot and bruising. Our teeth clash at several points, and I'm not sure where his tongue ends and mine begins. Under his weight, I sink deeper into the couch cushions. My legs wrap around his, my hands sliding into his hair, and I drown in all the strong feelings he brings out.

Hunter frees my lips and moves down to my neck. I actually moan when he licks me there, and my hips helplessly undulate against his crotch. He's already hard, and my fingers twitch to touch him. I blame it on curiosity, although it's not the driving factor.

"Do you want to know what *really* helps relaxing?" Hunter whispers against my ear. "What will definitely give your head a rest?"

I have the feeling this is yet another sex trap, but I willingly walk right into it. "What?"

"I know you don't like to bring up the first time we hooked up..." His kiss echoes in my eardrums. His hand works its way down the front of my body but doesn't go past my lower belly. "But do you remember what you were just about to do before you pushed me away that night?"

My breath hitches. I know what he's implying, I know where this is headed, and I could put an end to it if I wanted to. But I'm also burning up, so I add more fuel to the fire. "What was I about to do?"

His hot breath shivers into my ear. "Come."

I shudder, and seriously, it's like he has a direct line to my pussy whenever he whispers in my ear. Or when he does anything, really. Breathlessly, I say, "You are wicked. A demon sent to tempt me."

"Is it working?" he says, gently biting my neck. His hand is still on my stomach, heavy and unbearably hot. "Come on, Milla. Let me have another taste."

I blink up at him. "Another *taste?*"

"That night, after you left, I..." He doesn't say it, but his meaning is crystal clear. He must have licked his fingers after he touched me.

Why is this turning me on even harder?

"I take back what I said. You're not wicked. You're a full-on perv."

"For you?" He smiles as he kisses me. "Absolutely." His voice lowers. "You tasted good, Milla. Clean, and sweet. I liked it."

There's this way he has of twisting his tongue around mine that makes me melt instantly. He does it now, and my toes curl, and my insides clench. I become aware of the emptiness inside me that he could fill if I let him.

It's scary how much I want him to touch me again. I pull back and take Hunter's face in my hands. His blue eyes are half-lidded, his lips parted and swollen, his breath heavy, and he's staring right at me like...

"You look like you're about to ruin me," I mutter, tracing his cheekbones with my fingers.

"That's the plan." He trails the back of his hand just above the line of my shorts, and my insides melt while my heart races faster than an Olympian athlete on a one-hundred meter dash. I can't tear my eyes away from his. I feel his fingers on my zipper now, waiting for a word from me, and all I can do is remind myself that I need to breathe. And say something. Anything. But my throat won't open, and my lips won't move.

Helplessly, I look up at him with pleading eyes. Hunter shakes his head. "Tell me what you want."

He gets off on this, doesn't he? On making me squirm and whimper until I'm desperate and then stopping right when I'm about to lose it.

"You didn't have a problem with me not saying it before," I say.

"That was then. This is now." He traces a path along the inside of my thigh and plants a soft kiss on my lips. "What's it gonna be?"

I don't know why I hesitate. It's not like he hasn't done this before. It's not like I don't want him to do it. But being so open about these things is embarrassing and not something I'm used to.

The *yes* is on the tip of my tongue, but I can't bring myself to voice it. Maybe it's because I've already experienced it, and I know it will be good, so I'm afraid I'll get addicted or something. Then again, aren't I addicted to him already? At night, when I'm alone in bed, this is all I can think about. Hunter, me, our hands and mouths and bodies. Anytime my attention drifts, he's all I think about.

"Touch me," I whisper.

"I'm touching you already." He rubs his face on my neck. "You'll have to be more explicit."

The corner of my mouth lifts in a half-smile, and the way we're lying on the couch like this, my nipples tingle against his chest whenever I inhale. I don't know if he realized there was wordplay in what he said, so I tell him, "Then get explicit."

Hunter lifts his head to look at me, then reaches below.

My zipper slides down, and then he works the button open. His fingers slip into my shorts, curling underneath my panties, and I'm so wet it's embarrassing but...

A knock booms across the pool house. "Camilla, are you there?" Mrs. Beck calls from outside.

I freeze and look up at Hunter with panic in my eyes. He frowns, and with a groan, reluctantly takes his hand out of my pants. I hurriedly button up my shorts and get up from the couch while Hunter heads down the hall to stay out of sight.

"I'm here," I shout, rushing to open the door. "Good evening, Mrs. Beck."

She's in a gray silk cocktail dress, hair up, her face painted beautifully. "I'm heading out. Please give Harrison dinner and put him to bed."

An order, not a question.

I could tell her I'm technically off the clock right now and that I need to study—not that I *would* be studying, with Hunter waiting for me, but she doesn't need to know that. That she could have dinner with her son for once and put him to bed for once too. Looking at her, however, the anger gives way to sadness.

When you grow up with a mother who's rarely there for you, you can see when it's happening to someone else. And right now, it's happening to Harrison. He deserves better.

"Of course," I say with a tight smile. "I'll be over in a sec."

"Don't be too long," she says. "Harrison gets fussy when he's hungry."

A sigh escapes when I close the door, and when I go to my room to grab my shoes, Hunter's standing in the doorway scowling, arms crossed over his chest.

"That fucking woman," he says. "Were you even supposed to babysit today?"

"No." I shrug. "At least this way Harry's not spending the night alone." I've spent many myself, and if I can spare a sweet kid from that, then I will.

"I can do it," Hunter says, then kisses me softly. "Stay here and study."

"It's fine," I tell him. "I'm happy to feed him and put him to bed."

"Then let's both do it," he says. "Harry will love that."

"Okay."

My heart tightens, as if Hunter's dug his way further in and such a small organ doesn't have enough space to accommodate the space he takes up inside.

Chapter Thirty-Four

CAMILLA

When I enter the kitchen, I don't detect the usual lingering scent of my mom's cooking. She must have known I'd be dragged into this tonight and didn't bother making dinner before leaving for her next shift. Maybe she's the one who volunteered me to take care of Harry in the first place. Oh, well. We'll make do.

I check the fridge and take stock of what's available, then start pulling out what will take the least amount of work to put together: steak, mashed potatoes, and salad.

It's odd not to have Harrison trail my every move and step like he usually does, but he's currently playing Mario Kart with Hunter in the living room—and kicking his older brother's ass at it, if the screams I'm hearing are anything to go by.

After I put the potatoes in a pot of water to boil and the grill pan is hot, I place the steaks on it and throw a pinch of salt and pepper on top. While they're cooking, I get to work cutting up the romaine, cucumber, and tomatoes, and then dice some cheese. Sure enough, there's a box of artisanal croutons in the pantry to top it all off.

Harrison won't normally eat a salad, not if it's presented the way salads usually are. But I've learned he's more amenable if I plate it in a fun way. So I pour some ranch dressing in the center of a plate and then arrange the cucumber slices and cheese cubes around it so it looks like a flower. Then I add the tomatoes in a circle around that, using the romaine to fill in the background. I keep the croutons in a small bowl so Harry can dunk them separately. As for his steak, I'll cut it into small strips so he can dip those too. He likes his with ketchup.

The hairs on the back of my neck prickle, but before I can turn around, Hunter's voice is at my ear. "That is cute."

I jump and then laugh, shaking my head. "You have to stop sneaking up on me."

"Here I thought you'd be used to it by now." He wraps his arms around my waist, resting his chin on my shoulder. "How long until dinner? Prince Harrison would like to know."

"Where is he?"

"Went upstairs to get a game for after we eat."

I get one steak off the grill for Hunter and leave the other one to cook a little longer since Harry won't eat any meat unless it's well-done.

"Why are there only two?" Hunter asks, frowning.

Shrugging, I tell him, "I'll just eat at home later. I don't need anything fancy."

"Nope," he says, and it's the most affronted I've seen him. I watch him as he goes to the fridge and grabs another package of steak, then rips it open and slaps it on the grill. "You're having dinner with us."

"Okay," I say, touched by his insistence that we all eat together. "Let me just finish up the salad and potatoes."

"What's your plan for these?" he asks, looking at the pot of boiling water.

"If they're soft, they need to be drained and mashed with milk and butter," I say.

"I'm on it."

Minutes later, Harrison's approaching footsteps echo down the hall. He bursts into the kitchen with *Candy Land* in his hands and Roo under his arm. Noticing the three plates on the table, his eyes widen. "Milla's having dinner with us?"

"She is," Hunter says.

"Yes!"

We wash our hands and sit down to eat. The conversation mostly consists of Harrison telling us about the papier-mâché project his class is doing with all their favorite animals. He's making a dragon, since he's been on a *How To Train Your Dragon* kick. When Hunter says dragons only exist in stories, Harry happily informs us that they're really real, since there are such things as Komodo and bearded dragons.

As the meal goes on, I'm filled with this warm sense of...happiness? Belonging? I'm not sure. But I'm content to be with my two favorite boys, and I'm smiling at the littlest things. Especially when Hunter's foot and mine bump each other under the table.

Is this what it's like to have a whole family? If so, I like it.

Once we're through, I get the dishes in the dishwasher while Hunter cleans up the table and puts the leftovers away. Then we help Harrison set up the game, which isn't too hard since all that's required is unfolding the board, stacking up the deck of cards, and choosing our game pieces.

"I want green!" Harry says. "Which one do you want, Milla?"

"Hmm...how about yellow?"

"I'll be red," Hunter tells him.

Now here's the thing about *Candy Land*: it's a great game when you're six years old. After that? You realize it's based on the luck of the cards you draw, and there's really no strategy to it. Our session ends remarkably fast. Hunter draws two double square cards in a row and then takes a shortcut, leaving Harry and me in the dust. Two more rounds, and Hunter is at the ice cream castle.

The second round? Same thing happens, to the point I wonder if he's cheating at this basic-ass game.

"Your luck is unreal," I groan.

Hunter winks at me. "Don't hate the player, hate the game."

"I want to play something else!" Harrison demands, putting the cards back in the box. "Let's play something with dragons instead."

Hunter and I exchange a look. "Like what?"

"We can have a dragon, a knight, and a princess. The knight has to capture the dragon and rescue the princess," Harrison says.

"Why can't the princess rescue herself?" I interject, my feminist fire flaring up.

"I'm sure she can," Hunter says, quick to calm me down, "but maybe this is just a test the princess set up. So she can weed out all the knights who aren't brave enough to fight a dragon before she picks a suitor."

Harry frowns. "There's no fighting. The dragon will go live at the zoo." He points at each of us as he speaks. "Milla is the princess, I'll be the dragon, and Hunter can be the knight!"

Princess, me.

Knight, Hunter.

Of course.

I cross my arms over my chest, thinking that sometimes

I swear Harrison realizes more than he lets on. "You don't want to be the knight, Harry?"

"I'm always the knight at school." Harrison pouts. "I want to be the king dragon now! The one who sits on all the gold and gets to be in charge of all the other dragons!"

Hunter and I laugh. We move to the living room, where Harry tells us the couch is now a castle and everything else is his domain. After I take my place on the couch with Roo the "baby dragon" guarding me, Harry gets on all fours and proceeds to crawl all over the carpet, growling. It's extremely adorable and immensely funny, and since he's committing to this, I decide I should as well. Even Hunter gets in on it, laughing as he tries to make his way past Harry, who keeps throwing himself at his brother's feet and roaring.

"Oh no, whatever am I going to do?" I whine in a breathless, completely over-dramatic voice and place the back of my hand against my forehead. "Trapped in a castle surrounded by fields of lava! Is there not a single knight in all the kingdom who is brave enough to challenge the fearsome dragon and rescue me?"

"Rawr! The princess will be my dinner!" Harry growls, tiny hands wrapping around Hunter's ankle.

"Oh yeah?" Hunter tries to take a step toward me, dragging Harrison along the carpet. When the kid doesn't let go, Hunter says, "You leave me no choice but to use my secret weapon!"

"Your weapons won't hurt me! I'll make them melt with my fire breath!"

Hunter grins. "Who said anything about weapons?" Then he bends down, fingers finding Harry's midsection and tickling him.

He thrashes and kicks, begging Hunter to stop as happy tears stream down his face. "I surrender! I surrender!"

Hunter stops, but it seems smart-assery runs in the family. Harrison uses his brother's low guard to run, and then it all happens in a flash.

He tries to grab Harry, who wriggles out of reach, causing Hunter to lose his balance and fall right into me. We fall back against the couch together, his knee between my legs, his hand braced against my chest, giving him a handful of boob.

My breath catches.

I'm only vaguely aware of Harry running in circles around the room, yelling, "I win, I win, I win!"

We exchange a very panicked look before Hunter rushes to pull his hand away but doesn't climb off me yet.

"You okay?" he asks.

From the corner of his eye, Hunter checks out the ongoing victory parade. A mischievous smile twists his lips. It's the same expression he gets before he does something terribly inappropriate that's going to leave me all melty.

Dipping his head until his lips are beside my ear, he whispers, "Playtime isn't over, Milla." And yup, there it is. The tension. The melty-ness.

Suddenly, he's back on his feet, but only so he can lean over and hook one arm under my knees, the other around my back. As Hunter lifts me, I yelp from the shock of having the couch disappear from under me and automatically cling to his shoulders.

"Quick, princess, before the mighty dragon realizes we've escaped!" Hunter says, loud enough for Harry to hear, carrying me out of the living room, bride-over-the-threshold style. It takes me by complete surprise and draws a little scream out of me. I have no choice but to hold on tight to Hunter's neck.

As if I weigh nothing, he speedily takes us through the kitchen. Over his shoulder, I see Harry trying to catch up, but if I have to run to keep up with Hunter's brisk walking pace, a six-year-old has no chance. Hunter heads into the pantry, using his foot to nudge the door shut behind us.

"Noooo! Give me back the princess! Rawr! Rawr!" Harry yells from the other side. It's adorable and so completely ridiculous that I can't help but laugh.

"Never!" Hunter yells back. Then he looks at me, still in his arms, and starts laughing too. His eyes are the brightest I've ever seen, his expression completely unguarded.

Before I can stop it, one of my hands curls around the nape of his neck, fingers threading through his hair. I tilt my lips upward and Hunter meets me halfway.

Harry's protests from the kitchen fade into the background, so there's only Hunter, and me, and this moment. When I tug at his hair, Hunter groans softly.

My heart is full, so full of him, and it scares me. Especially in times like these, where I want to be with Hunter so much it hurts.

I pull away, scrambling for something smart to say. We're both breathing hard as I pant, "Your reward, sir knight."

Hunter lets me down gently. "What do you say we teach the dragon how to share?"

I let out a snort. "You need to learn how to share."

"I shared you for three hours. I'm an expert at it by now." His hands bunch on the waistline of my shorts to pull me back in, but Harrison starts beating on the door.

"Come on, Hunter!" he says, his voice pitching higher. "It's not funny anymore."

"You heard him," I say teasingly.

"Fine." Hunter lets me go. "But you owe me. Later."

"I can hardly wait."

Chapter Thirty-Five

CAMILLA

$\mathcal{A}$fter we all eat Toll House ice cream sandwiches for dessert—Harrison's choice—I send him upstairs to brush his teeth and get ready for bed.

"Can you read Harry a story while I put away the dishes?" I ask Hunter.

"Why don't we read him a story together?" he suggests.

I smile. "The quicker we get our chores done, the quicker Harry falls asleep, and the quicker..." My voice catches as heat spreads throughout my body. "You know."

"I see what you're saying," he says, a grin spreading across his face.

He heads up to his brother, and I turn back to the dishes. Just as I'm crouching down to play Jenga with a cupboard that's already full of pots and pans, my phone buzzes in my pocket.

When I pull it out, I see a text from Isabel, asking for my input on a dress she's designing and sewing from scratch for the upcoming spring formal (because at Oak Academy, homecoming, winter formal, and prom simply aren't enough). I answer that she should chill on the flower appliqués and that the bell sleeves look a little too medieval. Appliqués. Bell sleeves. These are things I know now.

Upon closing the chat, I realize I have a few unread emails, and I dive into my inbox to delete what I assume is my usual daily ration of news, junk mail, and spam.

But when I see one from admissions@stanford.edu, the sender name jumps out at me, my blood running cold. I tap it, biting my lip in the milliseconds it takes to load.

Please log in to your portal account to review your official admissions decision...

Heart pounding, I follow the link to the Stanford portal website, type in my username and password with shaking hands, and go to my official school inbox. Of all the college letters that have started trickling in so far, this one means the most.

Congratulations! On behalf of the Office of Undergraduate Admissions, it is my pleasure to offer you... I almost drop my phone as I squeal, and I have to re-read the email over and over again, blood rushing to my head as the first line jumps out at me.

I'm *IN*. I got into mother-effing Stanford. Yes!!!

There's no mention of a scholarship offer, which sucks, but there *is* a spot for me at my dream school if I can find a way to pay for it. The email reminds me to fill out the FAFSA application before the deadline in June, which I know is necessary. There's no way I can afford over $50,000 per year in tuition without financial aid. A lot of it.

The reasons why I haven't submitted the FAFSA already are two-fold. First, I need Mom to sit down and fill it out with me, which requires having her submit tax documents, and I'm still working up the nerve to ask since we haven't discussed college stuff except during arguments. Second, I was holding out hope that one of the schools I applied to would offer me a full ride. But if Stanford wants me, I'll do anything to make it happen. Even if that means taking out loans. That is, if I can get approved. A big *if*.

But something else gives me pause. The fact that Hunter still hasn't made any decisions about college for himself. I'm not even sure where he's been accepted so far.

If I'm at Stanford, which Hunter didn't even apply to, that puts me five hundred miles away from La Jolla. San Francisco State or UC Berkeley would both be less than an hour's drive from my campus, so if Hunter went to one of those schools it wouldn't be bad at all...but whenever I bring up making plans for where we'll be next year, Hunter changes the subject. I was putting off trying to force the issue, but now that I have my Stanford acceptance in hand, it's time for us to figure this stuff out.

The days are passing, the acceptances and rejections are rolling in, and we're getting closer and closer to the actual future. I understand why he'd want to avoid making any decisions in a hurry, but I wish I had a sense of what he was planning to do next year. The colleges we attend could be on opposite sides of the world, but I already know that I want to find a way to make us work. What if Hunter doesn't feel the same?

The thought turns my stomach, and I force myself to return to the dishes. There's no sense in dwelling over all of this right now. I'll cross this bridge when I come to it. And hopefully, if we're meant to be, Hunter will be ready to cross it too. Once they're done, I wipe my hands on a towel and sigh.

When I walk through the living room, I notice Roo on the floor. He probably got knocked off the couch when Hunter landed on me. I pick up the plushie, then head upstairs, where the hallway is dark save for the light coming from Harry's room.

When I get there, I stop at the threshold of the door. Hunter's lying in bed with Harrison snuggled up to him, a picture book open between them. I stay back, watching them quietly, not wanting to interrupt this adorably perfect brotherly moment.

I recognize what they're reading now—it's a little below Harry's reading level at this point, but I got it for him when I first started babysitting because I thought the illustrations were cute.

It's about a kangaroo, just like Roo, whose best friend, an emu, is moving away, and all the things the kangaroo does to try to make the emu's family stay. In the end, the kangaroo's mother sits him down and explains that although he and the emu might live in different places and not see each other as often, they'll always be friends. The book ends with the kangaroo and the emu exchanging email addresses and then planning to meet up at summer surf camp every year after that.

Like I said, super cute.

I basically know the book by heart at this point, and so does Harry, but this is obviously Hunter's first time reading it. He's trying to mock the text as he reads, saying things like, "Wow, how incredibly codependent," and the like. But I hear the catch in his voice and the hesitation in his page turning that tells me something else.

That innocent picture book is getting to him.

"Erwin put another toy in the box, and Kippy started to sniffle," Hunter reads. "He didn't understand why Erwin had to move away from the eucalyptus forest. Kippy didn't want to lose his best friend." He turns the page carefully, fingers twiddling with the book's edges, but he doesn't go on. He seems hesitant to continue.

Harry looks up at his brother, frowns, and says, "Don't

worry, Hunter. Erwin and Kippy go to the same surf camp. They'll see each other again soon."

I choose that as my cue to enter and head over to the bedside, Roo held out. "Hey, bud. You forgot this downstairs."

"Roo!" Harry takes his stuffed animal and hugs it to his chest as he looks up at me. The kid has unreal eyelashes, I swear, and uses them for maximum effect. "Milla, you're leaving next year, aren't you? Like Erwin. Where's your school gonna be?"

My eyes skim to Hunter, and I find him avoiding my gaze, looking at the book open in his lap, trying to seem like he's not paying attention to my answer. "I still don't know. Depends on how my scholarship situation works out."

Harrison pouts. "If you end up going real far away, will I be able to see you?"

His sweetness touches my heart and brings a smile to my face. "I'm hoping so. I'll be home for holidays at least, and maybe we can FaceTime."

I steal a glance at Hunter, and he's frozen, like a statue. He snaps the book shut before I can say anything and sets it on the nightstand. "Time to go to sleep, little man," he tells Harrison with a forced smile.

"But the story isn't finished!" Harry whines.

"We'll finish it tomorrow," Hunter says, and he sounds tired, as if he's been awake for two days straight.

I cross my arms and fight the urge to ask what's wrong. Instead, all I do is watch while Hunter tucks Harrison in, patting his head softly before turning off the light. There's anxiety in his steps when we walk out of the room together, and he lets out a sigh when he softly closes the door behind us.

I want to ask why he looks so sad. Is it about me leaving next year? Is it something else? Something I can help with?

Wrapping my fingers around his, I murmur, "Let's go to your room?"

In the dim hallway, his blue eyes fall to our hands, and his lips become a hard line. "I have to take care of some stuff," he says vaguely, slipping out of my reach.

My chest tightens, and for a moment, I consider minding my own business and just letting him go. But we're way past cold one-liners and rushed exits.

I follow him downstairs, where he's fumbling for his keys by the front door. "Wait. Where are you going?"

Hunter doesn't look at me as he laces up his shoes. "I don't know. For a drive, I guess." His voice is hoarse and breathy, a far cry from its usual smooth tone that exudes confidence. Worry instantly gnaws at my stomach.

"Is there something wrong?" I ask, then softly add, "You can tell me. Whatever it is."

He shakes his head, pulling the front door open. "I need to be alone right now."

"Hunter, stop, don't go—"

But he doesn't stop, and once he's closed the door behind him a little too hard, I give up on chasing him all the way out to his car. What would be the point when he clearly doesn't want to talk?

I wish I knew what I did or what's bothering him. He seemed totally fine thirty minutes ago, and now...this. Did that children's book really shake him up so bad?

As I watch his car drive down the street, a frown tugs at my mouth. Although both of us have been abandoned by a parent, the effects on us were completely different.

With me, I'm constantly looking to find my own version of the stability and validation I never had. Honestly, as much as I hate my dad for abandoning us, I really can't blame him for not being able to stick it out with Mom. I mean, most of the time I want to run away from her too, which is part of the reason I'm so desperate to go to college in the first place. That, and the fact that nothing seems more stable than having the ability to build my own life and make my own decisions. Plus, what could be more validating than a college degree? It'll open up a world of opportunities to me.

And as for my constant search for emotional stability, I guess I thought Hunter was giving me some of that. I was starting to rely on him as someone who'd be there not just a week from now, but for years, possibly even my whole life.

Maybe I was wrong.

Yet Hunter seems to have responded to his childhood trauma in the exact opposite ways. He doesn't seem to care about building his own life and finding his own stable path. It also seems pretty obvious that the reason he doesn't want to deal with any decisions about next year is because going away for school would force him to leave Harry behind. Maybe he thinks the best way to avoid uncertainty is to just stay exactly where he is, comforted by the routine of his life because it's all he knows. I get that.

And as for wanting to stay close to Harry, I get that too. Their dad's either doing the workaholic thing or too busy when he's at home to even pay much attention to them; Harrison's mom is the kind of Instagram influencer who seems to only spend time with her son when she needs to be able to post a picture of her happy family life.

What if Hunter is pushing me away because he's afraid I'll abandon him too?

As I pad back to the pool house, I realize some things I hadn't dared to before.

I don't want to leave Hunter.

These past few weeks have been like something out of a

dream. He's been sweet, attentive, and caring, and whenever I'm with him, I feel stable. Solid. Supported. Kind of like my feet are planted firmly on the ground, and I have someone strong to hold on to whenever problems threaten to uproot me.

My heart is full of Hunter because it's already his.

But left all alone now, with my thoughts and my worries and my doubts, it's like I'm missing a part of myself. He took a piece of me with him when he walked out that door and refused to tell me why.

Crawling across my bed, I plant myself face down in my pillow.

I wish Hunter would tell me what's really going on. I want to be able to help him. I want him to feel like he can rely on me the same way I'm starting to rely on him. But if he can't meet me halfway, then this relationship is going nowhere.

And watching him just walk out the door with no explanation and no look back, all because he can't even talk to me? That hurt. Just the thought of us breaking up makes my chest go tight.

It occurs to me that somehow, despite promising myself I wouldn't let Hunter jerk me around, I've let him gain way too much power over me.

What if I can't get it back?

Chapter Thirty-Six

HUNTER

*W*hoever said children's books are basic knows nothing about the gut punch a few words and drawings can pack. And when those words and drawings are basically a thinly-veiled version of the horrible events looming over your life? Yeah, no. I couldn't even finish reading the damn thing. Even my six-year-old brother is braver than I am when it comes to talking with Milla about her plans for college.

I don't want her to leave me. Leave this town.

Once she's gone, no one will be around to shine a light on my darkness. Everything will go back to the way it was before. I'll walk through my days like a zombie, not really living, not doing much of anything other than existing miserably.

But it's not as easy as she thinks to just walk away. I have to stay in La Jolla, to watch over Harry and make sure he's taken care of. He's too young to look out for himself, and I know firsthand what it's like to grow up with parents who don't give a shit. He's the most important person in my life, and he needs me. And yet...

247

How the hell am I supposed to get by here without Camilla? And when did I get so attached to her?

I tap a button on the touchscreen in my BMW and tell Siri to text Matt Mason and Tom, letting them know I'm going to Blackout and inviting them to join me for drinks. I leave Steve off the group text on purpose, since he's still being a little bitch about that time during lunch when I told him to watch his mouth. He can keep on nursing his bruised ego alone, for all I care.

After I park in the corner of Blackout's lot, I root around in my wallet until I find my fake ID. This isn't exactly the nicest part of town, but the plus side is that you can usually get in without door security trying to start shit or looking too hard at your driver's license. On top of that, the bartender is more than happy to keep the drinks coming as long as you have an extra hundred dollar bill to leave in the tip jar.

My friends don't take too long to join me, and soon enough, they're piling into the booth I'm at with a pitcher of beer and a few glasses.

"Rare to see you out alone nowadays, Beck," Matt says as he pours himself a beer. "Get in a fight with your little girlfriend or something?"

"Don't," I say sternly, taking a long slug of my gin and tonic. It's my second.

"This place isn't Camilla's scene," Tom interjects. "And besides, she's too much of a nerd to have a fake ID. No offense, man."

"You speak the truth," I tell him. I can't get offended either. Tom's right, and I know he isn't trying to be a jerk. If anything, he and Camilla have sort of become friends over the last few weeks, if their interaction at lunch is anything to judge by.

"I'm still sensing trouble in paradise," Matt says. "Given

the fact that you skipped the beers and went straight to gin, which by the way is nasty, bro."

"Nothing wrong with a nice G&T," I argue, gulping down the rest of my drink and signaling for another. "Even if you're right, I'm not in the mood to talk about it."

"No shocker there," Matt says, rolling his eyes. Because Camilla is the one topic that's been off-limits lately, even though I'm normally happy to share the details of my conquests.

The thing is, Camilla isn't a conquest. She's something completely different.

Matt and Tom soon get distracted by one of the flatscreen TVs, where a basketball game plays. I try to watch, but I can't focus. I'm not much of a fan. And all I can think about is Milla and how she might be walking out of my life, never to return.

As we continue to drink and bullshit, I keep going back over the events of this evening, and how things went from sexy to sour so fast.

What is it about this girl that has such a strong hold on me? When she's not around, the entire world seems duller, and I feel this urge to see her again as soon as possible, an urge that I can't shake. It's like an addiction. Even the gin feels especially weak right now, like my craving for Camilla is stronger than the numbing effects of alcohol. Everything has been better since she came along, but I can feel her slipping away the more attached I get. And the worst part is, it's all my fault. Because I'm too afraid to tell her the truth about what's really going on.

Even though a number of college reps have tripped over themselves trying to get me to accept their offers, and I've even had a few swimming scholarships thrown at me, I've refused all of them. It's not that I don't want to go to college, but someone has to look after my brother. Since it's not gonna be my dad or my stepmom, it has to be me. But I can't stay in this shithole of a town anymore either. All these different directions are pulling at me, and the only thing holding me together is Milla.

She's the only reason it's been bearable at home.

As I lift another fresh drink to my lips, I realize how little my so-called "friends" actually know me. No one does, really. I've gotten too good at wearing a mask—the mask of the popular guy who doesn't give a shit about anything but having a good time. Milla's gotten the closest to the real me, but even she doesn't know the depths of my miserable self. She'd probably run for the hills if she knew what was under my cool, detached exterior. I don't have my shit together, I don't have any kind of a plan, and I have no idea where my future is going.

So, yeah. She'd run real fast. That's not her speed at all.

There's a warm hand on my shoulder, and I look up to see Hillary, slightly blurry, though there's no mistaking the way she's pouting at me. "What's wrong, Hunter? You look sad." She slides into the booth beside me, getting indifferent head-nods from Matt and Tom. "Maybe I can cheer you up," she murmurs, giggling.

Under normal circumstances, I'd probably just go for it. Hillary's hot, and though we've only made out the one time, she's been after me for years, and I've heard she knows what she's doing when she's on her knees. I don't doubt that she'd be up for anything I might want, probably behind the bar even. This pain would disappear.

Thing is, she's not Milla. So there's no use trying to distract myself. And even if the pain did disappear, it'd be temporary. With my luck, it might even be worse after. Thinking of how Camilla would react to that kind of betrayal is an instant boner-killer.

I push Hillary away. "Nah, I'm fine." Not strongly

enough, it seems, since she returns and puts her hand on my leg, squeezing my thigh. My skin crawls underneath my jeans. "I'm not in the mood," I tell her, this time more forcefully.

"You're always in the mood," Hillary whispers against my ear. "Come on, Hunter. I can help you get over that servant girl—"

Servant girl. Right. Disgust washes over me. I'm well aware that the way they talk about Milla is on me. I started it, I enabled it, and I regret it every time I hear someone talk shit. But Camilla didn't deserve that, and she doesn't deserve this either.

I grab Hillary's wrist and fling her hand off my leg. "Seriously. Get. The fuck. Off me," I growl.

"What's the deal with you lately?" she screeches, dropping the cooing baby voice. "Ever since you started screwing around with that trampy little maid of yours—"

Anger erupts in my chest, and I slam my fist hard on the table. Hillary goes silent, wide-eyed at my reaction. Matt gets up and tries to make peace, gently pulling her away by the arm. "Come on, Hill. Let's go have a drink and leave Beck to his mope fest. He's not any fun tonight anyway."

They walk away, and I find myself shaking my head. The room's spinning.

"Dude," Tom says. "What was that all about?"

"She was being rude. About Milla." I can hear how I'm slurring my words, which is funny because the first few drinks didn't seem to have any effect on me whatsoever, and now all of a sudden it's like a booze train just hit me in the face.

I can't even remember the last time I got this impaired by alcohol. Freshman year, before I knew any better? No, wait, it had to be last year, after I won the CIF state championship. I have vague memories of a big-ass mansion up in Santa Barbara, sucking champagne off of random tits to the sound of cheers, jackhammering a girl bent over a pool table. God, I'm a monster. I can't offer Camilla anything decent or good.

Tom narrows his eyes at me. "Come on, Beck. Let's get you home." I let him haul me out of the seat. "You okay to walk? I'm calling an Uber."

"Whatever." I rub my face, but it feels numb. "Shit. Can I crash on your couch?"

"Always. But..." He frowns. "What's going on? Is it just girl stuff, or..."

Shit's truly gone belly-up if he's asking me this. "It's all good. I just don't wanna deal with my stepmom's comments in the morning."

"Okay, well. Stay as long as you want. You know my parents love you."

"Thanks, man," I tell him, stumbling a little as we head out the door.

It's hard to focus on anything with the entire bar spinning and whatnot. Once we get outside, I lean my back against the building so I have something solid to brace myself against. Fortunately, we don't have to wait long, and once we're in the car, I roll my window down for air and try to keep my eyes open so I don't puke.

The next thing I know, Tom's setting me up on his couch with a sheet and some blankets and pillows. "Night, dude," he says. "Text me if you need anything, or just come upstairs."

He leaves a light on in the hallway and sets out a glass of water and some aspirin for me. He's a good guy, I've never doubted that. Not all my friends are D-bags.

I force myself to drink the water and then throw myself

into the leather cushions, but even though my body is still, my thoughts keep spinning.

Camilla will be so pissed when she finds out I went to a bar and got hammered. Maybe I should text her.

I get my phone out, dim the brightness, and pull up our texts. But the way I walked out on her earlier comes rushing back, and I remember how she looked at me, how I had to leave before I did or said something I regretted. Like confessing that if she leaves me, she'll be ripping my heart right out of my chest.

Milla wants to go to college because it's her way into a better life. I get that. But I can give her that too. I could make all her worries go away, if she'd just let me.

It's not even about having her, though that's part of it. It's not about the sex either, though that's definitely part of it. Or at least, it will be soon enough. Shit, the things I want to do to her would put a lot of sex tapes to shame. I'm gonna own that ass. Give it to her so good she'll never even look at another guy.

But no. The truth is, as cheesy as it sounds, when she smiles, it makes me happy. She's kind, and smart, and she cares deeply about things, and she always does her best. She's an actual good human being, maybe even the best person I know besides Harrison, and I know I don't deserve her. Yet. I want to be worthy of her though.

Some day. Somehow.

As I start to drift off into a numbing haze, I realize the only way I can save us is if I pull out all the stops, find a way to make sure Milla stays. No matter what it takes.

And if I have to play dirty, then so be it.

Chapter Thirty-Seven

CAMILLA

For the first time since we started dating, Hunter's not waiting at the pool house door in the morning. Part of me wants to go to the Becks' house and check his bedroom, but I go out front first. His car isn't in the driveway, which makes it pretty obvious that he left for school without me.

Are we in a fight? I figured I hadn't heard from him last night because he was blowing off steam or something, but I'd been hoping we could talk it out in the car over a Pop-Tart. I guess he had other ideas.

Still, there's a sense of worry following me as I step onto the crowded city bus, and the entire way to school, my stomach is cramping. What if this is his way of dumping me? What if I have to hear about our breakup from the rumor mill, or worse, Hillary and her minions? I know I should just call him and ask what's up, but I'm too afraid of what he might say, so I decide to just wait until we're face to face. There's a better chance of us talking it out that way. Unless it's nothing.

Maybe everything's fine, and I'm just overreacting.

There are probably a ton of good, logical reasons why Hunter never texted me last night and why he would leave for school this morning without me.

Except I can't think of a single one.

When I get to my locker, I check my phone for the nth time, hoping Hunter texted while my head was in the anxiety clouds. He hasn't, so I fire off a message to Isabel to get my mind off things. I'm half super annoyed and half super panicked, which isn't a good mix. Plus, if anyone's heard gossip about me and Hunter, it'll be her, and she won't hesitate to dish it up and ask me to confirm or deny.

thank god this week's almost over, I text.

Isabel replies, *I can't wait to do absolutely nothing all weekend. I've earned it. Did I tell you I got into UPenn? Hello, Ivy. If only I actually wanted to study Biomedical Science lol.*

I tap out a rapid fire, *CONGRATS!!! I'm free Saturday if you want to celebrate. I'll make you any kind of cupcake your heart desires.*

Ooooob, she texts back with a grinning devil emoji. *Red velvet and a movie?*

Yes please, I write. I smile, thinking of the last few movie dates at Isabel's, where she whipped up some weirdly delicious popcorn flavors (one with hot sauce and parmesan, one with dark chocolate chips and black pepper) and kept interrupting the scenes with her commentary on the historical inaccuracies of the costumes. It was great.

Just outside the door of my first period class, textbooks crushed against my chest, I get one last text from her. One that makes my stomach drop.

FYI, just heard Hunter went to some shady dive bar last night and got so drunk he had to sleep on Tom Rice's couch. Did you know about this? Not cool.

My breath gets yanked out of me, and I lean against a

locker to write back. My fingers are shaking as I type, adrenaline coursing through me.

Last time we spoke, he said he was going for a drive. Around 9 last night. Haven't talked to him today. It's suddenly making sense why not. My heart is pounding.

Guess he drove to a bar, Isabel texts. *Tom had to carry him out and get them an Uber home. Hillary was there too, wtf? I can't believe you haven't heard from him. Sorry but that's shady af.*

I let out a sigh, relieved that at least Hunter wasn't driving drunk. I don't think I could ever forgive something like that.

But then I realize he gave me the cold shoulder last night to go get wasted. He was in such a hurry to rush out the door, and it was all so he could drink himself to oblivion with his friends. No wonder he didn't want to talk to me. Had he known Hillary was going to be there? I don't like that one bit. I trust that girl around Hunter as much as I trust Mom not to spend all our money on booze.

The bell rings, and I'm trembling with anger as I duck into my World History classroom and slide into my seat. Emmett gives me a little wave, but all I can manage is a terse nod back. I'm disappointed and furious and worried that Hunter hooked up with Hillary and is now avoiding me because he doesn't want to admit to it. Or because he's too chicken to break up with me after what he did. Maybe this was even his passive-aggressive way of getting me to dump *him*. By doing something so awful that I'd have no choice but to tell him we're over.

I'm not sure if it's a blessing or a curse that we have a test today, but I try to hit pause on all my musings and just focus on the multiple choice questions, the short answer responses, and the essays. Because I finish early, I ask Mr. Robertson if I can go visit the guidance counselor's office, and he's happy to let me go.

"Dr. Warren?" I ask, knocking on the door, which is already slightly ajar.

"Camilla!" she answers brightly. "Come on in. Take a seat. How are you?"

Before I know it, I'm blabbing about getting into Stanford—which I haven't even told anybody yet—and fighting back tears as I admit they didn't offer me a scholarship, and now I have no idea if I'll even be able to go.

"It's my dream school," I tell her. "Even if my FAFSA gets me some seriously solid financial aid, it won't be enough to cover $200,000 over the course of four years. My mom isn't giving me anything for college, which is fine, I have some savings, but between tuition and room and board and books, I don't know how I can afford it."

Dr. Warren lets me talk until I'm all out of words, nodding sagely and offering me a tissue when my eyes start to tear up again. She steeples her fingers and leans back in her desk chair, looking calm. "Camilla, we do offer a generous college scholarship each year to one special student here at Oak Academy," she finally says.

I shake my head miserably.

"I have over a 4.0 GPA, and I got a 1560 on my SATs, but Stanford didn't seem to care. There's probably just too many other qualified people fighting over the need-based scholarships. But, like...I don't know what else I can apply for. I don't do any extracurriculars. I've never played sports or joined a club, not since middle school. Not because I don't want to. My mom just moves us around so much that I never have a chance to get involved.

"I just...it's hard enough readjusting every time I start a new school." I start ticking off my other disqualifications because I've already studied the requirements for every scholarship I can find, and none of them ever apply to me. "I'm not in a military family, I'm not a future farmer of

America, I don't come from a marginalized demographic, I'm not a duck-calling champion..."

Smiling gently, Dr. Warren says, "That is exactly why this type of scholarship exists. It's not dependent on sports, or clubs, or how many fundraiser car washes you've volunteered for, or retirement homes you've visited. It's about your *potential*."

That pulls me up short. "Wait. If it's not about grades or community service, then how do I qualify for it?"

She goes over to a filing cabinet, riffles around in a drawer, and comes back with a sheet of paper, which she passes over to me. It's an application.

"It's called the Reed Scholarship. It's for students of character who don't necessarily shine on paper or have experienced academic setbacks or been the subject of disciplinary action in or outside of school, but are nonetheless deserving and worthy of pursuing a higher education, and wouldn't otherwise be able to afford college."

"Do I still have time to apply?" I ask, my eyes skimming over the deadline (which is Monday, yikes), the reward amount (up to $250,000 over the course of four years), and the application requirements. "It says I need two letters of recommendation along with a personal statement."

"I'm happy to recommend you if you can find another teacher to write you a letter," Dr. Warren says. "And I can tell you that the committee who decides on this is *very* receptive to rewarding those students who genuinely plan to make a difference in the world. Who are passionate about their majors. What do you plan to study?"

And there it is. The one question I've turned over in my mind a million times but still can't answer. I'd been planning on choosing something like English or psychology and then changing it once I'd taken a few general education courses and had a better idea of where my interests lie. But

Dr. Warren has a point. I have to make a case for why I deserve this scholarship and what kind of difference I plan to make.

"Child psychology," I hear myself blurt. And as I say it out loud, I realize it's true. I think of Harry, and Hunter, and even myself. "I want to help kids that have been through trauma. Help them be well adjusted. Make them realize how brave they are."

My voice cracks with emotion, and when I look up at Dr. Warren, she's nodding. "That's wonderful," she tells me. "I have to say, if you write about that in your essay, there's a very strong chance you'll be one of the committee's top choices. And I can also say that I happen to be on that committee."

"I can have the application in your hands by Monday," I tell her, adrenaline rushing. "I can do this."

"I believe you can," she says.

By the time I get to bio, my thoughts are going a mile a minute—and for once, it's got nothing to do with Hunter. My World History teacher, Mr. Robertson, happily agreed to write my second letter of recommendation for the scholarship, which he says he'll email to me over the weekend, and I've been mentally outlining my essay on why I feel so passionately about studying child psychology. Sure, I'll have to cancel all my weekend plans in order to get it done in time, but I know Isabel will understand. It feels like, for the first time since I started dreaming of going to Stanford, everything's finally coming together.

I know winning this thing might be a long shot, but it's the best chance I've got.

Chapter Thirty-Eight

CAMILLA

I'm leaning against my locker before lunch, tapping out a text to Isabel and Emmett to see if they want to eat together, when I feel a hand on my shoulder. Even before I turn, I know it's Hunter. He has this way of touching me that nobody else does—firmly but gently, almost the way you'd handle a precious piece of artwork.

"Hey," I say, looking over. And wow.

There's no doubt he went on a bender last night, so he better not even try to deny it. His eyes are sunken, his skin greasy and pale. Not the usual golden boy good looks I'm used to seeing. Massive hangover, from what I can tell, and although my heart softens a little, I remind myself that he ran out on me last night. To go to some gross bar that allows underage drinking with his dumb friends and Hillary.

"Hey," he replies, avoiding my very direct, very angry gaze. "How's it going?"

"Oh, I'm great." I yank my shoulder away and cross my arms over my chest. "But you look like hell. Guess you went on some drive last night."

Hunter winces as if I struck him, and his eyes dart up and down the hall, where a flood of students is in the process of chatting and slamming lockers and jostling each other on their way to lunch or classes. I'm sure they're staring at us, but I don't take my gaze off of Hunter's face to check.

"Don't have anything to say for yourself?" I taunt.

"Can we go somewhere more private?" he asks, his voice dropping low. "I don't want to fight like this in front of half the school."

"What's wrong? Afraid people will talk about you behind your back? I can't *imagine* what that must be like," I say, my voice icy and sarcastic. "Here's the thing. I'm not a toy, Hunter. You don't get to just pick me up and then put me back down whenever you feel like it. When you hurt me, there are consequences."

A muscle in his jaw twitches. "Camilla. Whatever you think I did last night, it wasn't a planned thing or me choosing anyone else over you—"

"But you did all the same," I cut him off.

Finally, he meets my eyes. I stare at him, unwavering. He deserves the same amount of consideration he gave me over the past twelve hours: none at all.

"I have to go," I say. I can't just stand here while he refuses to give me answers.

"Wait. Take a walk with me," he says. "Please."

My eyes are locked on his, and I feel my resolve weakening.

"Fine." I hate myself for giving in so quickly, but I can't hold out any longer. I'm not sure he's ever used that tone with me before. He actually sounds sorry.

Hunter is quiet as we head down the hallway, but as soon as we step outside the school doors, he lets out a long breath.

"Look. When I left last night, all I wanted was to go for a drive. That's all. Just drive around with my brain turned off until I could clear my mind. And that's what I did. I went in circles around La Jolla for an hour. Normally, that's enough to make me feel better, or at least less like I'm going to hit something. But it didn't work this time..." He trails off and doesn't continue.

"Why not?" I finally prod.

"Because...I guess because all I could think about was... losing you."

For a moment, I'm stunned into silence. This isn't at all what I was expecting to hear. "Losing *me*? How?"

He shakes his head. "Because you're leaving soon. For college. Don't deny it."

"That is my plan, sure," I say simply. "But that doesn't mean we're over."

"Yeah, right."

He sets off toward the corner of the parking lot where he always parks his car, and I follow. It's hard to keep up with his pace. He's clearly blowing off more steam.

When we reach his BMW, he whirls around. "Do you really think it's going to work out between us when you're eight hours away? We'll barely see each other."

"I'll come down every weekend—"

"No, you won't. Maybe at first, but then you'll get busy with studying and exams and you'll have to skip a weekend, and then two, and meanwhile, you'll be meeting new people, and pretty soon we'll just...drift apart."

"You can't predict the future," I tell him. "Why are you so convinced we'll fail? We care about each other, and we want to be together. So that's what we'll do. Everything will be okay. I promise."

"You're delusional," he scoffs. "And you can't promise that. Long-distance relationships never work."

"We'll make it work," I insist.

"The world isn't a fairy tale like you think it is!" he growls. "You see everything through purple-colored glasses, but that's not real life. You need to grow up, Camilla."

My eyes are blurring with tears that I can't fight back. His words have cut right to my core—not because what he's saying is true, but because it's all so wrong.

"My life has *never* been a fairy tale, Hunter. And honestly? You're the *last person* who should be telling anyone to grow up," I grind out, my voice cracking on the last word.

"It's not gonna work, Camilla. It's either me or Stanford. You have to choose."

It's an impossible choice, one he shouldn't be asking me to make, so I don't even attempt to respond. Instead, I spin on my heel and stalk back to school.

Minutes later, Isabel is hustling me into her car for an emergency French fry and Oreo milkshake run. All she knows is that Hunter and I had some kind of argument in the parking lot. Well, that and the fact that I can't stop crying.

"I'm not gonna push for details, girl, but let me know if you want me to kick his ass," she says as we idle in line at the drive-thru. "Happy to do it."

"It wouldn't fix anything," I murmur. "But thanks."

My eyes start to well up again, and I can't say anything more. I'm grateful that Isabel is true to her word and doesn't try to interrogate me about what Hunter said. Once we have our food, we drive back to school and spend the rest of our lunch period in her car, listening to Billie Eilish and sucking down our milkshakes.

I can't believe this is how it's going to end between me and Hunter. With him just giving up on us because he's too scared to try and fail. My chest feels like a black hole. I'm a combination of devastated and angry, utterly lost and disappointed.

For the rest of the school day, I keep anxiously checking my phone, hoping he'll send a text or leave me a voicemail in between classes, but there's nothing.

After school, I do my best to go through the motions babysitting Harry, but Hunter is nowhere to be found. Probably out joyriding around La Jolla again or hanging out with his bros, not a care in the world.

How could he possibly ask me to choose between him and my dream school? Not just my dream school—my future? And why am I so confused about it? It should be Stanford. Easily. It's *always* been Stanford. I shouldn't even have to think about it.

But the thought of losing him forever just feels...wrong.

That night, I cry myself to sleep.

Chapter Thirty-Nine

CAMILLA

The next morning, I wake up exhausted, drained, and nauseated. I can barely manage to choke down a piece of toast, my stomach is in such knots. I'm a zombie the entire bus ride to school. All I can think about is my fight with Hunter yesterday and all the things I wish I had said rather than just walking away.

When I see him in the hall before first period, I notice he's alone, just zoning out as he leans against his locker. He looks over at me, and I feel like I'm moving in slow motion as I head toward him. I can't just leave things like this between us.

"Hunter—"

"Camilla," he interrupts, all seriousness. "We need to talk."

No. I know exactly what this is. And I'm not going to give him the chance to break up with me before I say what I have to say.

"I know you're pushing me away to keep yourself from getting hurt," I tell him. "But it doesn't work like that.

You're obviously already hurting. You can't save yourself from this."

He nods. "You're right. I can't."

"Wait, what?" I'm completely thrown. He's actually agreeing with me? Why?

"Will you come with me?" he asks.

"I—I don't know. Where?"

"Just out to my car. Please. I don't want to fight. We still have ten minutes before first period."

"Okay," I say, letting him lead me to the parking lot. I don't doubt his sincerity. Still, I have no idea what I'm agreeing to. This better be good.

"I didn't get to finish telling you what happened the other night, when I took off..." He leaves the sentence hanging and rubs his eyes with the back of his hands.

"I already know what happened," I say. "You decided to go get incapacitated like an idiot, and you ended up crashing at Tom's. Everyone was talking about it."

"I'm sorry," he says. "I really am. I don't know what else to tell you."

Right. Except he's conveniently leaving out the most important part of the story, which doesn't give me a lot of confidence.

"And what about Hillary?" I prod as we walk down a row of student cars, my stomach dropping as I wait for his response. "What happened with her?"

But he's already shaking his head. "I didn't know she was gonna be there. I swear. When she came over to our table, I pushed her away. I mean, literally pushed. I'm lucky she isn't pressing charges."

"So you didn't touch her, except to push her," I say, keeping my voice neutral.

"Believe me, Milla. We didn't even kiss. We didn't do anything." He takes a breath. "And you know why not?

Because she isn't you. Do you get that? I don't want anyone else but *you*."

He's looking at me that way again, like I'm everything to him.

"How can you say that?" I ask. "You told me yesterday I had to choose between you and college. Do you have any idea what kind of position that puts me in? This is my one shot. I don't have opportunities falling in my lap left and right. I have to fight for myself if I want to have a good life. Nobody's going to take care of me except for me."

He stops and turns to me. "That's not true. I'll take care of you."

"Really? You're doing a great job of that so far," I say bitterly.

"I get that you're pissed at me, and you have every right," he says.

*W*e're at his BMW now, and Hunter unlocks it and turns to me. "But can you at least give me another chance?"

"Another chance for what?"

"For us." He gestures at the passenger door.

Assuming he wants me to get in, I reach for the door handle. But when I open the door, I realize what I didn't see through the tinted window: the entire seat is full of flowers. Purple flowers. Every color purple under the sun, from fuchsia to plum. I see irises and hydrangeas, asters and orchids and zinnias. More flowers I can't even name and don't recognize, their petals every shape and size imaginable. When I pull open the door, their fragrance surrounds me in a cloud. It's like a dream.

"I hope you like them. Harry told me purple's your favorite color," Hunter says. "A while back. But I remembered. I cut class this morning to hit up every florist in a twenty-mile radius. I promise next time I'll do better, but this is the best I could do."

"No. These are perfect. They're beautiful," I say, dazed. "Nobody's ever done anything like this for me before."

"Well, they should have," Hunter says. "You deserve all this and more. I'm the one who doesn't deserve you. I'm an asshole. And I'm so sorry I said that shit to you yesterday. Stanford is your dream, and nothing should stand in the way of that."

I feel like I'm going to cry. My chest is tight. My emotions are a mess. I don't want to forgive him so easily, and I'm still angry and upset with him, but I'm also overwhelmed by the apology and the flowers and the sincerity in his eyes.

Turning, I find Hunter's arms wrapping around me. I press against him and bury my face in his neck, just breathing him in, the smell of flowers all around us. I could stand like this with him forever.

"I want to forgive you," I whisper.

"It hurts when I think about you leaving," he whispers back. "I don't know what to do with that. I just...broke down. I lost it."

"Hunter." I pull back a little so I can look up at him. "You need to be able to talk to me when you're upset instead of just running off to hide and get shit-faced. That's not how relationships work. It's not how friends work."

"I didn't want you to see me like that. I felt pathetic."

"I don't care. I want to see *all* of you, however you are," I say. "Having feelings isn't pathetic, and I want to be there for you, for the good and the bad. You don't have to hide from me."

"I believe you." He inhales against the top of my head like he's trying to breathe me in. "I just don't want you to leave. I want things to stay the way they are." He brushes a lock of hair behind my ear. "I won't even know what to do with myself once you go away."

This pains him to say out loud, I can tell by the hushed way he's speaking.

"Me leaving for college doesn't mean leaving *you*," I say gently. "I told you, we'll work it out. I'll be back every weekend—"

"You'll find someone better up there."

"Stop." My voice trembles. "How can you even say that? I'm not—"

"Not what? You are everything, Milla. I'm nothing. And it's only a matter of time until you find someone smarter than me, and better for you..."

"You're the one who's going to find someone better," I say, exasperated. "I'm surprised you haven't gotten tired of me yet. You could have anyone. Someone who's prettier. Richer. Who gets along with all your friends."

"Not gonna happen." Hunter shakes his head, and there's something sad about the way he does it, and the way he looks at me. "You're it for me, Milla. You mean more to me than water."

Water. The thing he loves more than almost anything. The thing that gives him comfort, that reminds him of being safe. I look away. "Goddamn you."

"Well, if you're going to cuss me out for being honest..."

"You caught me off guard," I complain, but I'm smiling.

"I have something else for you." He goes to his trunk and pops it, then reaches inside. When he turns, he's holding a paper-wrapped bundle. "Happy college acceptances. Plural. I know they've been coming in already."

My hands are trembling when I take the gift from him, already sure what it is. "You got me books? You picked them out yourself?"

Hunter nods. "Open them."

I'm already touched before I rip off the flowery paper. Then I see them. Sturdy black hardcovers, one with red-sprayed edges, the other with gold. On the covers, beautiful illustrations and the titles *Six of Crows* and *Crooked Kingdom*.

The gasp that leaves me is completely authentic.

"You were looking at some bookstagrammer's account on your phone and sighing, saying you wanted to re-read the series, but the library waitlist was too long," he says, and though he's trying to be smooth, he's awkward, and it's adorable. "Now you don't have to wait any longer. These are both signed first editions."

"Hunter. I love them." Really, goddamn him.

I set the books on the car's roof and step back into his arms, burying my face in his chest. "We could've avoided all this if you'd just talked to me."

"I know. Please don't hate me. I'm sorry. I really am. And as for the other night, I swear I won't do anything like that ever again."

"You'll never get drunk with your friends again?" I say with a laugh. "I find that hard to believe."

"Fine, then how about if I want to do something like that, I talk to you first?"

I nod slowly. "Okay. And we'll figure something out when it comes to college. If we can't see each other physically every day, we can at least FaceTime—"

"I'm staying here next year. That's not going to change," he says firmly. "And I don't know if FaceTime is gonna cut it. I can't do *this* over the internet."

His arms tighten, and his mouth comes down on mine. It's soft, and gentle, and barely there, but enough to make a point. I get what he means. It's been only half a day since this last happened, and I already missed this. Hunter's warmth. His touch.

I've always said I wanted to go to Stanford because prestige goes a long way, but without a scholarship in hand, and with this Hunter situation throwing me for a loop, UCSD has been looking more and more appealing. At $15k a year, it's a hell of a lot cheaper. And closer. Hunter could be at my dorm in fifteen minutes, not eight hours.

"I got into Stanford," I whisper. "Officially." Instantly, I feel Hunter tense up.

"That's great," he says. "Congratulations. I knew you would. Didn't doubt it for a second."

"I was going to apply for the Reed Scholarship so I can cover the tuition, but...what if I just go to UC San Diego instead?" I say. "We could see each other every day if we wanted to. And we'd have every weekend together." And now that I'm saying it out loud, it feels like a real possibility, and I'm not taking it back.

"You're just saying that," he says.

"I'm not. I can't imagine being away from you for that long either." I cup the side of his face and rise to my tiptoes to kiss him.

When we part, Hunter's smiling. "Then maybe you won't have to."

Chapter Forty

CAMILLA

egardless of what I've decided—or think I've decided—about going to UCSD instead of Stanford, I'm not going to let the Reed Scholarship slip through my fingers when the award money can be used at any school of the recipient's choosing. So just as I'd planned, I tell Isabel I need to rain check our movie night so I can devote my weekend to getting all the required documents assembled (in between make-out sessions with Hunter, that is). Luckily, Mr. and Mrs. Beck have taken Harry to Anaheim to spend a few days at Disneyland, and they won't be back until Sunday, so I can devote every spare minute to my all-important scholarship essay.

I also fill up the whole pool house with the flowers he bought me, telling my mom they were from a school event and I'd rescued them from the trash. They're definitely keeping my spirits up as I do a last round of edits on this essay about my passion for psych, helping children, and being a force for good in the world. I even take Emmett's advice and give some explanation of my childhood and background, trying not to cringe as I write about feeling rootless and wanting so much to make a place for myself in the world.

When Mr. Robertson's letter of recommendation hits my OakAcademy.edu inbox Saturday night, I take a break to read it and am staggered at his praise. He talks up my studious nature, my intellectual curiosity, and the way I consistently go above and beyond what's in our textbook by exploring the topics on my own and expanding my breadth of knowledge. I'm practically blushing by the time I hit forward and send it over to Dr. Warren's email along with the rest of my application materials.

I can't believe it. I'm done! I made the scholarship deadline early and everything. Ravenclaws for the win.

My phone buzzes with a text from Isabel. *Otis or FIDM? Just found out I got into BOTH thanks to my costume design portfolio—TY for helping me put it together! Wasn't planning on having to choose between them...not that I'm complaining!!*

OMG!!! I text back. *They're both amazing, just like you :) I know wherever you go, they'll be lucky to have you in their program. So it's def one or the other?*

Yup, she tells me. *Gonna be matriculating in SoCal, what what!! You can come stay with me in L.A. whenever you want, so don't be a stranger.*

I smile at her enthusiasm and at the fact that our friendship won't be stressed by living thousands of miles apart. Not that I'd actually worry about that. Isabel is kind of my rock. Though I still wonder where Emmett will end up and if we "three musketeers" will manage to remain as close-knit as we are now once we're all at different colleges.

Speaking of which, I still haven't talked to my mom about the FAFSA application. Just the thought of it sends me into a panic spiral every time. No matter how much I tell myself it's no big deal, that it's something all parents do and that there's no reason she shouldn't do it for me, I can't help worrying that the topic will quickly snowball into a massive argument. Because I know her. I know how she is. And the subject of me going to college has never gone over well between us.

But if the Reed Scholarship falls through like the others have, I'm going to need lots of financial aid. The thing is, unlike scholarships, financial aid is not free money. Some of it is grants, smaller academic scholarships, and paid work-study options, but the majority of what's offered is actually massive student loans. Meaning I'd graduate with massive debts. Which I'd rather avoid, unless it's all I can get. Otherwise, no college for me.

Ugh. I just need to get this over with.

My bedroom door is closed, but I can hear my mom turn off the shower in the bathroom and then pad down the hall to her room a few minutes later. Now's my chance to pounce.

She's the type to lounge around in her robe while she's putting on makeup and picking out something to wear, so there's no chance she'll walk out of the house while I'm talking, and I'm hoping she hasn't started drinking yet if she's planning to drive somewhere tonight. Despite her issues, one thing my mom does not do is drink and drive. Not since her twenties, when she got into a car accident after drinking with friends at a house party. The damage to the other car was minor, luckily, but she realized she could have easily injured (or worse) a family with a baby in their backseat.

Knocking on her door, I keep my voice light. "Hey, Mom?"

"It's unlocked!"

Here goes nothing.

I go into her room, surprised at how neat it's looking. Usually her space is a lot more...chaotic. She's sitting at a vanity that's littered with cosmetics, her fluffy pink robe wrapped around her and her hair twisted up in a towel. I'm struck by how beautiful she is like this, still bare-faced after her shower and looking relaxed and in her element.

"What's up?" she asks, facing the mirror and carefully applying moisturizer.

There's a nice dress laid out on the bed, heels, and a purse next to it.

"You going out on a date or something?" I ask, trying to make light conversation and ease into this discussion as gently as possible.

"That's my business," she answers stiffly. "What do you need?"

So much for breaking the ice.

"Well, actually, I do need your help with something..." I take a deep breath to steel myself, heart pounding. This feels like the most important conversation I've ever had in my life. My future depends on her. "I wanted to talk to you about school next year. Um, so far I've gotten into Cal Lutheran, UC Santa Barbara—"

"That's a party school. You won't like it there." A snort curls Mom's nose. "And what makes you think you can even afford to go? I sure as hell can't pay for it."

"I also got into Stanford," I say, watching her face carefully for a reaction.

I never told her it's my dream school, but surely even she is aware that it's a really big deal for someone to get in. Part of me just wants her to say she's proud. Or amazed. Or that she knew I had it in me. Something. *Anything*.

"Well, you definitely can't afford to go there," she says dismissively. "What about city college? They have two-year programs, and they're free. You can get an associate's like I did. That's really all you need."

Her nonchalance has my blood boiling, and before I

stop to think, I say, "Yeah. If I want to clean houses for a living."

The words are out of my mouth, and it's too late to take them back. Both of us freeze. I feel my face go hot, and the floor seems to drop out from under my feet. Shit.

"Mom—"

She stands up now, pulling herself to her full height, eyes narrowing.

"You think you're too good to clean houses, Camilla? That you're so much better than me?" she hisses, glaring daggers. "You think getting some fancy degree is going to get you a job that pays a million dollars? Do you know how many people actually end up with a career in the field they majored in? Less than thirty percent. Look it up."

Her words are hitting me like gut punches, but it's not enough to deter me.

"I'm going to major in psychology," I tell her. "I want to help people. I need a *degree* to do that."

"Then get it at city college! The higher education system in this country is a con. It's elitist. Nobody gives a shit where you went to school."

"They do if you work in healthcare," I point out. But she's not even listening.

"Look at the Becks' son. That boy is a perfect example! His dad is going to hand him a real estate job that pays six figures as soon as the kid graduates, and then he'll be set for life. No college required. *That's* who succeeds in this world. Not the people who study the hardest or work the hardest. The sooner you realize that, the better off you'll be. Don't waste your time and other people's money chasing pipe dreams."

Blinking back tears, I shake my head. "*I'm going*. I'm not asking for money. I just need you to fill out the FAFSA so I can get loan offers. It'll be my debt, not yours."

Disgusted, she folds her arms across her chest. "Don't be an idiot. You want to be paying off student loans for the rest of your life? Trust me, you don't. And besides, you're wasting your time. I don't understand why you're being so stubborn about this when you have a perfectly good face and a decent figure, and there are plenty of men—"

"It's my life to live, and I'm not gonna waste it trying to get someone else to take care of me because they think I'm pretty!" I cut her off. "Please, Mom, just do this one thing for me. My savings will cover some of the tuition at least, and—"

"What savings?" She's gone stock-still, like a rattlesnake about to strike.

"My babysitting money," I say. "I have almost ten thousand dollars saved up—"

"Ten *thousand* dollars," she repeats, her voice suddenly ice cold. "You had *ten thousand dollars*, and you let us get evicted? Jesus." She shakes her head. "I raised you all by myself with zero help from your father, not a dime of child support, no free childcare. I thought you were using up all your paychecks on groceries and bills, and here you are holding out on me this whole fucking time! How could you be so selfish?"

The realization of where this is going hits me like a ton of bricks. She talks like I'm asking her to climb Everest for me, but all I need her to do is give me data for an online form.

I speak softly, trying to appeal to her logical side, worried my college dreams are slipping away right before my eyes. "Mom, I'll say this one more time. The only thing that I need you to do is fill out a form with me, and I'll help you every step of the way. That's it."

"Ah. So I guess little miss perfect can't do it all on her own. You still need me," she taunts. "God, I should've been like your father. Escaped all this. But no, I had to keep you. I had to raise you. You've already ruined my life, Camilla. I'm not going to help you ruin yours. Forget Stanford. City college is good enough for you."

In my chest, something breaks. The tears I've been battling to hold back well up again, full force. I hate her so much, and I can't do anything about it.

"I ruined your life?" I choke out. "How can you even say that? I'm your daughter!"

I never asked her for help with anything, and I worked hard all my life to help her however I could. So stupid of me to think this could've gone differently.

"No, you know what? You ruined your *own* life," I go on. "You ruin it every day when you fill that glass with—"

Her hand moves so fast I don't have time to react. Pain sears my left cheek, my face whipping to the side with the strength of her slap.

As tears slip from my eyes, all I can think is *leave*.

Chapter Forty-One

CAMILLA

*H*olding my face, cheek throbbing where my mother hit me, I turn around and run.

Out of the pool house, across the yard, into the Becks'. Rushing toward the one person who will hold me together while this pain tears my heart to shreds.

I burst into Hunter's room. He's in bed, in pajama bottoms and a T-shirt with his phone in his hand, but he sits up as soon as he sees me and tugs his earbuds out. A sob rattles my throat. Still near the door, I hesitate, chin trembling.

"Milla? What's wrong?"

He holds out his arms, and I run over, crashing into him on the bed.

"My mom," I sob, and then I can't stop.

Hunter holds me close, and I bury my head in his neck. The pain's still there, tearing a hole inside me, but being close like this lessens it somewhat. I can feel Hunter's warm, solid chest rising and falling beneath me, his steady arms around me. His presence reminding me that there *is* someone who wants me. That my mom is wrong, and I'm not the kind of person who ruins lives.

"What did she say this time?" he asks softly.

I've made some offhanded mentions of our arguments, and I know he's overheard a few of my mom's harsh comments, but I've tried to shield him from the worst of it. Not anymore though. I'm done trying to cover for her.

"That..." I do my best to sniff and stammer my way through it. "She's not going to help me with my college stuff. That I ruined her life. She said it's my fault we got evicted, and that...that I'm selfish. She called me little miss perfect, but I'm not."

I dissolve into tears again, equal parts relieved and humiliated.

"That's a lot of bullshit," Hunter says. "Shh. Don't cry because of her. You're the most unselfish person I know; she doesn't know what she's talking about. You're the best thing she ever did."

Warmth blooms on my temples, then again on my cheek. Hunter's kissing me as he speaks, putting my heart back together with his touch. I'm so starved for affection that it makes me cry even harder.

"But what about college?" I stammer. "I don't have enough saved up, and she won't do the FAFSA for me, and..."

"It'll be okay. I promise. We'll figure it out." He kisses the edge of my jaw and in my ear whispers, "I'm here. I'll always be here."

He says that last sentence over and over, like a charm, and I find myself holding on to the idea harder than I'm holding on to his body. I believe it when he says it.

It's between his arms and my tears that I realize the one stable thing in my life right now is Hunter. I finally stop crying and start to calm down. Contented to feel Hunter's warmth, I stay in his arms for a while longer, letting my tears dry. Finally, I excuse myself to go to his bathroom and blow my nose, splashing cool water on my face and rinsing my mouth out with mouthwash.

"Feeling any better?" he asks when I pad back over to his bed, brushing my hair back with his fingers.

I nod and climb back over to him, curling up in his lap. "Thank you."

"Don't mention it." He holds me tight in his arms but doesn't try to do anything other than trace my cheek with his thumb and look at me. There's concern in his eyes, and underneath that, genuine affection. Something I crave but have kept at a distance because I was afraid that we had no future.

But futures are uncertain. Only the present is real. Solid. Tangible.

And right now, I need to feel closer to him. As close as I can.

"Hunter," I say slowly, like a confession, as I adjust my position to straddle him. I grip his broad shoulders and then close the distance between us. His lips are soft against mine, and his tongue tastes of salt and sadness.

I feel his hands circle my waist while we kiss, and then one sneaks around to the small of my back, stroking the soft skin that's exposed where my shirt has ridden up. I don't want to leave this and go back to the pool house. Even if my mom is long gone by now, that's not where I want to be.

When we pull apart, I touch my forehead to his. "I don't want to go back home."

Hunter gives his head a small shake. "Then don't. Stay with me."

"Okay."

Our lips meet again, more aggressive this time. With

every touch, I sink deeper into him, surrendering more of myself, and with every kiss, I'm hungrier. The sadness I feel is still there, but something else is growing to devour it.

My fingers find the hem of his T-shirt, and Hunter barely has time to raise his arms before I tear it over his head. He does the same with mine, and with a flick, unhooks my bra and throws it aside.

Skin to skin, I wrap myself around him, kissing him harder until he flips me over. My back hits the sheets, and Hunter looms over me, eyes half-lidded, knee between my legs. "Milla," he says, mouth so close to mine our breaths mingle. "Tell me what you want. I need you to be really clear right now."

A shiver of embarrassment crosses my chest, but it's gone as soon as it appears. "To be with you," I whisper.

"You're already with me," he says, an edge of mischief to his lips as he brings them down against mine. He runs his thumb across one of my nipples, and heat pools in my abdomen. Under my fingers, the muscles on his back shudder. When I lightly bite his lip, Hunter hisses a breath, looking at me darkly. It's the look he gets when he wants to put his mouth and his hands all over me—and more than that, if I'd let him.

I want to let him.

"I want to be with all of you," I say, feeling lame, but it's what comes out.

"You want to have sex," he says, but I know it's a question. A question I have to answer if I want this to go any further.

"I want to have sex," I repeat, our eyes locking. "With you."

The Adam's apple bobs in Hunter's throat. For a moment, he doesn't seem to breathe, doesn't move, doesn't do anything other than pin me to the bed with his heavy body and his heated gaze. Then, suddenly, it's like I've unleashed an animal.

His mouth crashes down on mine, our tongues sliding against each other, and his hand moves lower to pop the button of my shorts and slide the zipper down. He wastes no time slipping his fingers down my panties, tracing my opening with his thumb before slowly dipping a finger into me.

Hunter only stops kissing me to say, "You're already so wet..." before his finger pumps deeper, in and out, and the sound of my wetness draws even more of a blush to my cheeks. My back arches, and I spread my legs wider to give him better access.

As he fingers me, his thumb brushes my clit, his mouth trailing from my cheek to my chin to my neck, finally planting kisses on the line of my collarbone. Moans and gasps slip out of me, my thigh muscles trembling, my hips grinding to meet his movement. The pleasure builds inside me, and I'm impossibly tight as the feeling grows and grows and...stops.

I look up at Hunter, and he has the wickedest smirk I've ever seen on him.

"Don't worry, Milla. You're gonna get something even better," he says, kissing me deeply until I'm out of breath.

Then he moves his hot mouth down to suck on both my nipples before heading lower, past my navel, and I suddenly sit up, shocked. His fingers going down there I expected, but his mouth? I don't know why I didn't prepare mentally for this, but I didn't, and now he's taking off my shorts and underwear in one easy movement.

"What are you...?" I ask, even though I know exactly what he aims to do. And as hesitant as I am to expose myself to him like this, the prospect of having his tongue there makes me even wetter.

"I'm going to eat you," he says. "Stop is your safe word, yeah?"

Before I have time to lose my nerve, he's grabbing my thighs and tugging my naked body toward the edge of the bed, sliding off and shifting my ass closer to the edge. Dropping to his knees with his face between my legs, he looks up and says, "I did tell you I wanted another taste."

Oh my God, I can't believe this is really happening, and then it is.

The first lick alone steals my breath, long and wet and slow, tracing a line all the way up to my clit. I let out a gasp that turns into a low moan, and Hunter laughs a little, his breath hot against my pussy, and says, "You're lucky we're home alone tonight."

After the second lap of his tongue, I'm clutching the comforter in my fists, head tilted back, eyes shut tight. Writhing is the only way to describe how my body's moving, my thighs squeezing his head as I try to stay in control. I can feel everything. Every shift of his lips, every twitch of his tongue, every soft suck.

"Oh my fucking *God*," I pant. I've never experienced anything like this.

Hunter pulls back, and I can hear the amusement in his voice as he says, "Wow. I don't think I've ever heard you curse before."

One of his fingers has been circling my entrance as he talks, but now he slips it inside me with ease. I immediately tighten, but slowly, gently, Hunter opens me up.

This is different than the times he's fingered me before. Deeper, less frantic. I'm wetter, hotter, and so close to the edge that I think I might actually come.

I look down my body at him, and our eyes lock, my heartbeat echoing in my ears. He dips his head, and his tongue and fingers—yes, it's plural now—are stroking and rubbing me just right. Tongue circling my clit, fingers pumping into me, faster, faster.

"Hunter, I'm..." I whimper. "I'm going to..."

"Do it, Milla." He bends his fingers, tapping some spot inside me that sends a flush of white-hot heat through my body, and then he whispers again. "Come."

I can't though. God. I can't let myself go, can't stop tensing up.

"I can't," I tell him breathlessly. "I'm trying."

"Then stop trying," he whispers.

With that, he switches to long, slow laps of his tongue, so slow I can feel myself clenching in anticipation between each stroke. The heat is building again, coiling tighter by the second. "*Oh my God*," I moan, drawing it out.

"Mm-hmm," Hunter moans, the sound vibrating against my pussy. "Mmm."

He moans again, but longer this time, louder, sounding almost as desperate as I am, and that's it. Heat is spilling out of me in an unstoppable rush, pleasure exploding from my center. My hips buck, and I'm grinding on Hunter's tongue, riding it as colors start to flash in front of my eyes.

"Hunter," I whisper, over and over again.

I thought it would feel the same as when I do it by myself, but somehow, it's so much better. Gasping for air, I'm whimpering helplessly as I finally come, in waves, all over his mouth and fingers, melting into a torrent of pleasure I never imagined.

Chapter Forty-Two

HUNTER

*C*amilla. I can't get enough of her.

The way she moans with her eyes half closed, biting her lip like that, makes me want to torment her even more, give her orgasm after orgasm until she breaks.

I have a lot of experience, yeah, but this girl is different. Camilla's giving herself to me because she trusts me, because she cares about me, because she wants us to be together in every way possible. It's not just to scratch an itch or to get her mind off of things. Actually, I guess this is new territory for me too.

I've never seen a girl come the way she just did. She totally lost control, and I could feel her cunt clenching around my fingers, so tight, squeezing in these hard little contractions. It was so hot, I almost lost it right along with her.

The aftershocks are still running through her when I ease my fingers out. Her breath is short and shallow, and then she's smiling as she takes in a big gulp of air, dark eyes glazed, hair in disarray. Sexy as anything, and she's not even trying.

A sweet sigh leaves her when I kiss the inside of her thigh and climb back up beside her, tucking a stray lock of hair behind her ear as I tell her, "That was really hot."

"You made me come," she whispers, sounding almost amazed.

I have to laugh. "Yeah. I did. You want me to do it again, or do you need a break?"

Without answering, she crawls on top of me and starts kissing me. Ravenously.

My dick's practically jumping in my pants with the way she's sliding her tongue around inside my mouth. Her body is warm against mine, and the muscles on my abdomen tense when she trails her hand down, under my pajamas and boxers, and grabs me. Her fingers are hot, her grip firm. All the time I spent licking her has taken its toll.

"Milla," I growl, a feral sound. "You don't have to—"

"I want to," she says, tugging my pants down, and I know she's thinking about the same thing I am. "Let me put my mouth on you."

She takes my cock in her hand, giving me a long lick from balls to tip, then wraps her lips around the head and starts sucking softly. When I let out a harsh breath, cussing softly, she pulls back, looking bashful.

"Was that wrong? I—I don't know what I'm doing," she admits.

I can't stop a quiet laugh from spilling out. "There's no wrong way, I can promise you that. Just, here." Gently, I move her hand down to the base and instruct her, "All you have to do is try to fit as much of me in your mouth as you can."

"Is that a challenge?" she asks.

"It doesn't have to be," I say.

"I accept."

With that, she opens up, lowering her mouth on me,

lips closing tight around my shaft. With a shudder, I hold her head in my hands and slowly pump back and forth, thrusting as softly as I can. Camilla's kind of right; she doesn't know what she's doing. But I don't care. This feels good because it's her. And I know she'll get better.

"Now suck it," I tell her, breathing hard, adrenaline racing through me. "Suck that cock."

Suddenly, she stops and pulls back.

"Are you okay?" I ask.

From the panicked look on her face, I suddenly get the impression she's trying to do the math of how we're going to fit together. Truth be told, I'm a little worried too. I've been with virgins before, but the last thing I want is to hurt her.

I brush the hair away from her face. "Talk to me. What are you thinking?"

"I'm too embarrassed," Milla answers, looking down, still squeezing my cock.

"It's okay. You can say it."

"It's just..." She swallows as she moves her hand up and down, treading way more dangerous ground than she realizes and making me groan. "Intimidating."

"Are you afraid it will hurt?" I can't believe what I'm about to say, but I'm not into having sex unless Camilla wants it as much as I do. "We don't have to do this, if you're not ready."

Milla shakes her head. "I'm ready. I want to."

I kiss her uncertainty away. "It's all right. Come here." I sit up and bring her to my lap, and when she's distracted from my kissing her, I slip a finger back inside her. "See?" I kiss her jaw as I add another finger. "You're already so wet. So soft."

I'm trying to reassure her, but it's turning me on beyond

belief. Her body's trembling again, and the sounds my fingers make inside her fill the room.

She buries her face against my neck and says, "You're a lot bigger than two fingers."

"Okay. Then how does this feel..."

I push a third finger in, drawing a gasp from her lips. Milla falls into me, and her teeth close on my shoulder, muffling her moan. I can't tell if it's a good moan or if she's in pain. I kiss her cheek, worried. "Is it okay?"

She nods, starting to move her hips in time with my strokes as if to tell me to keep going, clinging to me as she licks and kisses my neck. My hand's dripping with her juices now, and as I press her clit with my thumb, she groans my name.

Then she looks up at me with half-lidded eyes, lips swollen and parted. "I want you. Now."

"I want you too," I tell her.

I'm kissing her harder, my cock brushing the slick V between her legs. She's wetter now, even more ready, and she wraps her hand around me and asks, "Do you have a...?"

"Condom. Yeah."

I have never put one on faster. Once I'm ready, I pull her back on top of me, my tip pressed against her opening, my fingers digging into her hips. Although I want nothing more than to thrust up into her, I wait. And honestly, I should be getting a medal for this restraint because she's hot, and dripping, and her eyes are begging.

"Yes?" I ask, rocking my hips a little so my cock teases her just a tiny bit.

These things never meant much to me before, but I know if I do this, if I take her, she will be tied to me forever.

No matter what happens next, I will always be her first.

With a shuddering breath, Milla shifts her position, and I stop breathing as I feel myself start to sink inside her.

"Yes," she says, and lowers her weight onto me with a gasp.

I'm about halfway in when she stops, and I go still, holding her against me as she takes deep breaths. She's so tight, and I can feel her tensing up around my dick.

I kiss her to distract her. "Relax. There's no rush."

"Easier said than done," she whimpers. "I want to ride you."

She lets herself slide farther onto me, and this time I'm the one gasping.

At this rate, I'm going to come before I'm all the way in. I twist my hips, moving my cock side to side instead of deeper, letting her get used to the feeling. She feels good. So fucking good, but I know better than to lose control right now.

"Ooh," she moans, shuddering. Glad I'm doing something right.

Then, suddenly, as her tongue traces mine, Milla drops the rest of the way onto me in a flash, impaling herself on my dick. We both moan, and I close my eyes, not moving, not doing anything other than holding her, holding on to the single thread of control she hasn't cut. She's panting hard on top of me, and I let out a breath.

I'm finally fully inside her. She's mine now, all of her, and despite her fears, we fit like we're meant to be together.

I thrust up a little, testing the waters, and get lost in the sound of her moans. Lost in the way she feels, so hot and soft, and how her nails dig into my back, pleasure and pain mixing together in a heady cocktail. She says my name, and I say hers, over and over because she's all there is. We start to move together slowly, mouths meeting clumsily as little by little we find a rhythm.

She looks so dick-drunk, I have to ask, "How does it feel, Milla?"

"Good..." Smiling lazily, she pants, "You can go harder."

"Harder?"

"Yes."

And here I was trying to be gentle.

I shift our position so she's under me now, then lift one of her legs and slam inside her as hard as I can. Her pussy molds to me to perfection. It feels incredible.

"Good?" I ask.

"Yeah," she pants.

"It's so fucking hot inside you," I say, and she clenches around me like she's trying to milk me for all I'm worth, but I don't want this to end yet. I want to feel her more, to ruin her more. Through clenched teeth, I tell her, "Please. Try not to do that."

"I can't help it," she says. "It's too good, I can't relax..."

"You just have to—"

But whatever I was going to say gets lost when she tightens again. I let out a groan, and when she wraps her legs around my hips, I sink even deeper. She pulls me in for a kiss, and I can't stop myself anymore. I pump faster and harder, giving her what she asked for, looking down at her, lush mouth open, tits bouncing, moans pitching higher and higher, waiting for the moment she comes apart so I can follow.

"You're all I want, Milla," I tell her, feeling myself start to lose it. "Just you. I want to be with you. I—" There's more, but before I can say anything else, she's gasping my name again, so loud I'm relieved there's nobody home to hear us.

"Hunter," she says, digging her nails into my ass to pull me into her even deeper. "Hunter, yes, please, yes..."

"Come for me," I coax her, now that I know she needs someone to draw it out of her. "Come for me, baby, let it go, just come. Come."

She's looking up at me, meeting my every thrust as she takes the full length of me inside her. I'm barely hanging on when I feel the moment she tightens up, her eyes fluttering shut as she moans out her orgasm, bucking in my arms.

"I'm coming, Hunter." She's mumbling, gasping for air, back arching as the pleasure radiates through her, wave after wave. "Come with me."

I drive into her one last time, fully letting go, and I can hear myself groaning as I come inside her, harder and deeper than I ever have before.

Chapter Forty-Three

CAMILLA

*I*t's morning when I wake up in Hunter's bed.

My eyes open to sunlight streaming into the room, his solid body heat pressed against me from behind. His breath fans the back of my neck, and his arm is draped over my waist, holding me to him even as he sleeps.

Closing my eyes against the brightness, I let myself snuggle into this lazy Sunday comfort for a bit. Flashes of what we did last night replay in my head, and I feel myself blush when I remember it all. Though I'd assumed Hunter would know what he was doing, given the amount of practice he's had, I hadn't expected it to be the mind-numbing flurry of hunger and pleasure it turned out to be. I still can't believe I came with him inside me, looking down at me like I was a goddess. It was so intimate. So intense. It's still unreal when I think about it.

I already want to do it again.

There's a soreness between my legs, almost like a bruise inside, but the more I dwell on what happened, the more that soreness turns into a fiery ache. I need more of him, need to feel him inside. We're both still naked, and the feel of his warm skin against me is doing questionable things to my head.

I wonder if he's turned me into a sex addict just like I feared, if he's somehow awakened this singular drive to get my world rocked again. Either way, I'm ready.

Slowly, so as not to wake him, I turn to look at him. He looks unguarded when he sleeps, his lashes fanning his cheeks, his lips slightly open. Too appealing for me not to lean in and kiss him softly.

Hunter's arm stirs, and his eyes open lazily, focusing on me.

"Morning, beautiful. I think I could get used to this." A smile stretches across his lips as he touches them to mine. "Sleep well?"

The tips of our noses brush as I nod. "Better than I have in a really long time."

"Same." Hunter shifts to cover me and threads our fingers together. "We should do it again sometime."

"Sometime?" I repeat before he brings his mouth on mine again. His dick presses against the inside of my thigh, hard and ready, telling me exactly what he means by *sometime*. Reaching down to trace the tip with my finger, I tease, "What is this?"

"What did you expect? You were lying naked next to me all night." He kisses me deeply this time. His hand slips between my legs, where I'm shockingly wet already. Finding that out makes him smile. "Hmm. Seems like you want it too."

I slap his bicep, which was a mistake. He has really nice arms—he has a really nice everything—and all of that was wrapped up either around me or in me last night. And the way he's touching me now, stroking my opening with his fingertips, is reminding me of how good he made me feel, and how careful he was, how respectful.

"I'm ready for round two," I say.

He kisses the side of my neck several times, laughing a little. "Really?"

"Really," I moan. "And then let's eat something because I'm starving."

"Oh, you're starving all right," he jokes. His hands are traveling all over my body, lighting up a fire wherever they go. My body becomes unbearably hot, the tension ratcheting up, and I want to do the same to him, so I do what worked last time and squeeze that monster dick of his, brushing my thumb around the slick wetness at the tip. I still can't believe all of this was in me and I didn't break in two.

Hunter's breath catches, and with a serious look, he starts getting clever with his fingers on my clit, squeezing and releasing over and over again until I'm drenched and squirming, my hips undulating of their own volition. He's just rolled over to reach for the condom drawer when a knock on the door freezes the both of us. I watch, helpless, as whoever's on the other side jiggles the knob.

"Hunter, unlock the door," a deep male voice says from the other side. It has to be his dad. Shit.

The relief at knowing he's not walking in on us doesn't last long. We exchange a panicked look before jolting apart and diving to the floor to grab for our clothes. I find my shoes, top, shorts, and panties, but no bra. I frantically scan the room, but it's nowhere to be seen.

"Where did you chuck it?" I whisper, wiggling into my shorts.

"Doesn't matter, you need to hide." Hunter gestures at the bed and for me to get under. I shake my head. I feel like some shameful secret he's trying to hide. He comes over and grabs my hand. "Please, just get under. Five minutes."

"Get yourself up! It's past noon." Mr. Beck bangs on the

door again, his voice getting louder with exasperation. "We have to talk."

"Be right there," Hunter says, then nods toward the bed again with pleading eyes and pressed lips. Without much choice and not wanting Mr. Beck to catch me in here, I crawl under the heavy wood frame, still naked from the waist up. At least the blue carpet is soft on my back, even if it's a little dusty under here, meaning my mom hasn't been cleaning this place properly, and for some reason it pisses me off further than I already am. Hiding under the bed to hide from his dad—this is what my life's come to.

I hear a long sigh from Hunter before he turns the lock. "Morning, Dad."

There's a long pause. "You have to stop wasting your weekends sleeping."

"Yeah, well...long night," Hunter says and yawns. "What is it?"

I look at the bed frame above me, wishing they'd hurry up. The carpet is starting to itch, prickling against my skin.

Mr. Beck says, "I made a few calls after looking into what you told me about, and it's all taken care of. You don't have to worry anymore."

A crease instantly forms between my brows. The only person I can think of who Hunter worries about enough to bring his father in to solve a problem for is Harrison. Is something wrong? Is this about the marks on his arm? And if so, why didn't Hunter tell me anything about it?

"Can we discuss this some other time?" Hunter mutters, his words almost lost in the short distance between where he stands at the door and where I lie under the bed.

"There's nothing to discuss, son. It's a done deal. As soon as I let the committee know what you told me about Camilla's history at her last school, they immediately took her off the list." There's a pause, and I feel my chest crack under the weight of what I've just heard, my whole body gone ice cold. "So you can rest assured, the Reed will stay safe. It's like you try so hard to help the disadvantaged in this life, but then those are the exact people who try to manipulate the system and ruin things for everybody—"

"Dad, stop." Hunter's voice has gone steely. "Let's just talk about it later."

"Well, I just wanted you to know she won't get the scholarship."

I hear Mr. Beck's footsteps fade away, and I realize my future has just imploded. My hopes and dreams —destroyed.

All because of Hunter Beck.

*Things look bleak for Hunter and Camilla, but they aren't over yet. Read the next part of their story in **This Hurt.***

Camilla didn't know anything could feel like *This Hurt*...

Camilla thought she'd left her past behind. Leaving public school for the elite halls she walks now should have been her fresh start. Her chance to be the girl she wants to be, not the girl other people think she is—most of all, to be the girl for Hunter Beck.

But she can't seem to outrun the rumors that chase her, and she's starting to lose hope she ever will.

The year is quickly drawing to a close. The future she's been working towards seems farther away than ever before. Hunter and his father wield the power, she's always known that. Her mother never misses an opportunity to remind her, either. Fighting for what she wants while staying true to her heart seems impossible.

As her past and her future rush toward a collision, Camilla is no longer sure *what* her heart wants.

Should she leave everything behind and live the life she's been dreaming of for years?

Or should she throw it all away for the love of a boy she shouldn't trust—Hunter Beck?

Get This Hurt here.

ALSO BY JENNA SCOTT

This Boy

This Hurt

This Love

ABOUT THE AUTHOR

After growing up in the midwest, Jenna Scott moved to Los Angeles for the endless summer. As an introvert in the city, she loves to people-watch in coffee shops, writing down the stories she makes up about the other patrons. Besides her fiction habit, Jenna also enjoys photography and her collection of houseplants.

Made in the USA
Columbia, SC
05 January 2021

30387547R00183